Praise for *Blind Kiss*

"Carlino (*Wish You Were Here*) impresses and astonishes with this complicated, beautiful contemporary that shifts between past and present with devastating effect . . . [Her] sharp, incisive prose calls the traditional romance novel ending into question throughout. The expert characterizations and a constantly surprising plot are enthralling. Deep and complex, this heartbreaking and heartwarming tale will live in readers' memories long after the final page is turned."

—*Publishers Weekly* (starred review)

"*Blind Kiss* beautifully illustrates how destiny prevails over even the best-laid plans. You will love this story."

—Tracey Garvis Graves, *New York Times* bestselling author of *The Girl He Used to Know*

"A story of enduring passion, devoted friendship, and the undeniable power of chemistry, *Blind Kiss* asks the question: Would you wait a lifetime to be with the person you love? Renée Carlino's evocative prose is at once heartbreaking and full of hope, and the palpable spark between Gavin and Penny will touch the depths of your heart."

—Kristin Rockaway, author of *The Wild Woman's Guide to Traveling the World*

"*Blind Kiss* is Renée Carlino at her finest. The tension between Penny and Gavin leaps off the page. This is a romantic, tender, complicated love story. I found it heartfelt, honest, and simply wonderful."

—Taylor Jenkins Reid, author of *The Seven Husbands of Evelyn Hugo*

ALSO BY RENÉE CARLINO

THE
LAST POST

RENÉE CARLINO

ATRIA PAPERBACK

New York London Toronto Sydney New Delhi

ATRIA
PAPERBACK

An Imprint of Simon & Schuster, Inc.
1230 Avenue of the Americas
New York, NY 10020

First Atria Paperback edition August 2019

ATRIA PAPERBACK and colophon are trademarks of Simon & Schuster, Inc.

For information about special discounts for bulk purchases, please contact Simon & Schuster Special Sales at 1-866-506-1949 or business@simonandschuster.com.

The Simon & Schuster Speakers Bureau can bring authors to your live event. For more information or to book an event contact the Simon & Schuster Speakers Bureau at 1-866-248-3049 or visit our website at www.simonspeakers.com.

Manufactured in the United States of America

10 9 8 7 6 5 4 3 2

Library of Congress Cataloging-in-Publication Data is available.

ISBN 978-1-5011-8964-7
ISBN 978-1-5011-8965-4 (ebook)

For Gina . . .
Thank you for nurturing a sense of adventure in me

"You come to find love not by finding the perfect person, but by seeing an imperfect person perfectly."

—Sam Keen

THE
LAST POST

1. Jetpack

LAYA

"You want me to go to France this weekend?"

"Laya, it's Mont Blanc. It'll be like a second honeymoon. We'll do all the romantic things people do in France."

"Cameron, we've been married for a year and we've gone on three second honeymoons."

It wasn't hard for my new, beautiful husband to talk me into jetting off to exotic locations every week for his job, but I was still working in California, trying to finish my surgery residency. I didn't have the freedom to just pack up and go. But he was convincing; I'll give him that.

"There will never be enough honeymoons with you. I know you have to work. I promise, it'll be three days on Red Bull's dime. We'll hit Paris first—I'll take you to the top of the Eiffel Tower. I'll kiss you on le Pont Neuf."

"The new bridge?" I said.

"See, your French is spot-on. That's the literal translation, but it's actually the oldest bridge in Paris. It's beautiful. You'll love it! Say you'll go with me. Please, Laya?"

We were standing in our tiny kitchen in the San Francisco studio we rented. Cameron stared at me with puppy-dog eyes while I wiped down the counter. I wanted to go with him to France, but I had asked for time off once already that month, and I was still just a surgery resident at the hospital.

"What is the stunt you're doing?"

He came up and wrapped his arms around me from behind, brushing his lips against my neck. "Just gonna"—he ran slow kisses all the way from behind my ear and down to my shoulder—"do some . . . skiing," he said.

I turned and glared at him playfully. "Just some skiing, huh?"

Cameron did dangerous stunts for his sponsor, Red Bull. He also did dangerous stunts for fun, too. It was in his DNA.

"The Louvre," I finally said, straight-faced.

He kissed my cheek. "It's very touristy. It's where the *Mona Lisa* is. Kind of overrated, Laya."

"I know." I rolled my eyes at him. "That's my one condition. I'll get the time off if you promise to take me to the Louvre."

"*Mona Lisa*, here we come." He smacked me on the butt before turning and walking down the hall.

A week later I was racing to the airport to meet Cameron. My Uber driver was going at least ten miles an hour below the speed limit. I was scrolling through my phone, trolling Facebook, when a notification popped up.

CAMERON BENNETT to LAYA BENNETT

Waiting for you at the airport and staring at all your gorgeous pictures. Get your buns down here. Three. Two. One. See ya.

Every time I met Cameron at the airport, he would run up to me, yelling like we hadn't seen each other in years.

I saw him the moment I walked through the glass doors leading to our terminal. With his arms outstretched, he shouted, "Laya! Is that you? Laya Bennett? My god, you're as stunning as ever." He picked me up and swung me around. I was still wearing scrubs with my hair in a bun and no makeup on.

"Put me down—everyone is looking at us."

"Everyone is looking at you. Everyone is always looking at you 'cause you're so goddamn beautiful."

"Cameron, this is the last trip I can take with you for a while. I'm in hot water at the hospital."

"Okay, okay. I won't beg again. Or maybe I will." He was still holding me in the air, kissing every inch of my face.

"And, seriously, put me down."

He finally listened, but he dipped me first like we were doing the tango. When he popped me up, he said, "You're not excited to see Paris? You've never been. First thing we'll do is go see the *Mona Lisa*, and then we'll just hang out naked in the hotel room after that." He said the last bit with overexaggerated enthusiasm, well aware I wasn't buying it.

"I know you. You can't sit still in a hotel room for more than an hour, naked or not. Let's go." I yanked on his hand and pulled him toward the security line.

We had first-class seats on the plane. Red Bull spared no expense. Both of us were exhausted by the time we began taxiing toward the runway. We skipped the welcome champagne and fell asleep on each other's shoulders. My dream was vivid, more of a memory than anything made up. It was from the day Cameron and I had met in a tiny triage room at the hospital where I worked.

"How did you shatter your arm, Mr. Bennett?" I asked Cameron. He lounged on the exam table as if he were resting at home and not at the hospital.

"Skydiving."

"Do you skydive often?"

"As often as I can."

I popped Cameron's X-ray onto the light board and studied it. "So, did you have a rough landing?"

"Yeah, you can say that. I need to get back to skiing soon, though. What can you do for me? How long do you think the recovery will be?" He shamelessly winked at me and smiled.

"I'll need to check with the surgeon. We'll take X-rays over the next week to see how you're healing. You may not need surgery at all. I'll order an MRI. If the ligaments are intact—"

"I have a thing in two weeks."

"A thing?"

"A skiing thing."

I chuckled, then stopped abruptly when I realized he was seriously considering skiing with a shattered arm. "I'm sorry to be the bearer of bad news, but I don't think you'll be skiing anytime soon."

"Yeah, but I don't use poles, so you know, my arm's not

really a factor." He sat up, the white paper crinkling underneath him. "By the way, you have magical eyes."

"Okay, I'm a little confused. Do you think you're actually going skiing in two weeks with four fractures in your arm?"

"Hairline fractures."

"Ummm, not really."

His lips turned up at the corners. "Will you go out with me?"

I had started choking, and then a miserable coughing fit ensued, so he got down and started patting my back with his good hand. It was a wildly unprofessional scene. "Excuse . . . me."

"Was it something I said?"

"Mr. Bennett—"

"Cameron."

"Mr. Bennett," I reiterated. "I would really advise you not to do any sporting activities until your arm is fully healed."

"It's my job, though, *Doctor* Marston." He had emphasized the formality of my name as if to prove a point.

"I'm going to get your regular doctor to take a look at this and evaluate it." The moment I turned toward the door, my face broke into a smile. I was already putty in his hands, but I still tried for a while to hide it. We got married a year later.

WHEN I WOKE up on the plane, we were already making our descent into Charles de Gaulle Airport in Paris. I lifted my head and blinked against the sun beaming through the window. Cameron was awake and watching me.

"You were talking in your sleep. It was adorable," he said.

I laughed. "What was I saying?"

"You said something like, 'Just skiing, my ass.'"

"Ha! Well, I never did get full disclosure about the stunt you're doing this weekend. And if I recall, thanks to my dream, you lied to me the very first day we met about 'just skiing.'"

"It wasn't a lie. Maybe an omission, not a lie."

"Well, you've *omitted* some pretty important details."

Cameron chuckled. "I'm going to do a wingsuit flight after I ski off Mont Blanc."

My heart started racing. The wingsuit flights scared me, but I knew he loved them. He was the best at it, and I shouldn't have worried. I never wanted to second-guess him. He was a professional risk taker, if there was such a thing. I'd learned very early on in our relationship that Cameron practiced obsessively, meticulously planning every stunt he did, and he trusted his team.

"Well, okay."

"I know it scares you, Laya, but I've done it a million times here. It's a popular mountain for this. Low mortality rate."

"Is that supposed to make me feel better?"

He tried desperately to change the subject, but he was digging a deeper and deeper hole. "It's the highest peak in all the Alps. You'll be as close to space as you might ever get. Isn't that something to look forward to?"

He knew I loved everything involving space travel. It was an obsession I'd had since childhood. "We were closer to space when we were up in the air."

He tapped the side of my head with his index finger.

"Okay, smarty. How'd I land a doctor anyway? I can accept that I married a woman much smarter than me, if you can accept that I know what I'm doing."

I nodded.

"Then let's go see the Louvre," he said.

After going through customs and checking in to our hotel, we went, we saw, we stood in a long line to see the *Mona Lisa*. Not that it wasn't worth it, though Cameron did comment continuously on how small it was. I had already known that fact, and we enjoyed our time there anyway.

"What should we do after we see the new bridge?" I asked, as we strolled hand in hand through the beautiful Place Dauphine square toward le Pont Neuf. It exuded Old World charm with its gray architecture and cobbled road, contrasting against the people sitting in outdoor cafés, chatting on or scrolling through their phones. Other tourists took pictures, but Cameron and I were happy to just experience all of it.

We paused to let a bicyclist pass. "It's the oldest bridge, silly," Cameron said.

Just as we got to the sidewalk, he whipped me around and kissed me.

"I like romantic, Cameron," I said.

"Do you like me enough not to be mad when I tell you I have to get back soon?"

My smile faded quickly. I wanted to spend more time with Cameron, but he was always being swept off to this place or that by his team. There was little time in the hotel room—naked, as he had said.

The rest of the day was spent entirely on prepping for the stunt. Red Bull set me up in a little chalet near the base of the mountain, so I could do work on transcribing medical reports on my computer while Cameron practiced. I promised him that I'd be there at the top the next day when they planned to film him for the ad campaign. He said I was his good-luck charm.

The next morning six of us piled into a helicopter and headed for the top where Red Bull had set up.

Over the headset speaker Cameron said, "Two hours max and then we'll be back in that cozy little chalet."

When the helicopter landed near the cliff edge, Cameron hopped out with his skis. He reached out his hand to help me down from the helicopter bar. Right in that moment, a gust of wind came rushing at us. The helicopter pilot had to adjust the rotors, and in the process it kicked up a blinding cloud of powdered snow.

Cameron grabbed me and pulled my head into his chest while throwing his skis to the side at the same time. Once we were on more stable footing and the helicopter was gone, Cameron became eerily quiet. I hoped he was just mentally preparing for the stunt.

"Are you nervous? Was that a bad sign when we landed?" I asked him.

"No, Laya, I'm not nervous. I'm excited. I live for this." He pinched my cheek and smiled. "And you know I'm not superstitious. Stuff like that happens all the time."

I took him in. His wild blond hair was a stark contrast to his warm brown eyes. He blinked twice at me, then squeezed his eyes closed for a whole two seconds before opening them.

"Are you trying to wink at me?" I asked.

"No. I just want to make sure what I'm seeing is real."

"What are you seeing?"

"The love of my life."

"Quit gushing over me when you know I'm freaking out. It doesn't help." I leaned up and kissed him quickly.

He pulled away and stared at me for several long seconds before saying, "So I haven't convinced you yet? I got you to marry me, but you're still skeptical?"

"Are you fishing, Cameron Bennett?"

"I thought I already caught you," he said.

"You did. You're the love of *my* life. Is that what you want to hear?"

"Is it true?" he said with a knowing smirk.

"Well, I'm freezing my ass off on the top of a mountain with you, so believe it."

"Ahh, see . . . that does help, for me anyway. Now tell me you'll fix me up if I break my arm again."

I shivered, not because of the cold. "Please don't talk like that."

"Well . . . I'm waiting . . . "

"I'll always fix you up, you crazy man."

He made a spectacle out of kissing me for a long time in front of everyone. The crowd behind us, waiting for Cameron, all whooped and hollered. Someone yelled, "Get a room," and Cameron laughed.

After our kiss we were instantly surrounded by the Red Bull film team, who bombarded Cameron with questions. It was hard to have a moment alone with him when he was in work mode, but he tried.

At one point, I barked at a cameraman whose name I didn't know. "Can you give him some space so he can prep?" My anxiety was setting in again.

Cameron turned to me and said, "You lookin' out for me, doc?"

"That's what I'm here for."

He grabbed my chin with his thumb and index finger and said, "You're perfect, do you know that?" There was a solemn tone in his voice that sent another shiver down my spine. He knew I was nervous for him. In a weird, childish thought, I wished he were wearing a jetpack instead of a thin wingsuit.

When everything was set up and he was ready to go, he turned to me and smiled a big cheesy grin. I knew he lived for the thrill, but I wanted to cling to his warmth a bit longer. "See you on the other side," he said.

It was the same thing James Lovell had said to mission control on the Apollo 8 spaceflight just before they were about to disappear behind the moon. Cameron always said it to me before he did a stunt. But this time I scoffed when he said it. I don't know why, but it just didn't feel right.

"Count me down," he whispered, just loud enough for me to hear over the gusting wind.

"Three." I paused.

"Come on, Laya, you must be hypothermic by now. Hurry up."

"Two. One. See ya."

He winked, pulled down his goggles, and said, "See ya." Then he was gone. He took off skiing to my right, and I shielded myself from the snowy debris left in his wake. He smoothly descended downhill. Once he went off the edge, he did a backflip and released his skis before going into his wingsuit flight.

Everything was going as planned. I had seen him do the same maneuver more than twenty times. I was happy when he came back our way, skimming the mountainside in his bright red wingsuit with the big Red Bull logo on it.

I turned to his friend Jeremy and said, "Does everything look right? Does he seem too close?"

Jeremy shook his head, but there was something in his pause before he actually spoke. "He's got this." I tried to read his eyes, but he was wearing sunglasses.

As soon as Cameron rounded the sharp edge below, I blinked. He was gone. There was a loud sound, like lightning striking a tree branch. *Where did he go?* Then silence. Not even the sound of the wind could pierce my shock. *Where did he go?*

Moments later, I heard yelling, saw people racing toward the cliff edge. The cameramen were no longer filming. I followed them, walking dangerously close to the edge of the cliff, but Jeremy grabbed my arm. "No, Laya."

"I have to see," I mumbled.

"No, no you don't."

I yanked my arm out of his, inched forward, and peered over the top of the cliff face. My heart stopped. "What is that?"

Jeremy didn't answer.

"What is that?" I repeated in a higher pitch, but I knew. I just knew.

WHEN WE'RE TOLD "He or she died on impact," it's supposed to make us feel better, to stop our thoughts about our loved one suffering, alone. But is there a second just before the end that is full of agony and hell and hopelessness? If there is, I hoped Cameron didn't feel any of it.

In bed, when we close our eyes, sometimes we know we're about to fall asleep, but we still fight it. Like when you're watching a good movie and you don't want it to end, but you're so tired. Then you wake up in the morning and you can't recall the exact moment you actually fell asleep. For Cameron, I hoped it was like falling asleep without knowing you're falling asleep—a blissful moment and then you're dreaming about making love. About kissing, about touching your lover's body, about watching the sun set over the ocean . . . about promising eternal happiness with the person you'll end up being with for the rest of your life . . . his life.

2. Unmanned

LAYA

If you told me five years ago I'd be a widow at twenty-nine, I would have laughed in your face. Not because there's anything funny about witnessing your new husband die, but because I never thought I'd be married at twenty-nine in the first place.

My plan was simple. I'd finish medical school, become an orthopedic surgeon, buy a house on the coast with a lap pool . . . maybe get a dog. Simple, solitary, gratifying, and complete.

I lost my mom when I was three. My dad raised me alone. And he *was* alone in every way imaginable . . . still is. I had no model for romantic relationships, typical family life, marriage, or motherhood, so I didn't desire that lifestyle as an adult.

Though I was well cared for, and my father well commended by many for his ability to raise a grounded young woman on his own—the truth was, he did it with few words and even less affection. He was a broken man. I wanted badly to put all the wounded pieces of him back together with screws, bolts, and titanium, but he never let me get close enough to try. He devoted most of his energy to building a large architectural firm in New York City, where I grew up.

I only have one strong memory of my mother and father together. They were dancing in the kitchen to the song "Sweet Melissa" by the Allman Brothers. My mom had been cooking pasta sauce at the stove while I was at her feet. The smell of tomato, garlic, and basil took up the whole house.

She told me, "It has to cook for a long time, Laya. Good things take time and patience."

My father turned their old record player up, my mom smiled, he swung her around, she laughed, and all of a sudden no one else in the world existed but the two of them. What stuck out to me at only three years old, as I toddled around their feet, was that they were truly happy doing something basic. That was the only definition of love I knew. You create a tiny secret world inside a simple embrace while you're dancing in the kitchen. If that was all there was to it, I didn't need it. Beautiful, but unnecessary. Maybe because that realization came right before the moment I learned how quickly love could morph into excruciating pain.

That evening I had tugged at the hem of my mother's shirt to finally pull them apart. Three-year-olds are selfish. Later that night my mother had an aneurysm and died. I wished . . . I wished I hadn't pulled at her shirt.

My father wouldn't allow me at her funeral. My aunt,

his sister, told me later it was less about me seeing my mother's urn and more about not seeing my father broken. But I did see the urn, and I did see my father broken. So, when I learned there was a profession where you got to put people back together with nuts, bolts, screws, and titanium, I was in.

Marriage was the last thing on my mind. But then I met Cameron. I thought he would prove me wrong despite all the risks he took. He convinced me he'd always be there. I was dumbstruck in love for just a little while. And then he, too, was gone, and I found myself alone once again, doubting that love could ever possibly be worth the pain.

SIX MONTHS LATER

3. Architectural Symmetry

MICAH

You know those things we do to ourselves, where we challenge God, or our own existence? Like when you say I have to reach the door before it closes otherwise someone I love will die . . . or I'll die? My therapist said it was normal, a common game we play to convince ourselves we have control over our destinies. There was nothing normal about the way I played, though. I always added a twist to raise the stakes.

Sometimes, during lunch breaks, I would wander into an empty conference room and look out the window onto Sixth Avenue below, pick out a pedestrian, and think, *If that woman doesn't reach the curb by the time the light turns green, something bad will happen to someone I love.* I know now it's a sick and demented thought. I also knew my therapist was a quack.

Theoretically, after years of playing this mind-fuck game, I should have had no living loved ones left whose survival I could toy with, but I did. Which is how I was able to constantly up the ante. My creepy little omens never worked, thank god. I had no control.

In fact, I hadn't lost anyone I was close to. The only funeral I had been to was for my eighty-three-year-old great-grandmother, whom I didn't know and who didn't know me because she'd had Alzheimer's since before I was born. So that didn't count.

Now at my cubicle, I stretched my arms and blinked away the dryness in my eyes from staring at my computer screen for so long. My focus settled on the picture frames by my desktop. My twin sister, Melissa, was fine, living a granola life in Maine with her granola boyfriend. My parents were still happily married, living on the Upper East Side in a family apartment that had been passed down from generation to generation.

Lesley and Peter Evans took the meaning of retired to a new level. They got involved in the community, played tennis, had dinner parties, and knew way too many people who worked at Tavern on the Green. I wished I was closer to them like my sister, but I had always been an introvert with difficulty welcoming commitment or intimate, close relationships. At least that's what my therapist had deduced from the months we'd spent together analyzing my quarter-life crisis.

As if my family knew they were in my thoughts, my phone lit up, showing that Melissa had sent something in our group chat. Melissa was the only person I ever opened up to. I guess when you start growing in a tiny bubble and there is one person beside you, growing in her own tiny bubble, you get a built-in best friend. I wondered if we smiled at each other from our little embryonic sacs. Even if she often spent her free time thinking of new ways to torture me, I knew she'd always have my back. She tried to encourage me to be more expressive and less inside my own head, but I was never sure exactly how to do that.

My mother used to say I didn't like being held as a baby, and as a teenager I had difficulty expressing love. Every day she would ask, "Have I told you today that I love you?"

I would automatically reply with an, "I love you, too." It was her way of getting me to say the words out loud. When you grow up in a family like mine, it should be easy to replicate the kind of openness and unconditional love you're shown as a child.

My sister had no problem saying how she felt. She was extroverted and demonstrative. I didn't understand how she and I could be so different. Fear of rejection was ingrained in me for no apparent reason. I didn't even know it was a fear until I was much older. It made me wonder if I would ever find a person I could share my life with . . . a person I wasn't afraid to express myself around.

By the time I hit twenty-nine, being an eternal bachelor sounded like a nightmare. I hoped I wouldn't always be alone, but my life was currently at a standstill.

Years after I had graduated from college, I was still twiddling my thumbs, bored at my desk at Marston, Winthrop and Galem. The once successful architectural firm turned soul killer—its sad state mostly Winthrop and Galem's doing—made me regret spending hundreds of thousands of dollars on a Harvard education. Every weekend was just a new excuse to go out with the guys at work and have banal, meaningless conversations with female clubgoers.

I doubted if I would ever have the confidence to pursue more for my life and to get out from underneath the grips of what had become a dead-end job. Had I embraced my family and social life as it were, would I have been more successful or more determined to find love and take hold of the reins in my career?

I knew I had to get a grip, but it still felt like there was something missing . . . or someone.

I hated Shelly Winthrop, and I hated Steve Galem. "Hate" is a strong word, but when you work for moral criminals, you grow to hate them. They didn't break laws, but they took credit for many of the jobs they had nothing to do with.

As for Jim Marston, he started the company, was now in his sixties, and was nearing retirement, so he was hardly ever there. He was the only one I liked and admired, a good person, unlike Winthrop and Galem. Steve Galem had stolen four of my designs in the last year, and his wife, Shelly, had made a career of sexually harassing me on a daily basis. They assigned me the stupidest jobs and, on top of all of it, I was grossly underpaid. On the rare occasion Jim Marston would come into the office, Steve and Shelly would pretend the company was killing it on the architectural scene, but it was all a facade to keep Jim quiet.

I wanted to tell him what his partners were doing to the once amazing company he had built, but I thought if I said anything, it would diminish what he had accomplished back then. His legacy. He had dreams of his daughter, Laya, taking over, but she ended up in medical school instead. So, he left the firm in the hands of two people intent on running it into the ground through sheer complacency and shady business practices.

Getting up to walk to the break room, I noticed my friend and colleague Devin was at his desk in his cube, staring at his computer screen. In all the years I had known him, I had never seen a hair out of place on Devin's head. It was cartoonish. He was always clean-shaven and wearing perfectly tailored slacks and a dress shirt with crisp, ironed-in creases.

"What do Ding and Dong have you working on today?" I said to him.

He swiveled his chair around to face me. Squinting, he said, "Are you growing a beard, man?"

I ran a palm over my rough jaw. "No, I just haven't shaved."

Devin and I had gone to Harvard together. It supposedly has the best architectural program in the world, so why we were still jerking our dicks with Steve and Shelly, the two s-holes, I'll never know. I guess it was because Jim was still there and he was genuine and kind. In the beginning I thought Devin and I could swoop in and turn things around, but that dream was quickly fading.

I was twenty-nine, single, and barely able to afford the Brooklyn apartment I shared with Jeff, another friend from college. Everything was getting old: going out, drinking, one-night stands, my job, the two hundred grand I owed in student loans. I'm sure anyone could see why I'd found myself too often sitting around playing Kill Your Loved Ones instead of doing anything productive for the firm.

I hated that about myself. It made me feel like a bad person when I knew I wasn't. I was just in a rut and overthinking everything.

Devin said, "I was sketching for a while in the studio and then Shelly came in and started rubbing up against me, asking how my day was. You know she had breast cancer, right?"

"That's terrible. I didn't know."

"She wanted me to feel her breast implants; she said they finally felt normal. I actually felt bad for her, but I wasn't about to fondle her in the drafting room."

"Why?"

"Really, Micah? Because there were seven architects in there, including fucking Freedrick . . . hail Hitler Freedrick."

"That's actually not funny at all. What did you tell Shelly?"

"I said I couldn't touch her . . . that I was mammary traumatized because my mother breastfed me until I was eight."

"Is that a real thing, mammary trauma?"

"No, but after a while you get creative with Shelly," Devin said, smirking.

"Yeah, true. You want to head out and grab lunch?"

"No way, man. Marston's coming in . . . and Laya's in town. He'll probably bring her. You've seen her, right? The gorgeous surgeon? Nice body, too; I wish she'd operate on me," Devin said.

"I saw a picture of her on Jim's desk. I wonder why he never talks about her."

"I don't know, Jim's kind of a private person. He used to talk about her more. Do you think she'll go out with me?" Devin asked.

"No," I said straight-faced. "Anyway, it's your boss's daughter and she's a doctor."

He stared at me. "Yeah, and I went to Harvard, dipshit."

"Oh right, I always forget that." I smiled and walked away.

Devin was from Los Angeles, an only child with a very large and wealthy extended family. His parents, aunts, uncles, and grandparents all doted on him. His sense of entitlement knew no bounds, and needless to say . . . neither did his bank account.

New York had always been my home, other than the four years I spent at Harvard. Growing up, I went to private schools all over the city. I didn't have childhood friends or exes, really, but I still loved being in New York. I loved walking alone and staring at all the buildings I wished I had designed. I didn't mind sitting next to strangers on the subway or eating alone. But at the same time, the thought of being alone for the rest of my life scared me.

Later, on my way to the break room for more coffee, I noticed Shelly Winthrop heading toward me, so I slipped into Devin's cube again. "Still waiting for Laya to come in?" I said, hovering over him and trying to be inconspicuous.

"Why are you leaning over me?" he asked.

"Trying to avoid Shelly. She's coming this way." Thankfully she passed us.

"Of course, I'm still waiting for Laya to get here. I'm also planning where we're headed tonight."

"You and Laya? You're that confident?" I asked.

"I think the odds are in my favor." He laughed, and when I didn't crack a smile, he said, "No, I'm kidding. I was actually thinking about us and the boys . . . what club to hit up tonight."

I shook my head. "I don't think I'm going out. I think I have an ear infection or something. I might stay late and put some time in on the Glossette model."

"Why do you help Steve? That's his deal, not yours. We're not his minions, we're architects."

"We still work for him."

"Are you prepared for Shelly's Friday night routine?"

"You mean how she always comes back to the office drunk?"

"Yes, and how she flirts with everyone in here."

"I can deal with Shelly," I said.

"You should deal with her. You should sleep with her and get it over with. It's been a while for you."

"Shhh! No, I'm not sleeping with her, and no, it hasn't been that long. I'm just tired of the same type of women, standing in lines for watered-down drinks, my ears buzzing from the shit music until four in the morning. Tired of the whole scene. And honestly, if you plan on going out with Jeff, you guys should take it back to your place, not ours."

"Yeah, I thought you seemed a little peeved last weekend."

"I don't know who she belonged to, you or Jeff, but there was a naked woman in my shower when I walked in to take a piss. She screamed and threw a bar of soap at me in my own bathroom. So, yeah, it's getting old."

"Something's going on with you. I never thought I'd see the day where Micah Evans would be complaining about having a naked woman in his shower. You were the man in college."

"I wasn't the man, I just didn't take dating seriously. The

revolving door of women in our apartment never bothered me before. But that was college. I don't want to share my bathroom with naked women I don't know."

"Why not? That sounds amazing."

I shook my head.

Things were changing. I didn't mention to Devin that after the soap flew at me, I still brazenly peed in front of the woman while she tried desperately to cover herself with the plastic shower curtain. I smiled at the memory and laughed. "Yeah, I guess I didn't expect to feel this way either."

"Three weekends in a row now you've stayed home."

"I'm in a funk. You guys have fun."

I overheard Jim's voice in his office, talking to Steve and then a woman's voice I didn't recognize. "How are my boys, Steve?" Jim asked.

"Come and see for yourself."

I turned around to see them walking down the hall in our direction. You know those moments where you think, *I know I've never met you, but we know each other?* This was one of them. From Jim's office doorway, Laya emerged, walking behind Jim and Steve. I was transfixed. Frozen in motion and expression. I couldn't even smile.

Jim said, "Micah, come and meet my daughter, Laya."

My eyes locked on hers. Tunnel vision. I took her in. She had long brown hair resting in silky curls over her shoulders, insanely green eyes, full lips, and long eyelashes. She had on cute high-waisted jeans with a tattered NASA T-shirt tucked in at the front. My eyes traveled downwards to her feet . . . Converse.

I finally got ahold of my senses. "Hello," I said, offering my hand to Laya.

She smiled and shook it. I noticed there was a sadness about her, even in her smile, and I wondered why it was there.

When I pulled my hand away, there was an electric shock from her shoes scraping the carpet. "Whoa!" she said, laughing, and then she stopped abruptly and her sad smile was back. "You look familiar. Have we met?" She squinted like she was trying to find my face in her memory. She wasn't wearing a stitch of makeup; she didn't need to.

"I might just have a familiar face," I said.

"No, like someone I've met before. Maybe I'm thinking of one of my patients who looks like you."

"I'd remember if we had met. You'd be impossible to forget." *Oh my god, did I just say that . . . right in front of her dad, my boss?*

I think I saw a blush rise on her face, but she remained stoic.

"So, you're doing your fellowship in California?" I asked.

Jim interrupted. "She was. Now she's back in New York. Doing her fellowship here. Aren't you, Laya?"

"Yeah . . . I am," Laya replied, but she didn't seem all that convincing.

"Where's big D?" Steve asked.

I don't know why Steve gave Devin that nickname, but it felt silly to hear him say it in front of Jim and Laya. Something came over me where I had a burning desire to impress Laya. I ran my fingers through my hair. Combed a hand down the scruff on my face, thinking I should have probably shaved.

"Micah . . . Devin, where's Devin?"

"Oh yeah, he's right here," I said, pointing a thumb to the back. I had no idea why Devin was being elusive when he knew Laya was standing ten feet away. He'd been waiting to see her for hours. Then it hit me . . . he wanted to impress her by being aloof and acting caught up in his work. Devin always had the wrong approach.

"Devin!" Jim called out.

He jumped out of his seat and said, "Oh sorry, I was hyperfocused on this project. Nice to see you." He held a hand out to shake Jim's. "Hello," he said to Laya with a curt smile. God, we were all being so awkward.

"This is my daughter, Laya. She was in California for four years, but she's back now."

Laya nodded and said, "I did my postgrad work there." Her tone was almost robotic, like she had said the words a million times.

"That's impressive. Isn't that impressive, Micah?" Devin said.

"Yeah, very."

From my peripheral vision I noticed Devin glancing at Laya's left hand. My eyes followed his, where I spotted a simple gold band on her ring finger. *She's married?*

The four of us continued to exchange odd pleasantries while people in the office walked past the large circle we had formed in the middle of the hall. Every man did a double-take when he saw Laya. There was something about her look that intrigued me, and apparently everyone else. It wasn't childish, even though she was dressed like a teenager; it was more like she didn't care what people thought.

Jim asked about the projects we were working on. He

seemed pleased. When they walked away, Devin and I looked at each other, stunned just by Laya's presence.

I said to Devin, "Did you know she was married?"

"I had no clue, but that's never stopped me before."

I shook my head and started walking away. "You have fun tonight with the boys."

"Come on, just go with us!" he whined.

"No!"

LATE INTO THE night I worked on the Glossette model, which was one of Steve's shitty designs for an apartment building in SoHo. Steve would land an account based on a presentation we'd all put together, and then he'd draw up a design in three days and ask one of us to build a model for it. I always tried to spruce up the models, but his designs were uninspiring square sketches, with square windows that resembled prison blocks. There was no amount of little plastic trees or fake grass I could add to improve a building design that looked like a fourth-grader had drawn it.

Shelly stumbled back into the office around ten. As soon as I heard her singing in the hall, I rushed back to my desk, grabbed my messenger bag, and tried to sneak out the back stairway.

"Micah, where are you going?"

"I have to go, Shelly."

I left the building and walked all the way up Sixth Avenue until I got to Central Park. I roamed around the outskirts, trying to get a perspective of the surrounding buildings, but New York was suffocating me. I had to get out of there. I had no creative vision anymore.

There was a time when I could see building after build-ing coming to life in the city. I had dreams of restoring New York back to the charm it once held for me. For as long as I could remember, I was building. Starting with Lincoln Logs, then moved on to Legos, and finally computer soft-ware, where I'd sit for days on end creating one design after another. People took architecture for granted sometimes— living and working in buildings, but never realizing that ar-chitects had dreamt up the layout and the functionality with them in mind. Comfortable workplaces. Homes. Places to call their own.

In college Devin and I would stay up late sketching and building innovative designs, but now work just put me to sleep. Devin was especially talented, but he, too, was losing his edge.

I was standing in front of the Guggenheim. A museum, but a building that was art in itself. Why couldn't I channel Frank Lloyd Wright? I could hop across the street to another architectural masterpiece at The Met. All of these amaz-ing structures around me and I was building tiny, perfectly square boxes for Steve.

As I sat on the train heading home, I noticed an older man in his seventies staring out the opposite window. I won-dered what he was thinking. I thought maybe he was so used to riding the train home this late that maybe he was thinking about nothing at all. Once we were in the dark tunnel with virtually nothing to look at, I noticed his expression hadn't changed.

My dad always used to say, "Micah, what are you think-ing about?"

I'd reply, "Nothing."

"If you were thinking about nothing, you'd be thinking about thinking about nothing, or you'd be dead." He'd laugh and say, "Think about it."

I guess we're always thinking; for me, maybe too much, to the point where it would stress me out. The extreme lull in my life and lack of productivity as of late made me feel hopeless and directionless.

I remember returning to the city with some friends after college ended. I had felt invigorated, like she was breathing new life into me. The beautiful and diverse skyscrapers and brownstones, the people, the sun, and the colors that painted the sky. My friends and I talked about opening our own firm and taking over the architectural scene in the city, but nothing even close to that had happened. Pretty soon the sounds and smells of the city started grating on me, and I found myself roaming Central Park on my lunch breaks more often than studying designs or drawing plans.

Now I was sitting on the train visualizing my life as some giant novel with no meaning. Fuck that damn tome. I needed to rewrite it.

No one was home when I walked in, but clearly the boys had started the party there because empty beer bottles littered the counter. I cleaned the kitchen, showered, and collapsed onto my bed.

Dozing off, my mind wandered to unintentional places: me as a giant, watching the city, the cars, and the pedestrians below me; Shelly chasing me down a long, unending hallway . . . and Laya's face, a flash of her happy expression in the picture on Jim's desk, then that quiet, sad smile. My eyes shot open.

I couldn't sleep. My right ear was starting to ache and

I hoped it wouldn't turn into an ear infection. I texted Melissa. She had nothing better to do at midnight than to talk to me and eat chia seeds.

> Me: Do you think I have some sort of complex?

Melissa: Without a doubt.

> Me: Thanks.

Melissa: What'd you do now?

> Me: Nothing abnormal for me, just basically froze in the presence of a beautiful woman. What are you up to?

Melissa: I'm making overnight muesli.

> Me: I don't even want to know what that is.

Melissa: It's healthy, you should try it.

> Me: What do you think is wrong with me freal?

Melissa: I think you say *FREAL*, for one.

> Me: Stop, Melispa, I'm serious.

Mel had a terrible lisp as a kid, so naturally as her brother I wasn't going to let her forget it.

**Melissa: My-Cunt,
you stop.**

**Me: You are so vulgar.
Just flat-out crude.
I'm calling you.
Answer your phone.**

I dialed her number, putting her on speaker while I grabbed my guitar and started strumming. "Can you give me four minutes of your precious time and tell me what I'm doing wrong?"

"For starters, you're too nice, Micah. You need to get a backbone. It's like you turn into a pile of goo when it comes to women. Hmm . . . that's making me think. No, it's like you have a fear of disappointing them, and then you turn into a pile of goo. You weren't that way in college."

"I cared less in college. I just don't know what I want anymore. I'm not worried about disappointing women, Melissa."

"Disappointing them because you have a small penis— I mean, I saw it when we were kids—"

"I'm serious, shut up. I'm not worried about disappointing anyone. I'm worried about becoming a total shut-in. And you are not helping. I feel like everything is closing in on me. On top of all of it, I think I have an ear infection."

"Does your ear hurt?"

"Yes," I said.

"Oh my god, Micah. You need to go to the doctor; my friend lost his hearing from an ear infection."

"Really?" My stomach started churning. "Where should I go?"

"To your doctor, stupid."

"I don't even have a doctor, Melissa."

"What are you gonna do in this world? I can't hold your hand through everything.

"Just go to any doctor. As far as your girl problems, I don't know what to tell you, except maybe you could try actually dating and not hanging out with Devin the devil."

"What, like, find a date online? Tinder?"

"No, Micah, like meet someone at the gym, or doing yoga, or maybe if you see a girl at a coffee shop, approach her."

If I don't hear Melissa take a breath during this pause, she'll die tomorrow.

She huffed.

"Thank god," I said.

"What? Thank god for what? You definitely have something mental going on. I probably smashed you in the womb."

"Thank god you took a breath," I said.

"You're doing that thing again. The thing you went to therapy for, aren't you?"

"Don't you do it?" I said.

"No, never. Please stop praying I'll die."

"I'm not praying . . . wishing, maybe." That definitely was not true. "I don't know; I feel like my life should be different by now. Anyway, aren't you supposed to be an all-loving flower child? All earth love and shit?"

"That's Kenny. To be honest, I'm getting tired of his

whole hippie health thing. Like fucking eat a burrito, Kenny. Everywhere we go he's gotta find a goddamn tree to hug. You're not supposed to weigh the same as your boyfriend. His boxers are NOT cute on me the way boxers are supposed to be on girls. I can't roll over the top, you know?"

"Who cares about that? Kenny's a good guy. And that weight thing is shallow and not true. You used to be such a feminist."

"I know he's a good guy. Hell, he's more of a feminist than I am. I love him; I just want him to eat a cookie and some Fritos once in a while. We were out to dinner with friends the other night and my girlfriend offered him a bite of peanut butter pie. He acted like he was offended, then later said to me in the car, 'I can't believe you ate a bite of that pie.'"

"What did you say to him?"

"Wait, are you playing the guitar while we're on the phone, Micah? You know I hate that. It's distracting."

"I'm just practicing in case this architecture thing falls through."

"Practice later—talk to me now! It's annoying."

"I'm just strumming. It calms me down. Unlike you, I can multitask," I said. "Anyway, you're just jealous 'cause Mom spent seventeen thousand dollars on piano lessons for you and you can't even play 'Chopsticks.'"

She took a loud, irritated breath. "Yes, I can."

"Exactly, that's the extent of your musical ability and you're proud of it."

Melissa was a professional subject changer. "Why don't you cave and sleep with Shelly, poor thing. Isn't her husband gay?"

"Because I don't want to sleep with Shelly, I'm not attracted to her at all . . . and her husband is one of my bosses. It's not about that anyway. I want something real, something meaningful, like you always say."

"Wow, Micah, that's awesome, but what will Devin the devil do without his wingman?"

"Devin will be fine. He has Jeff."

"Oh, how could I forget Jeff?"

"Please do not talk about him."

I've walked in on my sister having sex exactly two times. Both guys were my friends. Before Kenny, Melissa was very . . . well, friendly. But the time with Jeff was the worst. It had just gotten dark, and he had texted me that he was going out. When I got home, everything was quiet. Apparently, my sister had knocked a wineglass off his nightstand in the midst of their coital exploits in his bedroom. I, of course, thought someone was breaking in, so I quietly opened the door while yielding a butcher knife, only to hear my sister's final orgasming words. I also saw him ramming her from behind. I threw up, literally . . . on the spot. I'm not exaggerating; I threw up right there on his floor and immediately dropped the knife. My sister started laughing while she extricated herself from my roommate.

She had said, "Get a nice show, perv?" For twins, she and I were not alike at all. I was passive; she was abrasive and crass, to put it mildly.

I pushed the memory out of my mind and our conversation was back to my love life, or lack thereof. "Then sleep with the husband," Melissa blurted out. "I mean, would you ever sleep with a guy? I get that you're straight, and wouldn't want to take it up the . . . you know, but if you'd give it to a girl in the heinie, why not a guy?"

"You think *I* have brain damage? Did you forget I was born a healthy seven pounds, and you were struggling to live at four pounds, eight ounces?" Sometimes Mel was incapable of being serious. Everything turned into a joke.

"Yeah, because you're a succubus, Micah. You suck the life out of me with your indecisiveness and the eternally pensive look on your face. Also, you took all of Mom's nourishment and her attention, too. You still do."

"A succubus is a female; also, that is the wrong definition. Did you get that from *South Park*? Anyway, it feels good to be loved by Mom." I laughed. I loved teasing her about being our mom's favorite.

"Good for you. Then what do you need a girlfriend for?" She yawned loudly into the phone.

"I'll let you go."

"Micah, Mom always says you're inside your head too much. You'll never be in a committed relationship because of that. Learn to let go."

I heard Jeff and Devin stumbling around in the kitchen.

"Jeff and Devin are back. Night, Mel."

I hung up and hoped the guys didn't hear me awake. I wasn't in the mood to hang out with drunk people.

Quietly, I crawled into bed and continued to overanalyze the state of my life until I was finally feeling sleepy.

Jeff burst through the door of my room just as I clicked the bedside lamp off.

"What's up, fucker?" he slurred.

"I'm sleeping."

"Doesn't look like it."

"Well, I'm trying to. Do you need something?"

A tiny blonde was hanging on his back. "We need a condom, and I know you don't use yours, so could you spot me one?"

I opened my nightstand, grabbed a full box of condoms, and threw it at his head. "Get outta here."

"He's a dick," I heard the little sprite say just as Jeff slammed my door, shaking our tiny shoebox apartment.

After enduring the porn-like moaning from the room next to mine, I finally fell asleep, envisioning myself at sixty, sitting on a park bench, deaf from an untreated ear infection, and alone . . . utterly alone.

4. Crooked Pillar

MICAH

Months flew by like I was living in a time warp. I had grown a very long and unkempt beard. Steve asked me to shave on more than one occasion and even started assigning me jobs where I wouldn't have to interact with clients.

"It's my artistic expression," I told him. "Just like how you wear khakis and tennis shoes every day."

"Will you at least groom it? Who knows what's living in there." He walked away down the hall toward his office.

I laughed and said under my breath, "Who gives a fuck?"

He turned on his heel. "What'd you say, Evans?"

"I said I'll take care of it right away, Steve."

"You better," he said in his boss voice.

I headed down to my cubicle. The one that had renderings of my dream designs tacked to every available space on the partition. None of the drawings had come to fruition. Not surprisingly, though, there were very talented junior architects who had been at the firm longer than me who had never even gotten a raise.

Devin said from his cubicle, "Do you know how much fecal matter they find in beards?"

"I don't understand how shit gets in my beard, man. I mean, I wash it, just like the hair on my head."

"Don't shoot the messenger; I read it on the internet. Dude, you're kinda starting to look like Kaczynski."

My head shot back. "The Unabomber?"

He shrugged and turned back to look at his computer.

I thought about it. My weekends consisted of hanging out at my parents' cabin in the Adirondacks, going to see my therapist, and continually analyzing the slow decline I was still on. I needed to shave the beard, but I argued my case anyway.

"It's cool now to have a beard," I said to Devin, whose back was to me. "You know that whole No-Shave November thing?"

He turned back around. "It doesn't mean a beard like that. And November is November. One month."

"I'll shave it, I guess. What are you doing anyway?"

"Looking at Laya's Facebook page."

I squinted. "Still going for that? Her complete indifference toward you, and, oh, her *wedding ring* wasn't enough to deter you?"

Devin didn't look at me. "Have you been living in a hole, man?"

"Kind of. Why do you say that?"

Lowering his voice, he said, "Steve told me all about her. She *was* married. It was like a whirlwind romance thing. Jim wasn't too happy."

I shook my head. "I don't know where you're going with this."

"She married Cameron Bennett," he said, opening his eyes wide.

"Doesn't ring a bell."

"Dude, he's that extreme sports guy who died a while back shooting a Red Bull commercial."

"Really? Jeez. Poor Laya. So, when she was in here . . ."

He nodded. "Yeah, he was already gone. She quit everything and came back to New York. She's kind of a mess now. Steve said she's living in one of Jim's rentals in the city."

"She did seem kind of, I don't know, despondent. I wonder why Jim never said anything."

"I think she saw the whole thing. That's what Steve said."

"Why'd you wait until now to tell me? I would have said something to Jim about it. Given my condolences or something."

"Jim wasn't too keen on the marriage. Not that he wanted the guy to die, but I think, like any dad, he wanted his daughter to be with someone who didn't have the high potential for death in his workplace. Some residual fear from losing his wife so early."

"Why are you looking at her Facebook page? You actually think she'd want to move on this soon?"

"No, this is the craziest part. Steve told me she sits in her apartment posting messages on Cameron's Facebook page like he's still alive. Jim's pretty distraught and I feel bad for her, but I'm like fascinated by the whole thing."

"What, like she's in denial?"

"No, like totally delusional," Devin said.

"What is she posting?" He rolled his chair out of the way, revealing the screen.

I bent over and read her post.

LAYA BENNETT to CAMERON BENNETT

Cam, do you remember the day we met? You told me I had magical eyes. You brought flowers to my work every day for a month while your arm healed. You said I fixed you. Where are you? Come back to me. I miss you. Three. Two. One. See ya.

"That's so fucking depressing."

"On some of these posts, Cameron's mom and sister are begging Laya to stop. It's painful to read."

I shrugged. "I guess if they don't want to see the posts, they can just stay off Facebook."

"This whole thing is so bizarre."

"It's sad, is what it is," I said, staring at Laya's profile picture. She was posing next to the sign on the top of Mount Whitney with who I assumed was Cameron. "Is that him?"

"Yeah. Look at the way he looks at her. That's how I'd look at her, too."

"Devin, she's a grieving widow in denial."

He smirked. "She won't be forever."

"I'm going to pretend you didn't say that."

She was looking right at the camera, glowing and happy, and Cameron was looking at her with pride.

"I wonder what she thought of his lifestyle?" I bent and looked at the screen again. "Did they want kids?"

"No clue."

She was a natural beauty. I couldn't take my eyes off her

photo. Standing there, staring at her profile picture, I tried to recall my entire exchange with Laya that day in the office. I couldn't understand why Jim and Steve acted as though nothing had happened.

On the subway ride home that night I thought about her. I was itching to read her posts. I wondered if she was all alone in her apartment. When I pictured her sitting in the dark, my heart sank. Her story had almost immediately put things into perspective for me. Here I was walking the earth, healthy, with a loving family, loyal friends, and a decent job, yet I had spent months whining and complaining inside my head about everything. I was playing Kill Your Loved Ones, while this poor woman was grieving her husband.

When I got home that night, I searched for Cameron's Facebook account. It was public. I was able to read everything and Laya had posted again.

LAYA BENNETT to CAMERON BENNETT

Cam, remember when we went wakeboarding at the Colorado River and I didn't know I was supposed to let go of the rope when I fell? You were screaming from the back of the boat for me to let go and then you buckled over laughing while I swallowed about seventeen gallons of water? Why didn't Sven just stop the boat? Anyway, that was funny. We should go back there this summer. Three, two, one . . . see ya.

No one liked or replied to her post.

My finger sat on the cursor for an hour trying to think of how I could contact her, or if it was even appropriate to contact her, considering I was giving Devin shit for basically the same thing. I thought about the day I met her and how sweet and polite she was, even as she tried to hide all that sadness. I wanted to reach out to her, but I didn't know how. Besides, I was no one to her. Did she even remember me?

My desk at home was empty other than my computer and a picture of me and Melissa from our high school years. She had it printed and framed, then left it on my desk without telling me. Probably to annoy me since I had a relatively severe case of teenage acne and her skin had always been flawless. Melissa was consistently able to provide that certain level of comic relief to bring me out of my head. Which was exactly what I needed now. I couldn't spend the whole night thinking about Laya Bennett.

I dialed Mel's number.

"Save me and send doughnuts in a discreet package" is how she answered the phone.

"I doubt Kenny would care if you ate a doughnut, Mel."

"You'd be surprised. What's up? What are you obsessing over now?"

"Hypothetically, let's say you wanted to contact someone on Facebook—"

"Are you sleuthing, Micah?"

"What is sleuthing?"

"Like spying on someone's social media."

"Looking at social media doesn't require spying." I took a deep breath. "There's a woman I want to get in touch with, and I just wondered if sending a private message . . . you know what? Never mind. It's a bad idea."

"Most of your ideas are bad."

"I love you, too, bye."

"Call me when you decide to climb out of the black hole you're living in. Kenny grew a new strain of pot and he wants you to try it."

I sighed. "I don't even smoke pot."

"He said it'll energize your chakras."

"I'm hanging up now."

"Stop, Micah, just come out this weekend. You never come to visit me."

"I'm gonna go out to Mom and Dad's cabin. I decided just now. I need to get out of the city."

"Awesome! I'll meet you there," she said.

I really just wanted to be alone and get away from Jeff and the guys, but I figured spending the weekend with Melissa heckling me every other minute would be a nice distraction.

"All right. I'll be out there early Saturday."

"Perfect, see you then, dork," she said before hanging up.

In the morning I made coffee and sat on my countertop, staring out the kitchen window onto a large, empty courtyard. I still couldn't get Laya off my mind. Some force pulled me back to my room and to my computer where I clicked on Facebook again and found a new post from Laya.

LAYA BENNETT to CAMERON BENNETT

Remember how my dad bought us tickets to see the Stones at the Garden and you were bummed because you wanted to stay in LA and see The National at the Greek? Well, I wish I would have told you then, I would have rather seen the The National, too. Three, two, one . . . see ya.

My fingers were moving of their own accord when I bought two tickets to see The National in Forest Hills on October 5. It was the following Thursday and I paid nine hundred dollars for the front row. *What am I doing?* I printed, left the tickets on my desk, and headed into work.

Once in the office, I tried to focus on work but found it impossible. I stared at the blank drafting table, wondering whether I should message Laya and ask her to the concert, to get her out of the house. But that was too coincidental. She'd get freaked out since it'd be clear that I was reading her posts. *Stalker,* said an inside voice that sounded suspiciously like Melissa's. Then how else would I slip the ticket to Laya?

I had to distract myself so I dove back into the Glossette model. I just needed to put the finishing touches on it. My hands were sticky with glue from placing sixty tiny trees around the very ugly miniature building.

"You have glue in that beard," Freedrick said as he walked by.

I don't care. Everyone called it "that beard" like it wasn't attached to my face. Like it had its own identity.

With sticky hands, a coffee-stained dress shirt on, and a sour look on my face, I took the model into Steve's office.

"What's that?" he said, sitting in his giant leather chair, his feet perched on the desk. Doing nothing—which wasn't surprising.

"It's your design for the Glossette building."

"It looks like an elementary school project." He arched his eyebrows. From the distance he was at, there was no way he could have actually gotten a good look at it.

Trying to contain the anger boiling over in me, I said, "I spent a lot of time on it, Steve, and—"

"Start over."

"But I followed your design and the blueprints to a T."

He looked around the room like he was bored before getting up and walking toward the door. "Make a new design then," he said.

"Steve, hold on. I want credit for my work."

"You'll get the credit, Mr. Harvard." He pointed to the model I'd spent hours on and said, "We can't take that to the clients."

If Steve wasn't five inches shorter than me, with baby-boy arms and a beer belly, I would have smashed the model on top of his head. Instead I followed him out of the room, bent the model in half, and shoved it into the trash. As he was walking down the hall away from me, I made a point of saying, just loud enough for everyone to hear, "If it's my design and my work, I want the credit." I was tired of doing other people's shit.

"Okay, Micah, do the work, then . . . and shave that damn beard!" he spat back. Now I was determined to go completely ZZ Top.

Later that night, in my room, while drawing sketches for the new Glossette building, my eyes kept darting over to the concert ticket receipt sitting on the corner of my desk. The only way this could work was if she didn't know that I was leaving it for her. I had to give it to her, but not directly. I tapped my pencil against my chin.

Devin said she was living at one of Jim's properties. Maybe I could leave it in her mailbox or on her mat. But I wasn't about to stroll into Jim's office the next day and ask him which property.

Maybe Mel could help me find Laya's address. She'd

always been good with the internet—well, at least better than me. *No, Micah, another one of your bad ideas.*

SATURDAY AROUND ELEVEN in the morning, I met Mel at our parents' twin-birch cottage overlooking Indian Lake in the Adirondacks. She was standing at the end of our long private dock with her head cocked to the side, staring at me as I came toward her. "What, did you walk here?" she said. She was wearing a giant wool sweater over our father's wading overalls and our mother's rubber boots.

I sat next to her and inhaled the crisp, cold air, free of the smog and dumpster smell I was used to in the city. "I had to borrow Jeff's car. I left at six this morning. Why are you wearing that?"

She shook her head—and ignored my question. "It's almost exactly the same distance from my house and I left at six. I've been waiting for you for an hour."

We never hugged; outward expressions of love were unnecessary for us. "Well, you must've driven a hundred miles an hour in that old Subaru Forester of yours. Again, why are you wearing that shit?"

She clapped her hands together and said, "We're going fishin', little brother."

"I just wanted to relax. And I thought you were a vegetarian."

"That's Kenny, not me. And fishing is relaxing."

"Okay, fine, but you'll never win. I still hold the record here."

She rolled her eyes. "If you're talking about that stupid little one-pound trout you caught when you were twelve, I hate to break this to you, but Dad made you hold it forward in the picture to make it look bigger."

"Whatever you say, game on. Let's go!"

Inside the tiny cabin with its stone fireplace framed by two creepy iron sconces, I studied the picture sitting on the mantel. Okay, it was a tiny fish . . . and I *was* holding it forward to make it look bigger. While Mel packed a lunch, I put my dad's boots on and set up his tackle box and poles.

"Just so you know, I'm not going to tie your line, or spend all day baiting your hooks every time you cast into the trees!" I yelled to Mel.

"I just spit in your peanut butter and jelly sandwich," she replied.

Moments later I was rowing our small white boat out to the middle of the lake while Melissa thumbed through a fishing guide.

"You studying?"

"I hardly brought any food, so you better hope we catch something besides pulmonary influenza," she said, shivering.

"That's a myth. You don't get the flu from being cold."

"Let's not talk to each other for a while."

"Sounds like a dream."

An hour into fishing, the score was tied zero to zero. Mosquitoes landed and lifted off the water surface. A few birds dove toward the lake before taking flight again, their search for food unavailing. My teeth were starting to chatter, but I embraced the cold. It made my thoughts feel more focused, and I realized, as I was waiting for a bite, that Laya hadn't crossed my mind in a while.

"We're never going to catch anything," Melissa whined.

"It's only been an hour."

"Tell me about the girl you're stalking on the internet." Did she read my mind?

"No, and I'm not stalking anyone."

Melissa casted her line again and it got caught on the back of my jacket just below my neck. "Shit," she said as she tugged on it, trying to free it from my clothing.

"Oh my god, you're the worst! Stop yanking on it; you're going to rip my ear off." The boat was dangerously rocking back and forth, and our yells interrupted a family of ducks floating nearby.

Forgetting her question about Laya, Melissa gave up. "We're not going to get anything here. Let's go." As I tried to pull her hook out of my coat, my sister grabbed the oars and started rowing us back to shore.

We spent the rest of the afternoon and evening reading and ignoring each other until Melissa finally said, "You can talk to me. Tell me about the Facebook thing."

I was wearing my dad's dusty argyle smoking jacket and had an empty pipe hanging out of the side of my mouth. Melissa was eating peach preserves straight from the jar and sitting in an old rocker near the fireplace.

"This is how my life will be. How terrifying," I pondered aloud.

"You look like Dad," she said. "That pipe is ridiculous."

"Well, you look like Mom . . . this is freaking me out."

"I'm kidding; get over it. Though I do spot some gray in that beard." *That beard.* I took the pipe out of my mouth, wondering if I should divulge any information about Laya to Melissa. Again, as if she could read my mind, she said, "Go after what you want and get it."

"I'm going to," I said in all seriousness.

"Just don't spend all your money and blow our inheritance before Mom and Dad kick the bucket."

"Thank you, Melissa, for always knowing exactly the right words to say. I'm going to bed."

"'Night," she said, smirking.

Melissa left early the next morning, and I spent most of the day sketching designs in the cabin. Without internet service, it's pretty hard to sleuth anyone. I was grateful for it and thought maybe I should live out my days in the old cabin on the lake. But the more time I spent away from the computer, the further I was getting from Laya and her thoughts—from getting to know her.

5. Time and Space

LAYA

When I left California, I told everyone I was going to complete my fellowship at The Hospital for Special Surgery in New York because I wanted to be closer to home. I never even applied. Even Dad bought the story, as if I'd be able to function normally. He kept telling me I was always stronger than he was. My psychiatrist actually gave me a grief timeline. Like in three months, I'd stop replaying the image of Cameron dying over and over in my head.

Three months flew by and I still thought I saw Cameron on every corner, in every grocery store line, and at every subway station. I got a lot of advice on how to grieve from everyone I knew, as if they understood. Some random Thursday I got drunk and walked seven blocks to a hypnotist. He said he was going to erase the memory of Cameron dying. Like the movie *Eternal Sunshine of the Spotless Mind* with Kate

Winslet, I would just magically forget Cameron ever existed. It didn't work.

Sitting around my dusty and dark apartment scattered with medical journals and unopened boxes, I cried every night. I forced myself to eat saltines and drink chicken broth like I had a perpetual flu. That's how grief felt, like a sickness.

I couldn't remember exactly what it looked like when Cameron hit the cliff. Maybe I had always made it up in my mind. I think I had closed my eyes, like I knew he was too close. I saw it coming. Everyone was pointing, the helicopter swooped by and headed in the opposite direction and I wondered what they were doing. I might not have seen it, the moment of impact, but we all heard it. I'll never forget that sound.

So, it'd been months. Measuring time was hard for me. I was supposed to be normal, but instead I'd sit there drinking vodka in the dark until it didn't taste like vodka anymore. The apartment my dad was letting me live in had floor-to-ceiling windows. I would stare outside all day, wondering how the hell I ended up jobless and alone.

Cameron's phone sat on the coffee table, endlessly vibrating as I dialed his number over and over again. I held my own phone against my ear, listening to the end of Cameron's outgoing message. I tried to hold on to his voice. It was something I did often.

When his phone would get to 10 percent, I'd pretend he was dying all over again. Ten percent—that was around the time we had met, when only 10 percent of his life was left. I thought about what I would have done differently in the short time we had together. He was twenty-seven and I was twenty-six. He only had three years of life left to go. When the battery would get to 1 percent, I'd think about our wedding day, about how we said forever, the rest of our lives, and it only actually meant one year . . . the rest of Cameron's life. Now it was forever for me.

Maybe he was the lucky one. I didn't want forever—not like this.

I sat with my back against my bed's headboard, thinking about the way Cameron said my name differently than anyone else. He put more emphasis on the last *a*, like my name was floating upward when it came off his lips. I wished I were floating upward toward him now. I looked down at his phone. Now it was finally at 1 percent.

His inbox would fill up soon, so I'd need to delete messages from his phone. I needed to make space to talk to him still.

"This is Cam, you know what to do, silly. Text me like a normal person."

"Hey, Cameron. It's me. Your friend wants to make a movie about you. A documentary. Ha! Should I give him all our footage? I wish you all would have turned that fucking camera off once in a while. I'm going to bed."

After sleeping with the phone still to my mouth, I woke up to someone banging on my front door. When I opened it, I saw Krista, Cameron's sister, standing on the landing with her hand on her hip.

"I came to get you out of the house." She walked past me into the apartment. "It's smells like booze and rotten food in here."

"That would be accurate."

It was hard to look her in the eye. Krista reminded me of Cameron, with those warm brown eyes and almost impossibly blond hair to match her fair skin. She was athletic, a daredevil like Cameron.

She was still planning to free-climb El Cap in the spring even though their parents had just lost one child. And for what? Some adrenaline? A Red Bull contract?

Krista started scurrying around, cleaning up dirty dishes and trash from the floor.

"Where are we going?" I asked her.

"Somewhere, the park, I don't know. Just get dressed."

"Is there something wrong with what I'm wearing?" I was wearing the same sweats I'd had on for three days.

"No. Maybe grab a sweater . . . " She paused from her cleaning to look up at me. There was sympathy in her expression. "Maybe run a comb through your hair."

She was grieving, too, but Krista was strong. Stronger than me, it seemed. "I didn't know you'd be in New York," I said.

"I'm only here for a few days. Your dad asked me to come."

"Why?"

"He's worried about you."

"So he called you? To keep track of me?"

She turned and scowled. "He called me because he knew I had seen the posts. He wanted me to talk to you about it."

"I don't want to talk about it."

"Everyone is hurting, Laya. Everyone!"

I hated that my dad thought someone needed to check

on me. I hated that Krista was here, seeing me like this. "Why are you doing it? Why are you *still* doing the stunts, even after your brother died doing the same thing? What are you trying to prove?"

"This isn't about me," she said harshly.

"You're right. This is about Cameron and the risks he's willing to take, despite the fact that we are in love. And the risks you are willing to take, despite the fact that people love you," I said in an equally angry tone.

Krista stared at me, blinking. Then I realized my slip-up, but I still couldn't correct myself out loud. I wouldn't say "he was" and "we were."

Her voice went soft. "Laya, please go brush your hair. We're going to leave in five minutes." Seeing the change in her expression suddenly made me feel like someone else — someone I didn't like at the moment. Krista was Cameron's sister. She was in the same boat as me.

I rushed off to the bathroom with both my phone and Cameron's in hand. What would Krista say if she saw that I still had it? Sitting down on the toilet with the cover down, I dialed his number again.

"Hey, Cam. When the fuck is this nightmare going to be over? Come back, please. I can't stand this."

I threw his phone in the bathroom trash can, combed my hair, and walked to the front door with my head down.

Krista and I sped through Central Park without saying much to each other. I had both hands tucked inside my sweatshirt, wishing I'd worn more layers. Krista, even being from California, didn't flinch at the wind tunnel that we came across. I'd forgotten how unusual a place the park could be—a place of silence compared to the taxis racing down one-way streets and people shoving past one another with their shoulders and elbows. The surrounding trees cut down the harshness of the sun. As much as I hated to admit it—and I wouldn't to Krista—I felt better being outside.

"Are you hungry?" Krista asked at one point.

"Does a bear shit in a toilet?"

"Funny. You need to eat. What are you living on, Top Ramen and vodka?"

"Just vodka."

"You need to stop with the posts. People are worried about you."

She stopped walking and looked over at the crowd gathering around the John Lennon *Imagine* mosaic etched on the ground. People had left him flowers and candles for his upcoming birthday.

"Did you know this whole triangular piece of land was designed by Bruce Kelly, the chief landscape architect for the Central Park Conservatory?" I asked. "That mosaic stone is modeled after the pavement that's all over Portugal."

"I didn't know that. I bet you know a lot about architecture."

"They call this section Strawberry Fields." I smiled wryly. "There are no strawberry fields here."

The sun went down behind the buildings, the wind kicked up, and the trees rustled around us. I shivered. Krista, in an uncharacteristic gesture, wrapped her arm around my shoulder.

"I never asked you: Why did you want to become a doctor, Laya? Why didn't you take over your father's firm? And don't give me some canned response like you wanted to help people."

I pointed. "You see that building right across the street?"

She nodded.

"That's the Dakota. The apartment building where John Lennon was murdered. They came over here to the park and they tried to put him back together with some trees, a few benches, some concrete, shrubs, and that mosaic. Ha! That's what my father wanted to do before he started designing condos. He wanted to design memorials. He thought he could put my mother back together with some stone and concrete pillars."

Krista took a while to respond, and when she did, her voice was clogged. "Maybe it's not about putting John Lennon back together. Maybe it was about putting the people who loved him back together. It's like filling a space . . . a void."

I looked up at her and noticed a stray tear running down her cheek. We walked closer to the *Imagine* circle and sat on the bench nearby, watching person after person kneel on the stones, leave gifts, and smile while someone took a picture of them. I thought, *Why are they smiling? The guy was murdered right across the street. Did they love him? Are they healed by this memorial?*

"Well, I guess you're right," I said.

"What?"

"I guess I became a doctor because I wanted to put together all the pieces of the broken people hobbling around, miserable and shattered like my father after my mother died." I inhaled shakily. "But I'm not sure that's possible anymore. I can't even put myself back together."

Krista placed a hand on mine before gripping it. I squeezed back. "When I climb, I look for space between the rocks. I fill that space so I can go higher and higher, but it takes patience, time . . . courage. The higher I go, the more courage I have."

I understood Krista. She wasn't a mindless fool just BASE jumping off buildings and risking her life for no reason.

"The only space I know is infinite," I told her. "There's no filling it."

"Just takes time, baby," she said, her words echoing Cameron's.

6. Wood Clapboards

MICAH

The break room smelled strongly of onions and sour milk.
I was retreating into myself again. Everything annoyed me:
the way Jenny, the admin assistant, slurped Greek yogurt off
the end of her spoon, to the way Devin removed a stringy
onion from his turkey sandwich, lifted it into the air, and
dropped it into his mouth like a baby bird eating a worm. I
walked by them both and held my breath.

"Dude, where have you been?" Devin asked, with a
mouth full of turkey. "You haven't been to work in days.
Shelly said you had the flu but Jeff said you haven't been
home. Are you ever gonna shave?"

"I was sick. I didn't want to get Jeff sick so I stayed out at
my parents' cabin," I said, which was half true.

I had lost time out there, which wasn't unusual for
me. I read and worked on sketches, but other than that,

not a whole lot after Melissa left. I didn't even shower or eat much out there; I just tried to focus on the Glossette design.

"Right, man. Was it that phantom ear infection again?" Devin was onto me, but he didn't push me. He knew if he pushed me, I'd retreat further.

"That was real. I had to put drops in my ears."

"Whatever you say," he said as I headed back to my cubicle.

It was true. The ear infection was real and exacerbated by my sister's overreaction. The flu, however, was just an excuse to take time off work.

The only reason I had come out of the cave, so to speak, was because it was Thursday and The National was playing in Forest Hills. I managed to get the ticket to Laya by putting it under her mat. I had checked my computer the day before when I got home from the cabin and noticed she had posted on Cameron's page just then.

LAYA BENNETT to CAMERON BENNETT

I'm going to Doughnut Planet to get your favorite square doughnuts. I love that even though you take such good care of yourself, you'll never pass up a doughnut. Three, two, one . . . see ya.

I hated feeling like a stalker but it was the only way I could find out where she lived. There was only one Doughnut Planet in New York and it was a half hour away by car—Jeff's car. He wasn't bugging me, so I guessed he didn't need it right away after I had come back from the cabin.

I couldn't take the chance of not catching Laya, so I

drove into Manhattan—without much traffic, miraculously—
and stood across the street from the doughnut shop. I felt like
a homeless person, with my scruffy beard . . . and I was sure I
smelled like a mixture of dusty cabin, old fishing tackle, and
pencil shavings from endless hours of sketching.

Luckily, I couldn't miss her even if I tried. Her beauty
was electric. She was wearing sweats, her hair was in a
messy bun, no makeup, just natural transcendent beauty.
She came out carrying a huge box like she was going to feed
doughnuts to the entire neighborhood. She looked thin, so
I doubted she'd had any fried dough lately. She walked fast
down two blocks and jogged up four moss-covered stairs to
a creaking door she opened, entered, and slammed shut. I
waited fifteen minutes across the street before approaching
the front door. On the buzzer, there was only one name . . .
Bennett. I slid The National ticket under the door, rang
the buzzer, and walked back to Jeff's car without turning
around.

Back at work, after the casual banter with Devin in the
break room, I sat at my desk and couldn't help but click on
Facebook. I read Laya's latest post and started shaking, like
Earth was crumbling beneath my feet.

LAYA BENNETT

To whoever left The National ticket under my mat . . .
is that your idea of a joke? Well, it's sick.

Damn! That was not my intention. Why was this affect-
ing me? Why did I care?

I jerked my head back when I noticed Devin peeking
over my shoulder. I quickly exited out of Facebook. "I didn't

think you went on Facebook," he said. He looked at me sideways and smirked. "You used to call it Fakebook, and say how everything on there is some person's way of making their life look better than it is. So why are you looking at it if you feel that way?"

He was right. I had always had that opinion, but I still had a compulsion to look at it daily since I had learned about Laya's posts. I couldn't look away from Laya if I tried. It was a secret and I was a hypocrite. All the posts from other people seemed so unrealistic; it made me think I was a shell of a person. I hadn't gone to the Bahamas and taken eight thousand selfies on the beach. I would never even think of posting a picture of a pretty salad I ate at a trendy restaurant. It all seemed so distorted.

Now Laya's posts were the most distorted of all, and yet I couldn't look away.

Is it because no matter the illusion, we can still see some truth? We can still see inside a person if we look closely enough at their insincere words, or their perfectly smiling faces. It was no different with Laya; she was posting as if everything were perfect even though we all knew the truth. Everyone knew the truth.

"I was just trying to kill time before Dickface comes in to look at my sketches." My response was good enough to distract Devin.

"He's out for the day. We're free!" He grinned.

"Is Shelly here?"

"She doesn't give a shit," he said. "Let's go get a slice at Roberta's."

"I'm gonna go home, I think. Work a little from there."

"Suit yourself." He shook his head.

I went back to looking at Laya's profile picture. Was she happy to be on that mountain? Had she sensed some kind of doom?

No one responded to her post about the ticket. I didn't think in a million years she'd show up, but I was going anyway. I had to see what she so badly wished she and Cameron would have experienced.

WHEN I GOT to the venue, I grabbed a beer and found my seat quickly. I had been to concerts alone before, but this time it felt strange. I rubbed my jaw. I hadn't shaved the beard. I didn't want her to recognize me. What if she did show up? I thought it would look odd, two loners sitting side by side, so I tried to strike up a conversation with the woman to my right, who was sitting with, I assumed, her husband. "You ever see The National before?"

"Yeah, this is our fourth time." She held up the universal *shoosh* symbol and smiled. I hadn't realized the opening act was on and I was trying to talk through it.

I heard Laya's voice before I saw her. "Excuse me, excuse me, can I get through? Also, thanks for the contact high, asshole."

She plopped into the seat next to mine and I couldn't bring myself to look over at her. When The National finally came on, everyone stood, including Laya. Most people screamed, but she was quiet. I finally glanced over just in time to catch a tear fall from her right eye, down her expressionless face. "Pure pain" were the words that came to my mind. I had to look away, but not before she glanced up at me. She didn't smile; she just stared.

I smiled anyway, then focused on the stage. I wondered if she had recognized me from months back when we met in the office. I only had scruff then, no beard . . . and she seemed pretty out of it, so I hoped my face wasn't sounding any alarms. About halfway through the set, when the lights were extremely low, I finally got the nerve to turn to her and say, "I'm headed to the bar. Would you like a beer?"

She squinted, confused, and then she said, "Sure, I guess. Whatever they have that's strong." She stuck her hand out to shake mine. "Thanks, I'm Laya."

"Bradley," I said quietly. I couldn't tell her my real name.

"Nice to meet you," she said.

"Likewise."

I finally caught a hint of a smile. It was pathetic that I was getting excited over a monumentally distraught woman smiling at me.

There weren't many choices at the bar, so I got her a white wine and when I returned, she stared at it in my hand. "There was nothing stronger so I figured wine? I hope that's okay."

She looked as if she were in a daze, or lost in a memory, or maybe she *had* recognized me. She finally shook her head and said, "No, it's great. Thank you." I could barely hear her so she had to lean in close to my ear. I could smell her lemongrass shampoo. The drums and guitars grew louder. I looked up to see the lead singer, Matt Berninger, hop off the stage, a crowd swarming around him. Everyone in the front-row seats where we were sitting moved forward into a herd, including Laya and me.

The band was singing "Graceless," one of my favorite songs, but the tempo was faster. Without even realizing it, the lead singer was heading in our direction, singing directly to different people. The crowd was bouncing up and down, including Laya. Matt moved toward her and shared the microphone as they both screamed the line, "Just let me hear your voice, just let me listen!"

She was smiling and laughing. It had to have been kismet. Were those the words she needed to scream out loud to a crowd? When the singer moved away and back toward the stage, Laya was still laughing hysterically. It had to be the most beautiful and genuine sound. Like maybe she hadn't laughed in a really long time.

"That was fucking crazy!" she yelled, moving closer to my ear.

"I know, right?"

"Hey, I meant to ask, how much do I owe you for the wine?"

I shook my head. "It's on me."

"No, really, I don't want you to buy me a drink." Her expression fell as she riffled through her purse for money.

"It's just a drink. Don't worry about it."

"Okay." She looked away and finished her wine in three large gulps. She was still happily bouncing to the music. I hoped she was able to escape her grief for a few minutes, but it wasn't long before everything shifted. The next song, "Vanderlyle Crybaby Geeks," was slow and somber. She sang the words, "Vanderlyle, crybaby, cry," while tears were streaming down her face. She tried to hide it. It was almost the end of the show when she darted out of the crowd and headed for the exit.

I followed her, hoping she wasn't going to run out and throw herself into oncoming traffic. She looked back and spotted me. Her pace sped up like she was trying to get away from me. I was still carrying half of my beer when she turned so abruptly that the beer cup shot out of my hand and landed on her shoes. When I looked down, I noticed she had two different shoes on. One dark-beige flat and the other black, but a similar style.

"Oh my god, I'm an idiot. I'm so sorry," I said.

She just stared at her shoes for several moments.

"I don't care," she replied.

"I'll replace them. Is that a style, like a new trend? I'll replace them," I repeated.

"It's not a style; I put the wrong damn shoe on," she said. "Are you following me?"

Our gazes caught each other and for a moment we were frozen. I was searching her eyes but they looked empty.

"No, I was going to offer to share a cab?"

Her head jerked back as though I had offended her. "I'll take the subway."

"I mean, it's late; you should get a cab."

"No, thanks. I'll be fine."

That was it. She spun around on her beer-soaked shoes and was gone.

Damn it.

7. Ground Control, Are You There?

LAYA

I rushed toward the E train entrance outside while dialing Cameron's number. On the subway platform, I took several long breaths while I listened to his outgoing message.

"This is Cam, you know what to do, silly. Text me like a normal person."

"Cam, I finally got to see The National. They were great. Wish you could have been there. The lead singer jumped down and sang right to me. I was alone but I didn't feel lonely for the first time in a while. Gotta go. Three. Two. One. See ya."

The subway was coming to a stop. I got on and was left only with my thoughts. I was oddly attracted to the man standing next me at the concert, and I felt guilty for that. He was tall, a whole head taller than me. It looked like I could fit my head right underneath his chin, like a perfect little nest. For being a thin guy, he had nice biceps and a broad chest. He smelled clean, just a hint of aftershave. He was dressed casually in jeans, sneakers, and a heather-gray T-shirt. He reminded me of someone. Then again, my mind was constantly playing tricks on me, especially when it came to seeing Cameron. I didn't know who I was seeing in everyone else's face. Sometimes it felt like everyone I came into contact with somehow knew I was self-destructing.

I fell asleep immediately after crawling into bed. It could have been the wine. It could have been the exhaustion from actually leaving my apartment.

LOOKING AT THE calendar, I tried to figure out what day it was. The National ticket stub had the date on it and I figured it had been two days since the show. I hadn't been out of the apartment or even looked at my phone. I'd barely done anything but sleep the entire time.

My room smelled and looked like a teenager lived in it, complete with my frilly peach comforter and bedside table and lamp to match. My father had whipped them out of storage the instant I'd said I was moving back to New York. My dad had even hung a poster from the space camp I went to as a kid. The only thing left that my room needed was a lava lamp and some Skittles.

The phone rang. The caller ID said it was Cameron's mom. I answered in two rings. "Hello, Carin."

"Laya. Thank you for the pictures. I do appreciate the gesture. It's so nice to see Cameron doing what he loved."

Her words stung. *He loved me and I'm not in any of those pictures.*

A week or two prior I had been sifting through a box of pictures. Mostly they were of Cam, only a few of us together. Tears soaked half of the stack. I didn't need any more reminders of him diving off cliff faces or scaling rock walls, so I sent half of them to his mom. I kept the few I had of him lounging on the beach, smiling. Or the two of him eating a giant steak. I don't know why, but I needed to remember that Cameron was normal sometimes. He wasn't always just a character in some daredevil video.

"You're welcome. You deserve them," I told Carin.

She started to cry. "God, Laya, I miss him so much."

Her tears should have moved something inside of me, but I was out of sympathy at the moment. I was sad, angry, and full of questions. I had never confronted her before and I hated to do it, but I needed to know. "Carin, why did you let Cameron do it? Why'd you encourage him to quit school and pursue this life? Why do you still encourage Krista? You know what could happen. Letting her free-climb El Cap is crazy."

Looking around my living room, I noticed that the layer of dust on every piece of furniture had grown so much my entire apartment looked gray. There was a sheet over the couch because I never sat on it, a toppled-over lamp, a box of rotten doughnuts, and a few pairs of dirty socks . . . and that was just one room. I guessed that if I walked outside for a few minutes and then came back in, I would notice the smell of a decaying animal somewhere.

I shuffled into my room while I listened to Carin cry on the other line. The right side of my bed had an indentation in it from where I spent many nights crying and drinking alone. In the kitchen, the sink was so full of dishes that I could see the stack spilling over the top lip from ten feet away. I had lost twenty pounds, so I estimated the stack had been built up over at least a month, probably since the last time I had talked to Carin.

Carin's cries started to subside. "Laya?" she asked.

"I'm here." My anger was quiet but still there. Carin and I had grown close in the short amount of time Cameron and I had been together, but because of the Facebook posts she had pulled away, told me I was delusional, that I was hurting everyone and needed to get help. I'd told her to stay off Facebook. I didn't think it was fair. I still needed a way to talk to him. Why couldn't she understand that?

"You know as well as I do that Krista and Cameron are adults who make their own decisions," she said. "I know what made Cameron feel most alive, Laya. How could I take that away from him?" She started sobbing again.

Who's delusional now? "Cameron *was* an adult. Do you want to say that about Krista, too?"

"I thought you believed Cameron was out there somewhere, even though you and all his friends and family paddled out and spread his ashes in the ocean?"

Not all of his ashes.

"I have to go, Carin. I'm sorry I can't talk about this anymore; I have things to do today." What a colossal lie that was.

"Laya, can you please call me back?"

"I have a lot to do, I'm very busy . . ." I hesitated, trying to hold back my own tears. "Carin . . . I wanted to make Cameron feel most alive, okay?" I hit *end* before she could respond.

I spent the better half of my morning staring at the same pictures of Cameron. I picked up his urn from the mantel, what was left of his ashes I couldn't let go of, and then I went to my computer and posted on his page.

LAYA BENNETT to CAMERON BENNETT

I was thinking about taking the subway to Brooklyn, like we used to do when we'd visit New York. I was thinking about the time you bought roses off the street vendor and all the petals fell off on the subway by the time we got to Brooklyn. There was a beautiful mess on the floor of the train. You're my beautiful mess, Cameron. Three, two, one . . . see ya.

Much later, on my way out to get some air, I paused halfway down the stairs and thought about that day. Cameron had stood on the very edge of the subway platform, past the yellow line. I had told him to step back, but he ignored me. It was like he was always missing the part of his brain that warned him of danger. Not only was he a daredevil, but he trusted everyone. He'd always say, "People are innately good and mean well."

When I reached the bottom of the steps going out to the street, I found six red roses and an envelope attached. The envelope had my name on it.

I tore it open, revealing a MetroCard. It was official: I had a stalker who was exploiting my husband's death to get close to me. I wasn't sure what to do. Shoving the Metro-Card into my pocket and leaving the flowers, I pulled my phone from my purse and posted on Facebook as I headed toward the subway.

LAYA BENNETT

Hey, lunatic. If your desired effect is to get arrested and charged with harassment, then keep doing what you're doing. If you're trying to help, you have a seriously fucked-up idea of helping someone.

Still, I used the MetroCard to explore the city. I wondered if the person leaving things on my doorstep really was crazy, or if it was a friend trying to make me feel better. I regretted my post, but left it up in hopes that I'd find the answer eventually.

After getting on the subway, walking a block, and getting back on until the twenty-dollar card ran out, I walked home exhausted and fell onto my bed, thinking about the day I took Cameron all over New York. It was a happy day. I estimated that he'd had only about 7 percent of his life left when he saw Times Square for the first time. I fished Cameron's phone out of the bathroom wastebasket. The moment I glanced at it, the battery went dead.

I plugged his phone in next to my bed and fell asleep, chanting in my head, *Come back to me.*

8. Exposed Rafters

MICAH

I shaved the fucking beard and put on deodorant. Progress. It was a Friday, and before I headed into the office I had to check Facebook, of course.

> **LAYA BENNETT to CAMERON BENNETT**
> Cam, it's Friday. I'm going dancing. I'm going to that club we used to go to when we'd visit New York. You know, the Top of The Standard? Maybe you'll be there. I need to get out. Three, two, one . . . see ya.

This time I was sure she would recognize me, so I needed backup. In the office Steve and Shelly were out for the day. Freedrick, the non-German, was being obnoxious, acting as though he was our interim boss. He did it because he'd been there the longest out of all the junior architects. I always went along with it. Devin didn't. Devin had actually learned to pull off a pretty decent German accent.

"Devin, what's the progress on those sketches you're working on?" Freedrick asked, while I eavesdropped from my cube.

"Vell, Freeed-rick, I do vonder vye you're asking me such tings, ven you're not even my boss. Rrrrr-move yourself from my space."

"Why are you talking like that?" Freedrick asked.

"Sheer boredom. Pure and simple," Devin replied.

Freedrick shuffled down the hall, mumbling something about respect. I stood and leaned over Devin's cubicle partition. "You want to go to The Top of the Standard tonight?"

He looked at me like I had two heads. Squinting, he said, "Micah, is that you? Did you come back to us?" His face scrunched up and he actually started fake crying. Why hadn't he become an actor?

"Shut up, man," I said, rolling my eyes.

"Dude, you shaved your beard, and it smells like you might have showered or at least put deodorant on. What's going on with you?"

"I'm just opening the blinds. I was in a rut," I said.

"Do you mean you might want to get laid after a year and a half?"

It should have been concerning that Devin knew how long it had been for me, but I tried to ignore it. "Huh?" I said with mock confusion.

He shook his head. "I'm shocked, Micah, honestly . . . in the way a person is shocked when they win the lottery. These are happy tears."

"Enough with the theatrics. Let's meet at your apartment at ten, okay?"

"You got it."

For the next two hours Devin sang that Michael Bublé song about it being a new day. I wondered if I had made a mistake.

WEARING MY WORK clothes sans tie, I headed to the Top the of Standard, where everyone was already drinking Manhattans and Old-Fashioneds, and Devin was blabbering about bottle service. I was just wondering how I would spot Laya. Again, in the back of my mind, I wondered if she would even be there. If I saw her, what would I say? Jeff was there with friends and a few guys they'd adopted since I'd stopped going out with them. They liked this spot.

When I sat down at the booth, they made a crude toast about me using my dick again. I laughed it off, but the toast just reminded me of why I had stopped hanging out with them to begin with.

After only being there for ten minutes, I spotted Laya standing next to the bar, alone and quiet. She was wearing a tight black dress. Her hair was pulled back. Nothing like the Laya I had seen before, but still beautiful. When she headed to the restroom, I got up and followed.

"Hey!"

She turned around and stared at me with no recognition. "Hello," she said.

"You're Laya, right?"

She stepped forward and squinted. "Why'd you say my name like that?"

"Like what?"

"You said the *a* differently."

I wasn't sure what she meant. "I didn't notice . . . I'm Micah, from your dad's firm."

"Oh yes, Micah, the golden boy. My dad always talks about you. Where's Devin, your prodigy sidekick?"

She didn't have much makeup on, just red lipstick. What was she looking for? She seemed a bit tipsy. She stumbled back awkwardly, so I reached around her waist and caught her. I removed my arm when I realized she was staring at it in shock.

"Devin is in a booth with some friends," I said to break the uncomfortable silence.

"Ahh." She raised her eyebrows and smirked. Her expression had changed to *what the fuck do you want?*

"Who are you here with?" I asked.

"I'm alone."

"Do you want to come and hang out with us?"

The music got louder and more annoying. The *unce-unce* beat was giving me a headache.

"Not particularly!" she yelled.

"Well, Laya—"

Her eyes widened. "There it is again. You say my name differently." She grabbed my shirt and pulled me toward her.

"What? What? What's going on?" I said, genuinely confused.

"Come with me."

"Where?"

"In here."

She pulled me down the hall into a dark alcove, then kissed me. I was dumbstruck. Her lips were soft; she tasted like wine but smelled like beautiful things, like what I imagined the ocean under a sunset would smell like. She went for the buckle of my pants and I didn't stop her even though in the back of my mind I knew it was wrong. I should have stopped her and asked her out on a date or for her number or for something normal, but I seemed to lose all self-control with her.

She was a passionate kisser, passionate everything. When she pulled away, she said, "My father always wanted me to be an architect. And to be with someone *like you*."

I wished the "like you" statement sounded less spiteful. She undid my buckle and hiked up her skirt, wrapping a leg around me.

"Whoa, Laya."

"Stop saying my name," she whispered, her breath hot against my ear.

"We're basically in public. What are you doing?"

"No one comes back here. Make me feel good. Please."

Her head fell back. She exposed her neck to me. I pressed my lips along her jawline. I cupped her breast, then kissed it through the fabric. Her hand was on me, touching me roughly. I groaned. She wasn't gentle and it made me want her even more.

Laya stopped kissing me and pressed her forehead against mine. Her eyes were closed and she was breathing hard, like me. That was all I could hear. I wondered if her senses were coming back to her, but my thoughts quickly stopped when I realized she'd moved aside her panties and was guiding me inside her. "I'm not wearing uh"—*she knows that*—"I don't have a—"

"It doesn't matter."

Was she losing her mind? She was willing to have

unprotected sex with a relative stranger in the hallway of a club. I hated to think how that made me look. Was I taking advantage of her vulnerability, or was I losing my mind too?

"Are you sure?" I asked.

"Yes!"

I moved and she moved with me, nuzzling my neck. I was surrounded by her smell, her sound, her touch. I justified all of this by telling myself that some part of me cared about her even though I barely knew her. I was just trying to make a hurting person feel better, though I couldn't deny how attracted I was to her.

Laya arched against me. Her legs started to shake; she was coming undone.

"You feel so good," I said as I quickly followed her.

She barely made a sound when I felt her trembling around me. Club music flooded my ears. We were back from our escape. Completely still and staring at the ceiling, she said, "Cameron." The music was loud but we were close enough that I could hear her soft voice.

I set her down and watched as she pulled her dress into place. She was crying. Again, her look was pure pain, longing, regret, and guilt. I was beginning to feel some of it. What we had done couldn't have made her feel any better. If anything, it probably confused her even more.

"Thank you," she said, wiping her tears.

I moved closer, but she stepped aside. "I don't understand. Why are you crying? Please, talk to me."

"I have to go."

"No, wait. Why did you say his—that name?"

"I don't know!" She threw her hands up in the air. "I don't know anything. I'm sorry."

She scurried away, out of my reach as I stood there blinking in disbelief. I began to buckle up, trying to wrap my mind around the past few minutes. What could I make of an incident like that? I looked nothing like Cameron; otherwise I would have thought she was reliving some moment they had shared, but that couldn't have been it.

Once I was back at the booth, the boys were sloshed. "I'm gonna call it a night," I shouted over the loud pumping music. I felt both tense and sleepy and just wanted to go home.

"There he is," Jeff shouted in an obnoxiously high voice. I still couldn't believe my sister slept with him. He was wearing a button-up shirt, but it wasn't buttoned up. He had a random girl hanging on his arm.

"Yes, I'm here," I said, deadpan. I threw back a shot glass from the table, and the drink burned my throat.

"We're not going anywhere," Devin slurred. "By the way, where have you been? Were you going number two in there?"

Nice. I just shook my head. "I'm gonna head home, guys," I repeated.

"Oh wait, no. The Unabomber is back. Are you gonna grow that disgusting beard again?" Devin said.

"I'm just beat. I worked a lot this week."

They all laughed, then ignored my comment and went back to fraternizing with the very inebriated girls they were with.

Heading out of the club, I scanned the room for Laya. She would be hard to miss even in a crowded room, but she was nowhere to be found.

In the cab on the way home I thought about what I had

just done and why she'd said "Thank you." What would happen if Jim found out? *Oh hey, Jim, I had sex with your daughter in the hall of a club. We barely exchanged ten words, then she pulled up her dress, we did it, she said thanks, sorry, and left.*

I imagined Jim's face turning bright red before screaming, "You're fired and I'm going to murder you."

9. Gravity

Rushing out of the club, I almost broke my ankle when the heel of my stiletto popped off. "Fuck!"

I had to get out of there before there was any chance of running into Micah again. I took off my other shoe, walked toward the bar and slammed the heel on the counter, successfully turning it into a matching flat, though in the process the heel went flying toward a bartender, practically impaling him.

"Hey!" he yelled.

"Sorry, I gotta go!"

Outside, I darted into traffic, hailing a cab in less than ten seconds.

What did I just do? I wished I could blame it on alcohol, but I'd only had one drink before accosting an employee of my father's firm. Micah said my name the way Cameron said it. In my mind, I was back in that French chalet begging Cameron not to do the stunt. Deep down, just like his mother said, I knew Cameron lived for it, and had I asked him not do what he loved, he would have resented me.

I thought, for just a few moments, I could imagine it was Cameron touching me in the club, kissing my ear, telling me I felt so good, but it was all Micah, and *he* felt different. He was tender and warm . . . and I wanted him. He was alive, tangible . . . passionate. When it was over, I said Cameron's name out of some deep sorrowful guilt I felt.

And when I looked up to see Micah's face, looking completely shocked, I felt even more guilt. I should have said something then. I should have told Micah I was just broken, and to stay far away from me.

Back in my apartment, I called Cameron's phone, but I didn't know what to say. I just sat there breathing, feeling ugly . . . feeling guilty.

MY FATHER ASKED me to go to his office and meet him for lunch the following Monday after the club incident. I felt it obligatory, as he had seen me in recent months only at my worst. It was like I had to check in with him every few days or he would get all fatherly on me. I knew I might see Golden Boy at the office. How humiliating. What did I gain out of Friday night? Possibly an STD. At least pregnancy was out of the question: I was still religiously taking birth-control pills. Even so, my stomach was churning when I entered the firm and headed straight to Dad's office.

"Darling," my father said, "you look healthy."

"Thanks, Dad." I remained standing. I glanced over at

the degrees and old accolades plastering his wall. There were only two pictures on his desk. One of me, the day I graduated from medical school, and one of him and my mom on their wedding day.

"Have you stopped with the Facebook posts?" he said with zero emotion.

Why'd he have to go there right off the bat?

I scowled even though I knew he would eventually bring it up. "Are you on Facebook now?"

"No, I'm just asking. Krista and I have talked about it."

"Yeah, about that—I didn't know you talked to Krista often. Krista is the one who plans to kill herself next month free-climbing El Cap, remember, so complaining about my Facebook posts is rich coming from her."

"She wasn't necessarily complaining. I called her because I didn't know who else to call."

"How come your desk is empty? It used to be covered with sketches and blueprints. Now it's just a couple of photos? And that?" I pointed to a paperweight of a rocket ship I had made out of clay when I was nine.

He smiled. "Laya"—his tone was one of calm frustration—"don't change the subject."

"I know you talked to Krista; she told me. That's what people do when others are falling apart around them. They talk so they can feel better about their own lives. It's called schadenfreude."

"Don't start, Laya."

I mimed zipping up my lips.

"Krista said she had climbed El Cap a dozen times. She said she had mastered it."

I scoffed. "She's never done it without ropes. There is no

such thing as being a master of climbing a cliff face without a rope. Do you know how many times Cameron had done the trick that killed him?"

My father looked down at his shaking hands on the desk. "Any of us could die at any moment, no matter how careful we are. Any of us could die of an aneurysm while standing at the stove making spaghetti sauce."

I bit my tongue. He was still in pain from my mother's death, and that was sad, but it was shocking he couldn't see how I was going through the same thing, and how what I really needed was for people to allow me to grieve in my own way. There was no manual, and he should have known that.

My father's eyes began to well up—something I'd never seen. I tried softening my voice, but I needed him to hear me. "Dad, I'm sad we lost her, too. But this is different." *Because he had more time with her.* "And I know you don't care that Krista wants to kill herself for a sports drink sponsor, but I do. You certainly cared what Cameron did." My father cleared his throat and straightened his shoulders but stayed quiet. "All of this aside, I thought you'd be the one to understand how I feel."

"But it's the posts, Laya. It's as though you think he's coming back. I never thought your mother was coming back. I never let myself believe anything but that she was gone forever."

"I'm trying to work through this. I am being realistic. Jeez, Dad! It hasn't been that long. I'm in fucking pain."

"Laya."

"I don't have a daughter to raise or a company to build," I told him. "I don't know what to do with myself."

"Get your residency and fellowship done. Focus on your

work! And sit down, for god's sake." I can't even remember a time when my father had raised his voice at me like that.

"No!" I slammed my hand on his desk. "I won't sit down. I won't just get over it."

"No one is asking you to *just* get over it."

Just then there was a knock on the door.

"What is it?" my father barked.

Micah opened the door slightly, clearly not expecting to see me and clearly not expecting to see my dad looking so pissed. His mouth dropped open. My dad's demeanor suddenly changed. His eyes lit up and all his previous anxiety was directly transferred to me, and probably Micah, too. Micah shot me a timid smile.

"Micah!" my father said in a much calmer voice. "How are you?"

"Good, sir."

"You know you can call me Jim."

I didn't know if Micah's formal greeting was compensating for what we had done only days ago or if he was terrified I might have told my dad everything.

"Um, you asked earlier to see these b-blueprints?" Micah said with a slight stutter.

He raised a long roll of paper.

"Oh yes, of course, son," my father said, shooting a look in my direction. "You know what? While you're both here—"

"Dad, I thought we were going to lunch?"

"You know, Laya, I'm rarely in the office anymore and I have a stack of work to do."

I knew exactly where he was headed, and I saw no stack aside from the blueprints Micah had set down. "I totally understand, Dad. I can take a rain check. We can continue this *uplifting* conversation later." I started backing away from his desk.

"No, darling, I was going to suggest you and Micah go to lunch. This kid never takes a break, and you can get to know each other since you're around the same age. I can order in and go over these blueprints while you two are out. And, Laya . . . you and I can continue our conversation later." It was like my dad was setting up a playdate to avoid seeing me get angry again.

Micah turned to me, expressionless, waiting for my answer. "You know, I suddenly feel nauseous," I said to my father.

Out of the corner of my eye I saw Micah's mouth turn up at the corners. He knew I was full of it, but he still tried to let me off the hook. "I have some work to do anyway," he said.

"Oh son, you always have work to do. You're a bona-fide workaholic." My father chuckled as he pulled his wallet from his desk drawer and placed a hundred-dollar bill on top of the blueprints. "Take her for some ramen; that always makes her feel better."

I was seething. My father did not pick up on our cues, or else he was pretending not to notice. Micah continued to stare at me, looking more sympathetic now.

"I could grab a quick bite, if you want?" He smiled sincerely.

"Fine," I said, and headed for the door without saying good-bye to my father.

Once I reached the hall, I heard Micah insist to my father in a low voice, "You don't need to pay, Jim. I got it."

"At least put it on the expense account."

Micah laughed and said something I couldn't quite hear. Back in the hallway, he whispered behind me, "We totally don't have to do this."

I ignored him and walked to the elevator. Once inside he looked like a deer in the headlights. I actually felt sorry for him. "Why do you say that? I think my father made it pretty clear he wants us to go to lunch." I wore a mask, not letting any emotions show on my face.

"*You* made it pretty clear you didn't want to go. I can just *say* we went."

"Why wouldn't I want to go have RAMEN with you?" When I shouted the word "ramen," he jerked his head back.

"Well, because of what happened Friday . . . at the club . . . remember?" He was timid and polite. Every time he said something, there would be a long pause afterward, but he'd never take his eyes off mine. He thought before he spoke. I liked that about him, and then immediately guilt washed over me for feeling that way.

"I don't know what you're talking about." Of course we were both completely uncomfortable about what had happened. I knew avoiding it wouldn't solve anything, but I was dying inside with regret and shame.

His eyebrows shot up. His magnificent blue eyes got even bigger and somehow bluer. Did the white walls around us make them stand out even more?

Probably noticing my stare, he took a step back, putting more space between us. For the first time he broke eye contact and looked down at his feet. "Well then, I know a good ramen place nearby. I was mistaken. I misspoke. I'm sorry; I didn't mean to imply anything happened. I had a long weekend, and I'm still recovering from it."

He was letting me off the hook . . . again. "Don't worry about it," I said.

The elevator opened to let us out, but neither of us moved at first.

"Subway or cab?" he asked.

"I thought you said it was close?"

"We can walk; it's just a little chilly out."

It was fall, but that day was windy and I didn't have a jacket, just a light sweater. We grabbed a cab without saying two more words to each other. I wasn't in the mood for small talk. I kept thinking about Cameron and what he would think of me riding around New York in a cab with another man. The man I'd had sex with a few days before.

I reached for my phone and quickly posted to Cameron's page.

LAYA BENNETT to CAMERON BENNETT

Cam, remember when we ate ramen at Momofuku and you told everyone you had the best ramen at Mama Fuck Yous? That was good ramen, wasn't it? Three. Two. One. See ya.

10. Colonnade

MICAH

I knew she was posting on Facebook. She looked out the window in silence. Pulling out my phone, the app already open to Cameron's profile, I saw she had mentioned Momofuku. I leaned forward and said to the cab, "First Avenue, East Village." I was so obvious, I annoyed myself.

"What?" Laya turned and said. "That's not even remotely walking distance. Why would you say nearby?"

"I'm spontaneous." Really, I wasn't, but I wanted her to think I was, and judging by what happened on Friday, she had to believe it by now. "I changed my mind," I said. "This is a better ramen place, Laya."

She grimaced. "Why do you say my name like that?"

Why did it bother her? She stayed silent and shook her head, then fixed her eyes on the front window. I studied her features. Her lips were full, her face smooth and olive, just beautiful even with the scowl she was wearing. Her eyes looked sunken, probably from lack of sleep, but her eye color, like absinthe, was the most stunning of all her features. Almost an impossible anomaly, one I had never seen. She was jaw-droppingly gorgeous.

It was in that moment I understood what falling for someone meant. It had nothing to do with sex, or wanting to feel good. I had already been there. Falling for someone is when you can't look away. When you know you would never forget what a person looks like. You would never mistake her for someone else. Her humility about her looks made her even more astonishing, mysterious, and vulnerable. But there was a strength behind her expression, too, one that promised if I said the wrong thing, she would punch me in the face.

I wanted to get to know her better, but at the moment I didn't think she wanted to get to know me. *Is she damaged goods? Is that even a thing? Do people heal from the kind of tragedy she has experienced?*

Her mother and husband died before she had even turned thirty. I couldn't grasp tragedy like that.

I tried another tactic. "Will you please tell me why you're offended by the way I say your name?"

She turned and glared at me. "Do you know?"

"No, I don't know. That's why I'm asking."

She rolled her eyes and looked away. I have to be honest: as much sympathy as I had for her, I was losing my patience. It felt like she was directing all her anger at me. She sat with her hands clasped in her lap.

"Okay, so I won't say your name anymore. Is there something else I can call you—perhaps Angry Bird?"

She tried not to smile. She was fighting it.

"Very funny." Her expression dropped. "I meant, do you

know what happened to me? Actually, not what happened to me . . . what happened to my husband?"

I nodded, and searched my mind for something to say that wouldn't piss her off even more. It was hard to know what to say when someone confronts you with a question like that. "I'm so sorry. I'm . . . I'm at a loss for words. I'm just really sorry you're going through this."

"Are you?" she whispered.

What did she mean by that? "Yes, I am . . . of course, I am."

She raised her eyebrows and chuckled a little. "It's funny how everyone says that. Did you murder him or something?"

"People say that because what else can they say?"

She slammed her hand on the glass partition, making me jump, and yelled, "Fifth Avenue is a nightmare right now, get over on Park. Jesus, this is going to be a forty-dollar cab ride." She turned to me. "We should have taken the subway. I would have taken the subway if I'd known we were coming all the way down here."

I took a deep breath and tried to compose myself, to keep myself from getting whiplash. My patience was dwindling very fast. The people who knew me well would say I had a very long fuse with a lot of explosives at the end. It felt like she was pushing me to that edge. *Why was she being so rude . . . to everyone?*

"You were saying that you don't like it when people say sorry."

"Yeah, I just don't get it," Laya said. "It's like a crap statement to avoid a conversation."

"What do you think people should say?"

"Nothing, nothing at all. They should just leave me the fuck alone."

"Whoa. I'm sorry. I didn't mean to offend you."

"There you go saying sorry again." Laya leaned back in the seat. "I'm clearly not in any condition to be going on lunch dates. This is ridiculous."

And that was when I lost it. "No one said it was a date. Pull over," I told the cab driver as I reached into my pocket, grabbed fifty bucks, threw thirty through the window, left twenty on the seat, and said, "Enjoy your ramen alone."

The cab driver followed my instructions, and right when I opened the door, right when I was about to walk away and give up—on all of it—Laya said my name. "Micah, wait. Please."

I turned to glare but couldn't. She was crying, and trying desperately to brush the tears from her face.

"What?" I said.

"Just get in and shut the door. We'll go? I'm sorry. I'm really sorry, for everything." Now *she* was saying sorry. I looked past Laya, at the cab driver who stared back through his rearview mirror. He shrugged and put his hands up as if to say, *What are you looking at me for?* A few seconds more and it would have been, *You're wasting my time, man.*

I gripped the top of the open door, trying to find the right words for Laya. "I can understand your anger, Laya, but I have no idea why you're taking it out on me. I haven't done *anything* to you."

"You're right. I shouldn't." She sounded tired. "Sometimes I can't help myself. You're a nice person—nicer than you need to be. Can we just start over? Please, let's just go."

The next few minutes in the cab were silent again. We couldn't look at each other, and I began to panic at the thought of a whole lunch date, me sitting across from her trying to read her mood. What if I said something wrong? Would she dump the whole bowl of broth over me?

Inside Momofuku, we sat side by side at the bar in front of the cooks. She quietly ordered the vegetarian ramen while I ordered the tonkatsu ramen.

"You don't eat meat?" I asked her.

She just shook her head.

"You can talk to me," I said, prompting her.

"I don't think I can talk right now. I'm sorry."

We watched the cooks drop thick, raw wheat noodles into boiling broth, deftly chop green onions in a blur, and cut delicate slices of marinated pork. Steam rose up in mesmerizing wisps, then disappeared into the vents above us. Every five minutes or so, to each new guest entering the restaurant, the chef offered coordinated greetings of "*Irass-haimase!*" It was busy, loud, chaotic, and probably exactly the right amount of distraction.

When our ramen came, I thought for a second that Laya's nose was running into her soup, but when I looked over, I realized she was crying. I put my hand on her back to comfort her.

She swiveled her stool around to face me and buried her head in my chest. She choked on her words and then finally said, "I feel guilty about everything. There are memories of him everywhere."

Her statement hit me like a five-ton truck. *Why did I bring her here?* All I was thinking was that I knew from her post she must like this place. I had zero foresight. How could I not see coming to this place was going to trigger a monumental sadness in her?

I held her close. "I'm not a psychologist, but I don't

think you can avoid all the places that are reminders forever. Don't get mad at me for saying this, but maybe one day you will be able to come here and smile instead of cry." Ultimately, it was what I had hoped for, but Laya wasn't ready right now and I should have known better.

She nodded as her tears soaked my shirt.

"I do remember last Friday," she said. "I didn't mean to devalue what we did. I tried to forget it because I felt terrible, and I felt like a slut."

I was rubbing her back in circles. She was still nestled in to me. "You are not a slut. And you have nothing to feel bad about. I didn't know him, but I imagine he wouldn't want to see you in pain," I said softly to her.

She sniffled. "The reason why it's hard to hear you say my name is because Cameron used to say it like that. He lifted up the *a* at the end, like Lay-uhh, like he felt good saying it. That's how I hear it coming out of your mouth. That's why it hurts when you say it."

Merely saying her name hurt her. I had to tread lightly. "It's a pretty name; it does feel good to say. But I can call you George or Fred if you want." She laughed finally. "Do you want to try to finish your ramen?" I asked.

"It's cold and too salty from tears and snot." She laughed again. It reminded me of the sound the wind chimes made on my parents' veranda. I had to stop thinking about all the different reasons she was so mesmerizing to me.

"Okay, I'll pay and we can take the subway. I'll walk you to your door," I said.

"You don't need to do that."

"I want to. We don't have to talk, but it seems like you could use the company."

On the subway I noticed Laya looked at everyone. She examined every person who got on and off. I would have gladly sacrificed a finger or toe to know what she was thinking, but I promised her no talking.

We climbed the stairway onto the street and that's when I totally blew it. I headed in the exact right direction of her apartment.

"Stop," she said. I turned and looked at her. There was obvious fear on her face. "How'd you know I lived down here?"

Recover, recover, recover.

"You live in your dad's rental, right?"

The fear left her eyes and her whole body relaxed a bit. "Oh yeah, I forgot for a second. I don't know how I could possibly forget that you work for my father. He basically forced us to go have lunch together." There was something peculiar about the way she looked at me, like maybe she thought I was lying . . . which I was. "Did my dad actually tell you I lived here?"

"No, I just figured because I knew it was vacant."

"Well, here we are, as you know. Do you want to come in?"

I couldn't believe she was asking me. It was a bad idea but I couldn't say no to her.

Her apartment was dark and messy. It smelled like old food. "I'm sorry. I haven't really had time to pick up in here," she said. She didn't sound sorry; she just said it like *it is what it is.* We stood in the center of the living room facing each other. I wondered what the hell to do.

"Do you want to lie down with me?" she asked.

This was a one-eighty from our earlier interaction, but it was a sign, I thought. She trusted me a bit more. I definitely couldn't say no now. "Okay."

She took my hand and led me into her bedroom. Inside I noticed it was like a time capsule. It looked like a thirteen-year-old lived there. We lay down side by side on our backs, staring up at the ceiling without touching each other. There were cobwebs draping the molding above us. I wondered how long it had actually been since someone had cleaned the apartment.

I rolled over on my side, propped on my elbow, and looked at her. If I reached for her, would she move away? I decided not to question it. I touched her shoulder. She didn't move. I ran my fingers down her arm. Her lips twitched upward but only slightly.

"When I fall asleep, can you leave?" she asked, sounding exhausted.

"Why do you want me here?"

"Because I need a distraction."

"I feel like a placeholder or something," I said in a low voice. I was half-kidding.

"Just stop talking. You're not an object." She nestled closer, and then she was dozing off. I watched her eyes until they fully closed, and when her breathing slowed to an even pattern, I realized my breathing was the same.

I sat up slowly. I took the quilt from the bottom of the bed and draped it over her. On my way out, I noticed a stack of pictures on her coffee table, nearly buried by other books and papers. I had a strong urge to go through them, but I didn't want to continue invading her privacy. I locked the door behind me and headed toward the subway.

New York looked dirty to me, even in the daylight. It was cold and hollow, probably the way Laya felt these days.

Back at the office, I tried to sneak past Devin's cubicle,

but he caught me. "Whoa, whoa, whoa. Did I hear correctly that you went to lunch with the boss's daughter?" He waggled his eyebrows.

"Are you kidding? Now she's the boss's daughter? I thought *you* were trying to land her?"

"So, you had sex with her?"

He was infuriating sometimes and I didn't want to make lying my new hobby, so I quickly found a way to skirt the issue since, technically, the club incident constituted having sex with her. "We went to lunch, man. We ate ramen."

"Why'd she choose *you* to go to lunch with?"

"She didn't choose me. I happened to be in Jim's office while she was waiting to go to lunch with him. Jim is the one who insisted I take her to lunch. She didn't even want to go."

"Well . . . "

"Well what?" I said.

"How'd it go?"

"We're getting married in July. She said she wanted to have ten of my babies and that I was the best-looking man she had ever seen. She did mention you, though."

"Ha, best-looking man she's ever seen, my ass. So, what'd she'd say about me?"

"I told her I was friends with you and she said, 'Oh you mean that talentless, blond asshole?' I said, 'The very same.'"

"Get outta here, I have work to do."

He turned his chair around and continued playing solitaire on his computer.

ON THE SUBWAY home, I scrolled through my phone. Laya hadn't posted anything yet. She was probably still asleep. I went through my news app, reading headline after headline. Nothing uplifting at all: a well-to-do couple was arrested for tax evasion, an old building near Wall Street was getting demolished; and just moments before I had opened the app, a report came in that the Q subway train had run over a guy on the tracks.

When I got home that night, I immediately called Mel. "What's up?" She sounded tired.

"Did you hear about that guy who fell on the tracks and got hit by the train?"

"Yeah, I saw that on the news. It's why I hate New York."

"You don't hate it; you just love Kenny and he hates New York."

"What's your point, Micah?"

There was Mel, so direct. "I don't know. Just that life is fleeting. It scares the shit out of me. I stopped doing that thing." She knew exactly what I was talking about. It's the twin telepathy phenomenon. I could have been talking about fishing or any number of things, but she knew.

"That's progress. I'm relieved you don't sit around wishing I were dead. When did you realize it was a totally demented hobby?" she asked.

"I just stopped."

"It's a relief you're no longer putting my gruesome death out into the universe."

I huffed. "It wasn't just you."

"Stop while you're ahead, Micah. So, how's your ear infection?"

"It's better. By the way, I met someone. That's when the epiphany hit me, Mel."

What I was trying to express to my sister, my twin, whom

I loved, was that life is out of our control; we can't always hold on to it. It *whoosh*es by us like a subway train that isn't stopping at our station. We all make so many mistakes in life, and most of them are forgiven, here and now with the people we love, the strangers on the street, the judge in the court. But does any of that actually matter? Maybe there is some entity out there tallying our mistakes, our actions, or the number of times we've hurt someone with words alone. When the page is filled with tally marks, we get hit by the Q train, Monday evening, headed home. Some onlookers are devastated, watching to see what's left on the tracks, and others are just impatiently wishing for the next train to pull in. Life goes on. That's it? No more chances for the man and no answers for the people he's left behind who are mourning.

Meanwhile, some idiot is sitting on the sixth floor of his posh office building playing Kill Your Loved Ones without any result.

I wondered if that was what religion was for. Maybe it's why we pray . . . in hopes that some of the little tally marks will be erased for ourselves and the people we love.

"Are you gonna say anything, Melissa? I said I met someone."

"I heard you. I thought you were going to elaborate. You've dropped quite a bit on me in one minute and thirty seconds." Her voice was low, like she was trying to prevent Kenny from hearing. I wasn't sure why.

"She's beautiful and smart," I said.

"Well, Micah, what's the problem, then?"

"She's been through a lot."

"Why are you being cryptic?" she asked.

"Why are you whispering, Melissa?"

"Because Kenny was complaining about how much you and I talk, and how close we are."

"You've got to be fucking kidding me. I've been hanging out with you since we were fetuses. Of course we're close."

"He's just being insecure because I've been on his case and now he's acting all weird. I'm just so damn tired of eating granola and goji berries. But we're getting off the subject. I asked you, why are you being so cryptic?"

"Because you know her, or at least about her, and I'm afraid if I tell you who she is, you'll start to lecture me."

"That's like a self-fulfilling prophecy. If you think I should lecture you, now I have to lecture you. Do you get it, Mr. Ivy League?"

"Yes, Miss Junior College Dropout."

"I finished junior college, dick."

"That's right. What was it? An associate's degree in horticultural studies so you could grow weed for Kenny?"

"I grow pot for dispensaries, okay? It helps a lot of people with cancer who are going through chemotherapy, and it supports us. I'm saving lives, too. Stop trying to change the subject."

"By the way that Marijuana Mac and Cheese you made practically killed Devin," I said.

"Wouldn't that have been a gift to the world? Back to the topic!"

"It's Jim's daughter," I blurted out.

"Okay, and . . . ?"

"She was married to Cameron Bennett." I was fishing to see if she'd know who he was.

"Oh my god, your boss's daughter was married to that crazy stunt guy?"

"You knew about him?"

"I remember it was all over the news. It happened right before your bizarre beard stage started."

"I shaved it, and anyway, Kenny has a beard," I said.

"Yeah, but yours was gross. Listen, I think you'd be walking on dangerous ground with that girl. Let me break it down: she's your boss's daughter, and she's a widow. I'm hanging up now so I don't lecture you."

"Go ahead. Hang up." But of course she didn't.

"I mean, can you do anything normal, Micah? You have a degree from a very prestigious college. You have a good job, you're all-right looking, I guess, and you go around sabotaging your own life. I seriously question whether or not you should be allowed to vote."

"You said you weren't gonna lecture me."

"It's impossible in this situation. That woman watched her husband die. Half of the world watched her husband die."

"There's something about her. Something I can't stay away from."

"You better try. Shut it down." Melissa was probably right, but I couldn't get my mind off Laya, and I'd never felt that way about a woman.

Melissa and I hung up. I went to my room, lay down, and closed my eyes.

I imagined being back in Laya's room, except this time she was running a hand down my arm, timing her breathing to mine.

I didn't remember the moment I fell asleep.

11. Cosmonaut

LAYA

I spent another late night unable to sleep so I called Cameron's phone and listened to his outgoing message over and over, thinking of what to say.

> "Hey, Cam. I don't know why, but I think leaving you these messages and posting on your page will somehow reach you. Or maybe you're floating around in space like some cosmonaut receiving my signals from a giant satellite.
>
> "I went to Momofuku today with a man who works for my dad. I cried in my soup and he hugged me. Wouldn't Dad have been so happy if I'd married that clean-cut architect?
>
> "Your sister still plans to free-climb El Cap and your mom is supporting her. I used to admire all of you. Your family, and the sense of adventure you all have. Like watching your mom ski moguls at sixty, and your dad skydiving, your sister climbing cliff faces with nothing but a bag of chalk, and of course you! Flying in that bright-red wingsuit. I love you, but I think you're all nuts.

"I'm conflicted, Cam. You always said if I wasn't living then I was dying. But aren't we already dying? No matter how many times you jump out of a plane and land safely on the ground, you're still dying. That's what life is: you're born and then you die. But you can't deny that what you and your sister are doing, even your dad sometimes, is just speeding up the process. Why? Why, when you had me? I was never enough, was I? How come I couldn't see that?

"Cam, I'm attracted to the man I went to lunch with. He's shy. He's polite and kind and loving and I was awful to him. When will you stop making me be awful to myself and other people?"

The voicemail cut me off, so I went to Facebook and posted. I had to get back to a good memory of us.

LAYA BENNETT to CAMERON BENNETT

Cam, I loved when we first started dating and we went to that fancy movie theater where the seats recline. It was like ten in the morning, and we were the only people there. We brought a blanket and made out like teenagers the whole time. Remember? I was wearing that scarf and you kept smelling it. I had sprayed a tiny bit of perfume on it. It was the perfume I always wore. You asked if you could have the scarf. I gave it to you, kind of reluctantly, and thought it was a strange request. But then the first time I went to your house, I saw it on your pillow. Three. Two. One. See ya.

After I wrote the post, I cried, then finally fell asleep.

12. Roundel

MICAH

It had been six weeks since lunch with Laya. I tried to stay off Facebook but found myself trolling it when I was bored. It made me feel like a creep. I got into a political fight with some guy I didn't even know. I got asked out on a date in a private message from a twenty-year-old, and I bought six stupid things from China.

I finally sent Laya a friend request. Mel caught me online and sent me a message. . . .

> What are you doing on here? Shouldn't you be working? Who are you stalking?

I ignored it.

I looked at Laya's last post from six weeks ago about the movie. I wanted to have that kind of moment with her. Instead of creeping her out by hiding tickets under her mat,

I decided to ask her properly. Well, at least in a Facebook private message. I wasn't good on the phone. Always too quiet. I also wasn't the most technically savvy when it came to social media, and didn't realize she wouldn't get the message until she accepted my friend request.

I wrote:

> Hi Laya. I hope you're doing okay. There's a movie I've been dying

Shit, I can't write "dying."

> There's a movie I was really hoping to see. It's called "The Shape of Water." It's about this fish alien-god thing that—and this mute woman . . . oh never mind. I was wondering if you wanted to see a movie with me this weekend? No pressure.

When I stood to stretch and walk off the anticipation of waiting for her reply, I noticed Devin was in his cube playing solitaire on his computer again. "Hey, don't you work?" I asked him.

"I'm taking a mental health break. What's up?" I was going to ask him to lunch but realized there was already food all over his mouth and he was eating hummus with a spoon.

I gagged. "Don't you have pita bread to dip in that? A cracker? Anything? A carrot maybe?"

"Micah, do you need something?"

I didn't know what possessed me to say it, or what sort of cosmic somersault Earth did in that moment, because

Devin was probably the worst person to share my feelings with, but I suddenly blurted out, "I think I'm in love with her. And I don't even really know what that means."

"Aw, poor baby. Who the hell are you talking about?"

"Laya, you idiot."

He pinched his eyebrows together. "Laya, like in—"

"Yes! That Laya."

He clicked his mouse a few times, seemingly in deep thought. "That's really . . . neat, Micah. It's . . . cute."

"Cute?" I said, pinching my eyebrows together.

"Well, I don't really know what to say except she's off limits if you're thinking serious girlfriend. She's your boss's daughter and has too much baggage. I don't think you're her type anyway, unless you pick up some kind of extreme sport."

"Is it your goal in life to insult me on a daily basis?"

Devin grimaced. "I'm not trying to, man. I think the whole situation is totally complicated."

I sat back down. My body felt heavy, but I also felt a twinge of annoyance. If Devin was talking about any other girl, I'd probably listen to him. But this was about Laya. "I like Laya. I like that she's complicated," I said, "And 'baggage' is kind of harsh, don't you think? It's not like she's a single mom with twelve kids." I heard my computer *ding*. "Never mind, I shouldn't have told you anything."

He shrugged. "I just think it's pointless to even try with her." He paused and looked thoughtfully at me, though I knew his next words wouldn't be so considerate. "I'll take you out this weekend if you want. Maybe you can find another girl instead of one you know can't commit."

"Just forget it."

Sitting down at my computer, I went straight to Face-book. That was the *ding* I had heard. She had accepted my friend request and responded to my message.

She wrote:

Micah, sure. That movie sounds interesting, if not completely bizarre, but what the hell? Why not?

Am I responding too fast? Who cares.

Laya, great. I'll pick you up on Saturday at six.

She replied immediately.

Sounds good.

It wasn't exactly the most enthusiastic response. Still, I wasn't sure why I hadn't tried harder, sooner. I knew she needed time and space, but I felt a connection to her, and I think she felt it, too. And . . . life really is short.

THE WEEK WENT by like I was pushing seventy pounds of molasses up a hill. I actually worked hard through it all and managed to stay off Facebook for the most part.

Saturday, when I arrived at Laya's and rang the buzzer, she took her time coming down. For a moment I didn't think she was going to show at all.

"Hi, Micah."

"Hi, George. How are you?" She looked stunning, even though she was wearing sweats and a beanie. She did have a scarf on, though, and I found that interesting. I remembered her last post.

She laughed at the George comment and gestured to her clothing, "I get cold in movie theaters. That's why I'm dressed like this."

"Do you know why movie theaters are cold?" I asked as we walked toward the subway.

"To prevent the screens from overheating."

I smiled. "I just can't get one past you, can I?"

"You can keep trying. I like it."

This was a different Laya. A more playful and less sullen Laya. I hadn't checked my Facebook in a while, but I wondered if that whole business of posting on Cameron's page had stopped. I couldn't exactly ask her.

"Do you think you'll go back to being a doctor again?"

"No," she said quickly. "I want to be a dog groomer now."

I laughed. "That's funny."

"I'm actually serious. I want to do something mindless. You know, just wash the dogs and dry them. No high expectations. No potential for killing someone." I nodded. "Or I was thinking grocery store checker. I used to play grocery store with my friend when we were little. You know, the beep, beep, price check on aisle two . . . it's all pretty fun and gratifying."

Downstairs, Laya swiped her card—maybe the one I had given her—and went ahead through the turnstile first. I wanted to ask her if checking out groceries would actually be more gratifying than saving lives, but at that moment Laya had turned around, gesturing for me to hurry up. She was smiling. I didn't want to ruin the mood by asking serious questions.

We waited downstairs on the platform. A busker was playing a cover of an Aerosmith song on a banjo and something made from a rolling pin and washboard. He had a Brazilian flag hanging on the column behind him. The tourists—their fanny packs and sneakers (dead giveaways)—weren't the only ones listening. Even the New Yorkers, easily distinguished by their brisk pace and impatient expressions, seemed to enjoy the momentary entertainment.

I turned to Laya, who was nodding her head along to the music. "So . . . ?" I asked.

"I've been well. If that's what you're wondering. I'm trying to figure things out. I'm as well as can be expected. You know, being a doctor was a lot of pressure. I was working really long hours while trying to balance a social life . . . and a marriage."

"I can understand that. Luckily, your dad has given me a lot of freedom to work when I want to. I almost make my own hours."

"But how can you stand Tweedledum and Tweedledee?"

"Yeah, Steve and Shelly are a lot to handle."

"I meant Devin and Freedrick," she said, deadpan.

I couldn't help but laugh.

"You know I'm joking," she said.

"Are you?"

She smirked. "*It is* really Steve and Shelly who are the problem. I think they've taken advantage of my dad. I wish I had a sibling to shoulder the burden because I feel like the old man's going to lose a lot in a company he built from the ground up. Steve and Shelly have contributed nothing."

"I'll help look out for your dad. Steve knows I don't like him and Shelly just wants to sleep with everyone in the office."

"Have you?"

"Are you kidding? No."

She looked up at me with sincerity in her eyes. I almost felt embarrassed, like she was staring at something inside me. "That's really nice of you to offer looking out for my dad, and the firm."

I wasn't trying to score points with her. I meant it. I didn't want to see Jim's company destroyed. "Well, I'm there all the time and—"

"I know you don't have to. I know it's because you care." The Brazilian busker ended his cover and bowed as people clapped, us included. "Do you have any siblings?"

"I have a twin sister, Melissa. She lives in Maine." I already knew more about Laya than she knew about me, but I did notice she was wearing a NASA space camp sweatshirt. "Do you like NASA?" I said.

"I like space," she replied. "I went to space camp every year from the time I was six to twelve years old. When I was eighteen, my dad took me to the Kennedy Space Center Museum. I was so disappointed I cried like a five-year-old. All those childhood fantasies went up in flames." She was laughing so I knew she wasn't serious. "I thought I was going to see a rocket ship take off, or some other cool shit, but it was just a museum."

Her childlike wonder was endearing.

"Space is totally fascinating," she said.

"So why didn't you become an astronaut?"

She winked and said, "I just told you. The damn Kennedy Space Center Museum. It ruined me. Dream shattered."

We started laughing so hard my stomach hurt. "You're something else," I said. She locked her arm through mine and I nearly jumped at the unexpected touch. This Laya was drastically different . . . and I loved it.

"So, tell me about Melissa."

"Well, Melissa is complicated."

"Like deep?"

"No," I said without humor. "She's kind of the opposite of deep. I love her, but she's blatant and crass and crude and—"

"Wow, sounds like you have a very high opinion of her."

"No, no, I really, really love her. She's . . . it's hard to explain; maybe you'll meet her someday." That didn't cross my mind until now, but I liked the idea of it. Laya could hold her own against Melissa in a way that might even make my sister shut up for once.

When we got to the subway platform, Laya walked past the yellow line. "Laya, what are you doing? Laya, stop!" One of those trains that was not meant for our stop flew by and forced her back another step. I grabbed her from around the waist and pulled her flush to my body. The wind was strong from the train and the noise was loud. I heard a gasp from an onlooker. As I held her to me, she stared into my eyes. It was like I could see right into her soul. I couldn't look away from her—she suddenly appeared so tortured and innocently sad.

"Why did he want to do that?" she asked, and then she kissed me. A full passionate, long kiss with her hands grabbing the hair at the back of my neck. Her eyes were completely closed. She was giving me all she had, but I was still confused.

When she tried to pull away, I held on. I didn't want it to end. She was a mystery to me. I didn't know why she stood on the edge of the platform and put herself in danger. I didn't know why she had kissed me, but I knew I didn't want to let her go. I said, "It's me, Micah."

"I know," she said very seriously.

"What did you mean when you said, 'Why did he want to do that?'" I asked her.

She shook her head, breaking her fugue state. "Cameron always stood so close to the edge in everything he did. I never understood it. I still don't."

It was hard for me to talk to her about Cameron. I felt like at any moment I could fuck it all up and say the wrong thing.

"Maybe he just wanted to feel. Maybe it made him feel alive, like the way you make me feel." I didn't realize the admission I was making until the words were already out of my mouth. The timing might have been bad, but I needed to tell her how she made me feel.

She was wearing a small, tight smile. "Maybe you're right. Do you think I wasn't enough . . . to give him that rush . . . that thrill?"

I shook my head. "It wasn't about you . . . at all. He was already that way long before you were in the picture."

"What about me makes *you* feel alive?"

"Sometimes I feel like a nobody, but not when I'm around you. You must have that gift. You command my attention, too." We stared at each other while the crowd moved around us. I smiled and she smiled back, her eyes crinkling at the corners like she was still searching for the meaning in my words. "Laya, we just missed our train." I hadn't even noticed until it was pulling away.

"It's okay; there are other trains," she whispered.

"You make me feel alive because there's nowhere else I'd rather be than right here, talking to you, missing one train after another."

"Cameron was always skiing, flying, rappelling away from me. I was always waiting around for him to come back . . . even in our short life together. It's hard to be the one waiting and watching from the sidelines."

"I'm not Cameron."

"I know that."

I don't know how many trains we missed before we finally got on one. She sat close to me. It felt right.

13. Aliens

LAYA

The movie, although strange, was about something so simple: two people who understood each other because they were alike. Cameron and I were polar opposites. I thought it made us a good couple. He was outgoing; I was shy and introverted. I could be outgoing and social when I needed to be, but I preferred to be alone most of the time. Cameron was always surrounded by people who adored him; I didn't need that. I glanced over at Micah in between a scene. Were *we* better for each other because we were alike?

We reclined our seats. It felt like we were lying together in a bed. Micah might have felt my stare because he turned and flicked the end of my scarf, whispering, "I like this."

"My friend knitted it for me. It's made from Mongolian silk."

If he's says it smells good, I'm going to get up and walk out.

"That's really cool. She must be crafty."

I smiled. "Yeah, she is."

During a touching part in the movie, the mute woman put on a record for the fish alien, god, whatever he is, and he swam gracefully in circles in the water. I rested my head against Micah's chest. His heart was beating fast as he held me. "Are you nervous?" I whispered to him.

"No, this film is moving."

Micah touched my stomach under my sweatshirt and moved his hand way up. I held my breath but didn't stop him from slowly moving further. He was reassuringly warm and tender, and it wasn't long before I felt relaxed even though I wasn't wearing a bra. He caressed the underside of my breast, and then he leaned in and kissed me, very gently. I remembered back to the club, how he was so rigid, maybe uncomfortable when we kissed. Now we were taking our time.

"Was that okay?" he whispered near my ear.

"It's okay," I responded, but realized I could have said more. I could have told him I liked it. We focused back on the movie—or I tried to, at least. All of it was so hard to navigate. How do you get married and then a couple years later start dating someone else? Were we even dating? All I knew was that I was making out with him in a movie theater. I'd had sex with him in a club. I'd cried on his shoulder at the ramen place. I wasn't rejecting him, but I still felt a tremendous amount of guilt for Cameron. I couldn't remember if he'd really, sincerely told me I should move on if anything happened to him. What if he didn't want me to move on? What if he were rolling over in his grave while I was getting felt up in a movie theater?

The movie ended, and I blinked to adjust to the bright lights. Micah stretched and waited for me to get into the aisle first. It was impossible not to compare the two men. Cameron would have laughed at the movie. He would have thought it was silly. He would have jogged down the stairs laughing and jokingly teasing about being my fish alien god.

The fact was, the movie *was* touching, and well-made, and it had a beautiful sentiment. It was about a lot of things, but one piece was about being scared to lose someone and to make a sacrifice to save them. I wasn't given the opportunity to make that sacrifice for Cameron.

Cameron was brave and I was always fearful; even when I wore the mask of proud wife or strong doctor, I was terrified. Scared of not performing, scared of being hurt. Scared of dying at the stove while listening to the Allman Brothers on the record player.

For a short time Cameron had given me a glimpse into the mind of a brave person and what it was like to face your fears and embrace adventure. But then he skied off that slope with a smile and within seconds confirmed all my fears again.

So, the fish alien god was misunderstood and the mute woman was, too. They were the same. They fell in love because words didn't matter to them. Sometimes I thought words shouldn't matter to anyone. They are just words, after all. Actions, mannerisms, movements, embraces, and sacrifices . . . simply put, added up to love, right?

Micah pulled me close as we walked back to the subway, and I let him. He was a gentleman. He walked me to my place, kissed me on the cheek, and said, "That was a weird movie, but I kind of got it. If you feel like lunch, come into the office. I promise I'll keep Devin away from you."

LATER THAT NIGHT, after cleaning my living room and washing the pile of dishes in the kitchen, I called Micah because I had forgotten to say thank you. He bought my ticket and popcorn and I didn't even thank him for it. Sometimes it felt like I was out of touch with other people's feelings, or out of practice with how to be a human. I would ask someone a question, like "What are you up to?" or "How are you doing?" and not even give a shit about their answer. I was so swept up in my own crap, I didn't care. I was always making excuses like, "I'm sorry I hurt you by not calling back, but I'm depressed and my husband just died." As though that gave me license to mistreat people.

Micah picked up on the first ring. "Hi. What are you doing?" I asked.

"Actually, I'm at a little dive bar with a friend from college and my sister. Hold on, let me go outside."

I heard music and people laughing. I looked around my living room and saw that cleaning it highlighted just how much space I had to myself. Too much that it made me feel suddenly alone. "No, I don't want to interrupt," I said.

"It doesn't matter. My sister is sitting at the bar talking to some guy about chia seeds, and my friend is hitting on a girl way too young for him. Hold on." This time I actually cared what he had to say.

When he came back on, he said, "Hey."

"Hey?" That was it? What did I expect? I was calling him out of the blue at ten at night.

"I don't know why I called. Yes, I do actually, I called because I forgot to say thank you for today. Sometimes I get in these moods where my mind is somewhere else."

"It's understandable, George." He chuckled, his voice deep and low.

"Have you been drinking?"

"I had a little gin. I have to drink to be around my sister, sadly. She's a lot."

"Well, thank you anyway for today. Have fun." *All right, that's enough, Laya.*

"I will. You can call me anytime. Just so you know," he said.

"Thanks, I'll keep that in mind." I ended the call. I wished he had invited me. Micah seemed to be the only person who could get my mind off Cameron at the moment, even if it came in short little bursts. I didn't know how to be forward and ask if I could meet up with him. And I still got the sense that he was treading lightly with me. Who could blame him; my moods were all over the place.

I thought I'd clean my bedroom, but thoughts about Micah kept me from doing anything productive. I wished I were at the bar with Micah, his sister, and his friend. It would have made things seem so normal, but instead I was at home.

Before I knew it, I'd called Cameron and was leaving a voicemail.

"Cameron, when are you going to let me go? I need to be a real person. I can't do that if you're popping into my mind every thirty seconds."

I dozed off without finishing my thought. In the morning, I woke up to my phone ringing against my ear.

"Hello?"

"Sorry, I know it's early." It was Micah. Our date and that late-night conversation came to mind and I wondered if he'd bring it up.

"Yeah, what time is it?" I tried to check the time, but I still wasn't fully awake.

"It's six a.m. I just couldn't sleep and I thought I'd get your voicemail so I planned to leave you a message."

"What were you going to say?" I sat up, running a hand through my hair—glad that no one could see me now.

"That I'm sorry I didn't invite you out last night. It wasn't much fun—we were kinda just sitting there. I didn't think you'd enjoy it. I didn't realize it until later but I should have invited you anyway, but—"

"You're rambling. It's okay." But it wasn't. Sure, he was saying all the right things, but still, he didn't invite me out, and I was alone, here, in my apartment.

"I don't know exactly how to be in a relationship," he said.

"I'm not sure I would call this a relationship . . ."

"Well, anytime you're interacting with someone, even on a semi-regular basis, it's a relationship."

"You know I'm not ready—"

"But *you did* want to come and meet me at the bar last night?"

"Well, I um . . . um . . ."

"Laya, we're in a relationship. Call it whatever you want. You can say we're just seeing each other."

"I didn't say that." *Are we really arguing about whether or not we're in a relationship?*

"I like you and I think you like me, and we are seeing each other, which qualifies as a relationship."

"Then why didn't you invite me last night?"

"You're right. That's why I'm calling you now to apologize."

"It doesn't matter. Let's just forget it, okay? I'll see you around."

"Are you kidding? See you around? You might as well had said 'have a nice life.'"

"Have a nice life, Micah."

"Laya, this is crazy."

It was true . . . I was annoyed he hadn't invited me. It all seemed so childish. Neither one of us knew exactly how to navigate what was forming between us. We were emotional babies. I was an injured baby; he was a newborn. We were just stealing Cheerios from each other on the playground and pretending it was foie gras.

"I'm going back to bed."

"What?"

"Yes, it's six a.m. on a Sunday. We'll talk later," I told him.

"Okay, I guess," he said, irritated.

Almost immediately after I hung up, I went to my computer and posted to Cameron's page. Afterward I shut it down and crawled back into bed.

LAYA BENNETT to CAMERON BENNETT

I just want to run. I don't know how to do anything. I want to get out of here. Let's go to the Adirondacks. Remember when we did that and swam in the freezing lake? I want to go again. But does it really matter what I want? Three. Two. One. See ya.

When the phone rang a few hours later, I had a feeling it would be Micah again. I didn't answer with a hello. I said nothing at all.

"Laya?"

"I'm here."

"I read your post on Facebook. Do you want to run from me? Is that what you meant? I'm really sorry about not inviting you last night."

"That post wasn't about you," I lied.

"It seems like you turn on a dime. One minute you're nice, attentive, talkative, and the next you're despondent and short?"

"I don't know, maybe because my husband died," I said.

"What am I supposed to say?" he said. "I don't know how to act, Laya. Your husband died tragically. I don't think anyone could get over that and I won't pretend to know what you should do or how you should behave. The only thing I know is that I don't think you want to find yourself alone, depressed in a cabin somewhere, growing a disgusting beard. Take it from me."

I laughed. I gave myself permission to laugh for just a moment. "That's funny, Micah, if not totally strange." *Hm. So he had had a beard.*

"I just wanted to clear the air and make sure you were okay," he said.

"I think I am okay," I said even though I still felt tired after sleeping for so long. "Hey . . . I have to go."

"Okay, I hope you feel better. I am sorry, okay? Um . . . well, see ya," he said.

I cringed. "Bye," I choked out.

14. Crumbling Bricks

MICAH

I immediately called Mel after my conversation with Laya. I needed to process the conversation with someone else.

"What's up? What kind of life havoc are you creating now, drama queen?" she said.

"I'm not dramatic."

"So, were you calling me to see how the weather is in Maine? It's cold as fuck."

"Mel, do you think I'm selfish?"

"Yes, unequivocally."

I swear, why do I call her?

"But you said I was nice."

"Yeah, like in a *you want everyone to think you're nice* kind of way."

"That's not true!" I said. "Last night, when we went out, Laya called."

"I know. I remember. I was there."

Mel was infuriating sometimes.

"Well, you were swept up in that chia-seed conversation."

"Move on, Micah."

"Anyway, after I thought about it, I think she wanted me to invite her, so I called and apologized."

"Why didn't you invite her?"

"I didn't really think about it at the time."

"Is that totally true, Micah?"

"No, I didn't think she'd want to meet us."

She paused, which meant she was either going to say something really mean and vulgar or heart-wrenching and profound.

"Well, you can't know if you don't ask. You can't sit around, overthinking someone's motives or wants or needs. Sometimes you just have to ask."

"It's hard for me to find the right words. I'm not as expressive as you."

"I think it's because you're afraid you'll say something stupid and not live up to your Ivy League persona."

"I'm not like that at all. I resent that."

"Well, then I don't know what to say. You asked for advice so I'm giving you some. Quit your obsessing." And just like that, after her tough love, she switched topics. "Hey, I'm going to Mom's in two weeks for dinner. I'm leaving Kenny at home, otherwise he might comment on her use of food preservatives. Do you want to go, too?"

"How come they don't invite me? They don't visit me at work anymore either. They make excuses, like 'Dad's tired.'"

"Well, now you know how it feels to *not* be invited somewhere and then to hear about it later. Just come with me."

"Are you saying I do that?"

"I'm saying you did it to Laya. And by the way, Mom and Dad hardly ever invite me over. Okay, I gotta go harvest some carrots and weed with Kenny in the greenhouse."

I really needed to reevaluate why I turned to Mel for advice. Walking from my room to the kitchen, I noticed Jeff's door was open. I heard a female say something in an irritated voice.

"Hey, Micah?" Jeff yelled.

Oh great, what does he want?

"What?" I yelled back.

"Come in here; we need a third-party opinion."

I wasn't in the mood to play mediator for Jeff and whoever he had in his bed, but I went anyway. When I poked my head into the doorway, I saw a naked woman lying unabashedly next to Jeff in bed. I looked away. "This is Lonnie. She's not shy."

"Hi, Micah," she said before pulling the sheet up, probably for my benefit more than hers.

"What's up?" I said.

"So, Lonnie here is from Chicago. There seems to be a strong desire in all Chicagoans to argue with New Yorkers about who has better pizza and hot dogs."

"New York pizza and Chicago dogs," I said.

Jeff looked shocked and Lonnie just smiled. "We're even," she teased Jeff.

"How can you say that, man? It's such a betrayal." Both Lonnie and Jeff were laughing and I was just staring, unamused.

"Is that all you need?" I asked.

"What's wrong?" Jeff said. "You having woman problems?"

Lonnie sat up. "Maybe I can help." She pointed to the

edge of the bed, covered herself more and sat against the headboard. "Sit. I'll give you some advice."

"Really?" I said, wondering why I continued torturing myself by listening to other people's opinions about my love life.

"Tell him how it is, honey," Jeff said. I was fairly certain Jeff had just met Lonnie and he was already calling her honey, but who cares?

"I'm seeing a girl. It's complicated. I barely even know her and I keep fucking things up." I sat at the end of the bed, making a concerted effort to ignore the fact that my roommate and the woman he was with were naked under the covers.

"But you have feelings for her?" Lonnie asked.

It was true. I did have feelings for Laya. I was intrigued by her, her beauty, her unselfconsciousness, her talent and wit. I didn't know if I wanted to pursue anything with her or if she was even emotionally available. It seemed like every encounter ended strangely. I knew she was lonely, but I didn't pity her. Maybe I was being selfish to keep trying. Maybe I just wanted to prove to myself that I could somehow make a woman who once had a charismatic, successful, good-looking husband fall in love with me.

"Yes, I do have feelings for her," I told Lonnie.

"All women want is to be wanted, appreciated, and respected. At least the good ones. Yeah, there are bitches out there who want Gucci bags, drink expensive champagne, and feel loved by receiving material objects, or being married to the rich guy. Then there are the women who talk incessantly about themselves and need constant praise and validation regardless of who it's coming from. But I promise you there are also women out there who just want to experience another person, have a connection, bring meaning to their lives by exploring life with someone who gets them."

I looked to Jeff. "Who is this woman? She's like the Einstein of emotional intelligence."

"She's also good in bed," Jeff said.

Lonnie rolled her eyes at Jeff. "I was just in a relationship for ten years, then I dated a total asshole who would never tell me where he was, or what he was doing. He didn't understand communication is a necessary component of respect. He felt entitled, like 'Why should I tell her? I don't owe her anything,' but that's the thing. He only cared if there was some chance we'd have sex that day. Every other day he was too busy. He made me feel insignificant. What I'm saying is, if you like the girl, ask her questions, tell her about your life. Share personal details with her. Don't fuck around with other women while you're trying to get to know her. At least wait until you have that conversation."

"There aren't other women," I said.

"Okay, it's easy." Lonnie spoke softly. "Take it slow, then."

I nodded. Who would have known I'd get profound, if not slightly abrasive, advice from the stranger sleeping in Jeff's bed?

"Thanks, Lonnie," I said as I headed into the hallway. I wished I lived with her instead of Jeff.

"Anytime!" she yelled back.

15. Command Module

LAYA

My phone rang, jolting me out of sleep, "Hello?"

"Hey, it's Izzy."

I hesitated. Izzy was my only friend from grade school, actually my only childhood friend period, but it'd been a while since she and I had talked. Correction, she'd been calling me, but I ignored her. I had basically shut out everyone I knew after Cam died.

"Hi. How are you?"

"Good. How are you?"

"I'm okay."

"Listen, I'm sorry I didn't make it out to California for Cameron's service."

"It's okay." I couldn't blame her. She'd only met Cameron once or twice.

"Why haven't I heard from you? I've left so many

messages on your phone. The only reason I knew you were alive was because I called your dad's office and asked. He said you were just busy. Are you back at the hospital working?"

"I *have* been busy," I said. Busy with my thoughts, but she didn't need to know that.

"Well, I hope not too busy to grab lunch with your old friend."

"Um, okay, sure. When?" I knew I needed to get out and face the world eventually.

"It's just that I pick up Alexander from nursery school around lunchtime."

Didn't she just ask me? "We can go somewhere kid-friendly."

"Yeah, but Alexander is only two and you know how two-year-olds are."

I had no idea. Why would I know that? Sometimes people just want you to know how busy they are and how fulfilling their lives are.

"Well, when you figure out a time that works, let me know. I'm sorry I didn't return your calls. I was trying to get my head straight," I said.

"Laya, I've seen your Facebook posts."

"I gotta go. Call me when you want to grab a bite . . ." The thought of juggling friendships was exhausting to me. I went to my computer, almost mindlessly, and posted. I don't know why I did it.

LAYA BENNETT to CAMERON BENNETT

Hey, Cam, do you think we should have kids? I mean, with your lifestyle? Do you think that would make sense? With the risks and all? Would I have to give up my job? Could we balance it all? See ya.

Three. Two. One.

Later that day I went to my dad's office. I had questions and felt like we were just skirting around issues all the time. I felt like he scrutinized me for grieving when I thought that of all people, he should know how it felt.

Micah wasn't there. Devin saw me walking in and waved me over. I didn't even ask Devin about Micah, but apparently they talk about me because he said, "You just missed Micah. He went out to meet with clients."

"Good to know. Thank you." I waved, and scurried down the hall toward my father's office.

In a sense, I was relieved Micah wasn't there. Our last conversation hadn't exactly ended on a pleasant note.

As I made my way down the long hall, I stopped outside the gallery room where they kept all the models from buildings the firm had designed in the past. It was beautiful to see all their creations in one room. I stared blankly, wondering how my father had pulled it all off after losing my mother. *How did Dad do it? How did he build this place from the ground up while swimming in grief?*

Since Cameron died, I felt naked when I walked down the street. Everything reminded me of him. Everyone was giving me timelines, and all that did was bring up old wounds. I would lie in bed and smell him, but he'd rarely sleep in that bed. I had gotten rid of all the stuff we had bought in California with the exception of that bed. Everyone suggested more grief counseling, but every time I went, I would talk about Cameron and sob and sob. It wasn't cathartic at all for me. It didn't help me. Even the crying just exhausted me and made me feel fatigued for days.

I shuffled past a few other offices and into my father's as he was just ending a call. He hung up and smiled at me lovingly.

"What's going on, baby girl?" he said as I sat down across from him. His question ignited something inside me. He knew the answer, yet he asked anyway. My eyes fell on one of the frames on his desk—the one of him and Mom at their wedding. I picked it up and traced Mom's smiling face with my finger.

I didn't want to bring up more pain, but it had been far too long that he had avoided this conversation with me. "Why don't you ever talk about Mom? Why didn't you move on and remarry?" My voice grew louder. "Why didn't you explain grief to me?"

Dad leaned back in his chair, not answering right away. He was stoic and seemed resolute. "Which should I answer first?"

I nearly scoffed in disbelief that he was finally going to open up to me. "Answer this: How long did it take you to stop being mad at the universe? How long did it take you to get over it?"

He looked me in the eyes and said, "I've been waiting for you to come to me and ask questions."

"Why didn't you come to me first? You're my dad."

"I wish I had. I know I wasn't a perfect father. I'm still not, Laya. Watching you go through what I went through brought so many buried feelings to the surface." My father was never a good liar—or someone who would readily admit he'd done something wrong. Tears welled up in my eyes and his were soon to follow. "I wouldn't wish this relentlessly horrible feeling on anyone."

"I just want to know when I'll stop feeling like a broken tooth walking around with exposed nerves constantly hitting the freezing air. I feel like my skin has been peeled off." When I started crying into my hands, my father quickly handed me a box of tissues. He got up from his seat and sat down in the chair next to mine.

"I wish I could tell you that it will all go away. That someday you'll wake up and not think about him. You may not want to hear this, but the answer is *never*. I never got over losing your mother. It changed, but the grief never went away." Dad squeezed my hand in a rare show of affection. "Someone once told me a story. He said, 'I've lost friends, best friends, acquaintances, coworkers, grandparents, mom, relatives, teachers, mentors, students, neighbors, and a host of other folks.' He went on and said, 'I wish I could say you get used to people dying. I never did. I don't want to. It tears a hole through me whenever somebody I love dies, no matter the circumstances. But I don't want it to *not matter*.'"

"I don't want him to not matter," I said.

"You probably couldn't if you tried."

"Who told you that?"

"Oh, some old man in one of those grief support groups."

"You did that?" I asked, surprised. "You went to support groups?"

"I did everything, Laya. I was trying desperately to function as a father without losing it every five minutes. I knew that I needed to think of you, but it broke me every day knowing you'd grow up without a mother."

"What else did the old man say?"

My father's hand was shaking, so this time I squeezed back. I realized he had always been there for me, in his own way. He might have had a hard time being affectionate, but there was never a moment when he'd let me down.

"He said, 'Scars are a testament to the love and the relationships I had for and with each person. And if the scar is deep, so was the love. So be it. Scars are a testament to life.' Losing Cameron has left a scar that will always be there."

My mind instantly wandered to being in the operating room. Meeting patients concerned about their actual scars. I had said almost the same exact words. Scars *are* a testament to life.

My father went on, "The old man taught me a lot about grief that I will never forget. I remember it clearly. He said, 'It comes in waves. When the ship is first wrecked, you're drowning, with wreckage all around you. Everything floating around you reminds you of the beauty and the magnificence of the ship that was, and is no more. And all you can do is float. You find some piece of the wreckage and you hang on for a while. Maybe it's some physical thing. Maybe it's a happy memory or a photograph.

'In the beginning, the waves are a hundred feet tall and crash over you without mercy. They come ten seconds apart and don't even give you time to catch your breath. All you can do is hang on and float. After a while, maybe weeks, maybe months, you'll find the waves are still a hundred feet tall, but they come farther apart. When they come, they still crash all over you and wipe you out. But in between, you can breathe, you can function. You never know what's going to trigger the grief. It might be a song, a picture, a street intersection, the smell of a cup of coffee. It can be just about anything . . . and the wave comes crashing. But in between waves, there is life. Somewhere down the line, and it's different for everybody, you find that the waves are only eighty feet tall. Or fifty feet tall. And while they still come, they come farther apart. You can see them coming. An anniversary, a birthday, or Christmas, or landing at O'Hare. You can see it coming, for the most part, and prepare yourself. And when it washes over you, you know that somehow you will, again, come out the other side. Soaking wet, sputtering, still hanging on to some tiny piece of the wreckage, but you'll come out.

'The waves never stop coming, and somehow you don't really want them to. But you learn that you'll survive them. And other waves will come. And you'll survive them, too. If you're lucky, you'll have lots of scars from lots of loves. And lots of shipwrecks.' That's what he said to me . . . and it was true."

By that point I was sobbing. "I don't know if I'll be able to move on," I cried.

"Laya, I have had other loves in my life. I have loved and lost since your mother. I never shared my private life with you because I didn't think you needed to know. It was my own storm to weather. I think the only thing you can do right now is try to stop being mad . . . mad at me, mad at Cameron, mad at yourself. Try to keep yourself busy. That's all you can do."

He stood, pulled me up by my arms, and held me tight. I rarely hugged my dad, but I needed to this time. I cried into his shoulder. He didn't move; he just let me cry.

"I wish I had known how to love you better, sweet pea.

I wish I hadn't stayed bitter about your mother for so long. Please consider that."

"I will, Dad."

"What are you going to do now? Where will you go from here?"

"I don't know."

"You know your surgical fellowship is waiting for you?"

"I can't even think about that right now."

Dad finally released me and held me at arm's length. "You were an amazing surgeon. You are, I mean. Did I ever tell you that?"

I managed to smile. "No, you didn't, Dad."

"Well, I should have."

16. Legos and Blocks

MICAH

"Kenny is bugging me so bad. I think I need to break up with him," Mel said as we climbed the subway stairs heading toward our parents' apartment.

She had met me at my apartment in Brooklyn, which I sort of dreaded, praying she didn't have a run-in with Jeff, especially when she was talking about leaving Kenny. I always liked Kenny, even though he was a little preachy about the health thing. I thought he was good for Mel. But nothing really lasted long with her . . . which made me constantly wonder why I ever considered her dating advice.

"I like Kenny," I told her.

"Whatever. You only like him because he wants you to design an upscale tree house for him."

I laughed. "I already have the drawing for you. You'd have your own wing on the weakest branch."

"Thanks. So, doesn't your girlfriend live up here?" She peered over my shoulder, as if Laya's apartment was in sight.

"One block over—and she's not my girlfriend. In fact, I haven't talked to her for days."

"Oh, since you blew it and didn't invite her out that night. I want to see her apartment; let's go by it."

"No, you'll do something stupid. It looks like every other apartment on this side of town." I moved to block her, but she dodged me easily.

"I don't care. I want to see it. I want to see where this mystery mess of a women lives."

"Fine. And please don't call her that."

We walked over one block and stood on the opposite side of the apartment. "There it is, right across the street."

"How about we ring her doorbell?" Mel asked.

"No, that's creepy."

"Said the man stalking her."

"I'm not stalking her. Now you are!"

Mel shrugged and grinned before darting out into the street to cross. She turned at the last minute, calling for me, "Come on! Don't lose your nerve—"

The next moments happened in slow motion. I yelled at her, tried to warn her, but it was too late. I've never seen anything like it. The cab hit her from the right, and Mel crumpled against the bumper before hitting the windshield with a force that sounded like a gunshot.

I screamed and yelled and cried and a part of me felt like it was dying. "Help!" The cab driver got out and started saying something about her crossing without looking. I didn't care. My twin was on the ground now, bleeding from her head and nose. She was murmuring, but her eyes were still closed. "Get help!"

The driver nodded, then fumbled for his phone.

"Mel, Mel!" I kept screaming. I gave up on the driver and dialed 911 first, then Laya's number. "My sister and I were walking. We're in front of your building." I was breathing hard and could barely get the words out.

"Wait, what happened, Micah?"

"She got hit, everyone is standing here, I don't know what to do. Please, I don't know what to do."

She hung up, and a minute later she was next to me on her knees applying pressure to a cut on Laya's head. "Melissa, try to stay awake. Do you hear my voice?" Laya said.

While she was talking to Melissa, she was scanning her body.

"Is she going to be okay?" I asked.

"We can't move her until the ambulance gets here. Melissa, what hurts? Tell me."

"Everything," Melissa mumbled.

The driver was just standing there, dumbfounded. His skin was ashen. There were onlookers, also frozen in shock. The only one who was alert and moving was Laya. She pointed to a man and said, "You, direct the traffic north. It's crowded; the ambulance can't get here unless you clear up the street.

She looked to me and mouthed, *She's gonna be okay. I promise.* Her words reached me like a reaffirming embrace.

I trusted her. My heart slowed and I stopped hyperventilating. Melissa was part of me. My other half. I knew undoubtedly that I loved her and it wasn't a sibling love where we just tolerated each other. I literally was made with her.

I was formed at the exact moment she was, and it created a bond I didn't know I needed until that moment when its existence seemed to be in peril.

My head was aching. Was I feeling what Melissa was feeling?

"You're gonna be okay, Melissa," Laya said.

The ambulance arrived and paramedics started to stabilize Mel's body. I watched their expressions, trying to read them. I was looking for a tell that either things were bad and Laya was sugarcoating it for me, or that Mel would be fine, but the first responders were just working stoically to take care of her.

When Mel finally became more coherent, she looked at me said, "I'm sorry I fucked Jeff and Ian." That was how I knew Melissa would be okay. She was nothing if not consistent.

It was still a dire situation. When the paramedics asked what happened, Laya did all the talking. They were telling Melissa to relax and not move so they could put her on a stretcher.

Laya and I both got into the ambulance. She held pressure to Melissa's head while the other paramedic was hooking up the electrode stickers. Laya looked at me and said, "It looks like it's just her knee, and she probably has a pretty serious concussion."

"She has a hard head."

Melissa actually laughed at that, and then said, "Ouch. Don't make me laugh."

"See," Laya said, "I think she's gonna be fine."

I shook my head. "Mel, you just got hit by a car."

"I know. I was there, dipshit."

Laya looked at me again and smiled.

Thank you, I mouthed back.

When we got to the hospital, they ran a bunch of tests on Mel. They did a CAT scan on her head and X-rays on her body. She'd torn a ligament in her knee, but other than that, just bumps and bruises. I thought about how much worse it could have been. I couldn't imagine losing Melissa. Her humor and love were always so grounding for me even though she could be wild and obnoxious at times.

Kenny showed up and brought a large bag full of holistic medicines.

"Get that shit away, Kenny," Mel said. "They're giving me morphine. It's so much better."

"Melissa," Kenny said. "Just listen to me—"

"No, Kenny, I just got hit by a car. Don't push your arnica bullshit on me. I'm in pain."

"Kenny," I said, jerking my head toward the door. "Can we have a talk outside?"

"Sure, man."

Laya was still in the hall, talking to one of the doctors. Before Kenny followed me out, I took Laya in, the way she looked and talked and held herself with confidence. Her shoulders were squared, her eyes were clear, and it was like she had this absolutely glowing and resolute look on her face. She was definitely in her element at the hospital. She turned and held a finger up toward me as if to say *one minute*.

I nodded. Kenny came out and said, "What's up?"

How do I get through to this guy? "I love my sister. I saw her get taken out by a car today. I know you want to be as healthy as possible but, man, I want my sister to be happy. And she can only be happy if she's alive. Let the doctors do their work. I think she feels a lot of pressure to be something she's not when it comes to you two. And bringing that stuff in here when she needs real pain medicine and surgery doesn't make anything better."

He stared at me, blank faced. "One of my friends who is a yoga instructor gave it to me to bring. I was only trying to help. You know Mel asked me for a break?"

"She did?"

"Yeah, but she took it back half an hour later. She gets frustrated with me a lot. Even when I'm not doing anything to her. She has a fit about my lifestyle on a daily basis. I thought she loved who I am. I want to love her but she makes it so hard."

I actually felt sorry for him as he stood there in his green khaki shorts and Crocs. He had a T-shirt on with a tree holding a sign that said "Free Hugs."

"Then love *her*," I said. "You don't need to bring all of your interests into the relationship. You guys can be different people with different interests. Hell, Mel and I are twins and we don't even like the same food. Trust me, I know she's not a walk in the park, but I wouldn't change a thing about her. And you know what? Eat some goddamn Fritos, Kenny, they're not gonna kill you."

Kenny was so innocently literal. With excitement and determination, he said, "I'll get her some Fritos and maybe M&Ms. I'll go right now." He turned and walked quickly down the hall.

I went into Mel's hospital room. "I love you, shithead. I heard the whole conversation with Kenny," she said.

"He's a total dweeb but he loves you. He said your yoga friend gave him the stuff to bring."

Mel rolled her eyes. "Figures. She's always nosy-ing around in our business. I know exactly who he's talking about and she needs to go away. She's just a reminder of how not flexible I am."

I glanced down at her wrapped-up knee and said, "You're definitely not now."

"God, I hate New York."

"And you love Maine? You're always complaining about it. You're as New York as they come. I honestly can't believe you went all the way with this whole hippie phase."

"Do you really think it's a phase?"

"Well, let's see . . . with your last boyfriend you cut a mohawk into your head and dyed it purple. With the guy before that, you almost joined the army. So, yes, you tend to take on the persona of whoever you're with. Just be your-self."

"Atticus and Andrew were great guys."

"You change your mind more often than you change your underwear. I know that; I grew up with you," I said.

"You're funny. I love you, Micah."

"You're so hopped-up on morphine. I wish you were like this all the time."

She laughed loudly. "Ouch, don't, Micah, don't make me laugh. My body hurts."

"It's how I show you I love you, by inflicting pain."

It hit me that I had almost lost her, and my smile quickly faded. My sister looked at me and frowned, probably think-ing the same thing.

"Hey, Micah, do you really like that girl?"

I turned around, expecting Laya to be right there. "Yeah, I do."

"Good," Mel said. "She's awesome, by the way. Kind of out of your league, though, dickwad."

I sighed. "Annnd you're back." I kissed her forehead. When I turned around, Laya was actually standing in the doorway. I had a glimpse of Laya as a surgeon then. It was easy to imagine her in a white coat, checking on her patients.

"Hey," she said to Mel. "How do you feel?"

"Kind of like I got hit by a cabby."

"Try not to play Frogger next time you visit New York, okay?" Laya smiled.

She nodded for me to talk to her outside. When we got into the hall, she said, "So she's gonna be fine. I figured that much." She smiled sincerely.

I smiled back. You know it's hard to look at someone for longer than ten seconds without saying something, but that was the second time it had happened with us. I pointed to her head. "I wish I could climb in there right now."

"Oh, it's just a bunch of trash, cobwebs, and buttons that don't work."

"I still think I would like it in there. You know you have a beautiful smile?" She blushed. I didn't peg her for the type to blush easily. "But you know it's a muscle, though, smiling? If you don't use it enough, it just turns into goo."

"Did you learn that in a medical manual, Micah?"

"I just noticed something. When you say my name, you push the *a* and *h* up, like it's floating away."

She frowned and whispered, "Like the way you say my name?"

"I guess, yeah. Anyway, thank you for everything you did for Mel." I took Laya's hand, squeezed it, and then kissed her cheek.

"I guess I should say thank you for trusting me when you called."

"Even though your head is filled with cobwebs and probably baby spiders?"

"Definitely baby spiders."

I looked in on Mel and she was nodding off, so I turned my attention back to Laya and said, "So, what were you talking to that doctor about? You looked really happy."

"I asked who I should see about finishing my fellowship here." She squinted. "My dad suggested it, but I wasn't sure until today."

"Why today?"

Her eyes welled up. "Because it felt good to know I could help. I've felt powerless for so long."

Here is where I thought I would blow it because the words just spilled out of my mouth. "Laya, you can always help. You helped me and I wasn't even the patient."

She stood there, staring at me for a long time. "I never thought of it that way."

When my parents showed up finally, my mother was in a tizzy, running down the hall toward Mel's room. Laya stopped her before my mother went in, and though Laya was still wearing her street clothes, she tried to calm my mom by saying Mel's injuries were fairly superficial. Laya didn't realize she appeared to my parents to be a complete stranger commenting on Mel's wounds.

My mother blew up at her. "Who the hell are you?"

"Mom, this is Laya Bennett. She's a friend of mine who

happens to live on the street where Mel got hit. Laya, this is my mom, Leslie, and my dad, Peter."

Mom looked her up and down. "And what makes you an authority on my daughter's health?"

"Mom," I said. "Laya is an orthopedic surgeon and helped when Mel was hit. I don't know what we would have done without her."

My parents exchanged a look; I could see my mom calming down. "Well." She shrugged. "Thank you, I guess."

Very humbly—more than my parents deserved at the moment, Laya said, "You're welcome." A professionalism I had never seen before in her came out.

My mom and dad went into Mel's room, waking her from near-sleep. I leaned against the doorframe and watched my mother rest her head on Mel's bed and cry. Mel had some bandages but it wasn't like she was in a full body cast. I looked in and saw my father stroking her hair, kissing her forehead over and over. Then he said, "What were you thinking, Melissa? Did I not teach you to look both ways?"

Mel just smiled up at him.

I said, "See, they do love you. I have no idea why." My mother shot me a look of irritation, but I just chuckled.

Right at that moment Kenny walked in with Fritos and placed them on Mel's nightstand before saying, "I'm sorry."

Mel's eyes welled up. Buy her Fritos and she turns into a ball of mush. My parents looked confused by the exchange, but they didn't say a word.

From behind me, I heard Laya say very quietly, "Can I talk to you again, Micah?"

I stepped out into the hall and followed Laya to a spot

where it was just the two of us. She leaned back against the wall and looked down at her feet.

"Uh-oh. Should I be worried?"

"No."

"What were you two doing in front of my building?"

"I swear, Laya, we just happened to be walking by."

"It's just strange." Her eyes were probing mine. Apparently she didn't find what she needed because she switched directions abruptly. "I'm not scared of being alone, Micah."

That surprised me. "I didn't think you were. What are you trying to tell me?" I put my hand against my chest in a defensive gesture. I recalled our last conversation about where our relationship was going. "I'm not trying to pressure you into anything. The last thing I want to do is push you away by rushing you into this."

"There isn't a *this*, Micah."

I shook my head, disagreeing with her. There *was* something, but neither of us had a name for it. "Laya, I just want to get to know you. I thought we connected at lunch and at the movies, and then the argument the other day was just out of the blue. I thought about it for weeks. I didn't mean to make this a thing we need to attach a label to. All I know is that I called from the street because I knew you could help. I thought of you immediately."

Compassion flooded her face. Again, like we had done before, we were staring at each other without scrutiny. I considered myself passive and closed off, but something about Laya made me want to open up to her.

No one walked by for several moments; it was just the two of us. There was no escaping each other. We had said our piece, but there were still so many unspoken feelings left swirling around us in the silence. Questions about the night in the club hung thickly in the air. I was torn and confused about what had happened. It was not that I regretted what we had done . . . I regretted not telling her how I felt that night. I should have told her she was the most beautiful woman I knew. I should have acknowledged her pain and expressed an understanding instead of coming off as an opportunist.

Finally, I broke the silence. "Why the club?"

She shook her head. "I'm not sure. I've thought about it a lot."

"What'd you come up with?"

"I guess I needed to feel something. You seemed safe to me, but I wasn't using you. I swear."

"I'm less concerned about my feelings than I am about yours."

"We hardly knew each other. We hardly know each other now," she said.

I took a step toward her and ran my thumb down her cheek. "Don't say that. It felt good to be with you . . . even if the circumstances weren't ideal." I was still curious as to why she said Cameron's name that night in the club. It was hard not to think she was imagining being with him and not me, but I couldn't exactly ask her about it. "Your feelings were all muddled up. I get it. I wasn't trying to take his place."

"I wasn't thinking about him; I was thinking about you. But then it hit me and it crushed me to think he was gone and there I was, seeking out some release or affection from someone else." She seemed to stop herself from saying more. "Listen, I need to go. I'm not feeling well. I'm glad your sister is okay."

Just when I felt like we were making progress, she got scared.

"Don't run."

"I need to go."

"Let me get you a cab?"

Her eyebrows pinched together. "I'm very capable of getting my own cab, Micah."

"I didn't mean it like that."

"How did you mean it?" she asked.

"To pay for it, to return the favor in some small way."

"It wasn't a favor to help your sister. You owe me nothing . . ."

"Can I see you soon?"

She shook her head. "I don't know. I have to get my head together."

"Why won't you let me help you?" As soon as the words came out of my mouth, I knew it was the wrong thing to say.

"Help me? Help me what?" She was shaking her head, looking past me down the hall. "I don't need your help. I need time."

"I have feelings for you."

"That's what I'm questioning. Why would you have feelings for me? I'm damaged—don't you see that?"

"I don't think you are."

"Micah, are you there?" my mother called out from around the corner.

"You need to go, and I need to go, too," Laya said.

She started to walk away without saying good-bye. I was frozen in place, trying to find the right words that would make her stay. When she made it to the elevator and pressed the button, it occurred to me that I might not get another opportunity to talk to her . . . to convince her to give me a chance. I walked quickly toward the elevator. As she stepped in and turned around, our eyes locked. I prevented the door from closing with my arm.

Laya spoke first. "I'm scared."

"Of what?"

"Of everything. I'm scared to let him go. And . . . I'm scared to fall in love."

"I'm scared, too."

She closed her eyes. A tear ran down her cheek. I reached out and wiped it away with my thumb, but she stepped back.

"Go be with your family," she said.

Stay with me. We can be scared together.

I kept my eyes on her as she stared at the floor. Just as the doors closed, she lifted her head, meeting my gaze with a gut-wrenching sadness in her eyes.

17. Habitat

LAYA BENNETT to CAMERON BENNETT

Hey, Cam. What are you up to? Get it?

Remember when we would visit my dad, and we'd go to the East Village first and go to Grace Church and light candles? Or I would anyway. It was for all your friends who went diving off cliffs or out of planes and ended up dying? I haven't done that for you yet, because you didn't believe in it. Frankly, neither did I, but I thought it would help you mourn. I've learned other people can't help a person mourn. Three. Two. One. See ya.

My text pinged right before I got into the shower. I realized there were several built-up texts I hadn't seen. The first was from my father.

**Dad: The chief of surgery called
me and asked if you were ready.**

My dad knew a lot of people at the hospital. He kept in touch with the doctors who had worked on my mother. I think because my father had to eventually give the order to pull the plug on my mother, he felt like he had left a part of her there. After her death, he'd designed a wing and donated money to the hospital.

My father and Richard Wellington, the chief at The Hospital for Special Surgery, were good friends. I didn't want my dad calling in any favors on my behalf. I wanted my accomplishments to be my own, so it made me sad that Richard had to call my dad to find out if he could trust me.

Still, I remembered the sensation of being back in the hospital—how familiar the sterile scent was, how thrilling it was to have adrenaline rushing through my body again. I welcomed the certainty in my actions after grappling with so many unknowns.

Me: What did you say?

Dad: I said "undoubtedly," honey.

**Me: I am ready.
Thank you, Dad.**

Dad: It's not going to be easy.

Me: What is ever easy?

**Dad: Come and see me
this week.**

I thought about seeing Micah again and my stomach dropped but I knew I couldn't avoid the office forever.

> Me: I might have to get all
> my ducks in a row before
> I start the fellowship.

Dad: Got it. Soon, though?

> Me: Okay.

The next four texts were a string from Micah.

Micah: Again, thank you. Mel
is on the mend, being the normal
smartass that she is.

Micah: My parents are not easy
people to deal with. I think my mom
wants me to stay single for the rest
of my life.

Micah: I didn't mean that I was
implying . . . never mind. I saw your
post. I'll go down to Grace with you
if you want to light a candle.

> Me: No, thank you, Micah.
> It's personal for me.

Micah: Of course.
I didn't mean to intrude,
just thought you might
want some company.

I didn't respond.

At Grace Church, I put one penny in an envelope, stuck it in the slot out of spite for Cameron basically killing himself, and then I walked outside without lighting a candle because I was thinking his soul could be sitting at the bottom of that ravine. It's terrible that my thoughts for Cameron had gone in such a pitiful direction.

I was constantly vacillating between being angry with Cameron and missing him desperately. I wished I could stop feeling sorry for myself. I wished I hadn't made every day of the last several months all about him.

Outside, I sat on the freezing steps and cried. Why were Cameron and I still punishing each other when we loved each other?

An old man sat down next to me. He had bushy eyebrows and wild hair, Albert Einstein–style. He didn't say anything at first, but he was sitting uncomfortably close to me, especially considering that I was crying into my hands, soaking my sweater and jeans.

Looking up at him, I said, "Hello," as tears poured from my eyes.

"I know someone," he said.

"Oh yeah?" Alarm bells should have been going off in my head but they weren't. There was something particularly warm about the man. He might have been in his seventies or eighties; it was hard to tell.

"Yeah, I know someone."

Maybe he's a few sandwiches short of a picnic.

"Who do you know?" I asked. My tears had subsided.

"I know God. The man, the master, his holiness, the creator, the divine being, the holy spirit, the almighty."

"Do you now?"

He raised his eyebrows, shot me a tight smile, and nodded. Had he not smelled good, and looked fairly put together, aside from his gray, long disheveled hair, I would have thought he was homeless or crazy. Crazy was still up for debate, but I was sure he wasn't homeless.

"Has he mentioned anything to you about me?" I asked.

"No, he hasn't said a thing." He shrugged as if to say *sorry*.

"So, it's definitely a him?" I said with a frown.

"Well, hmm . . . more like an it."

"That doesn't sound very pleasant."

"What's your name? I'm Henry." He stuck his hand out to shake mine.

"Laya." His hand was remarkably warm for how cold it was outside.

"You know, it's just semantics; it doesn't really matter whether it's a him or a her. It's all around us . . . him, her, us, them, we . . . that's God. That's what I believe anyway."

"What are you trying to sell me on, mister?"

"I saw you inside."

I was becoming very suspicious. I wondered if the man worked for the church.

"Did you see me only put a penny in the envelope? Is that why you're talking to me now?"

"That's not why. Of course not. I saw you didn't light a candle, though, and I did wonder. That is sort of the point of the donation, regardless of the amount."

"Are you the candle police?"

He actually smiled when I said that. "Why are you so angry? Are you angry at God?"

I shook my head. "I'm not sure I even believe in God."

"Then who are you angry at?"

"Well, Henry, I guess I'm angry at my husband for killing himself."

His face fell. "Your husband committed suicide? I'm so sorry."

I felt awful for saying that about Cameron. That's not really what happened. "He didn't actually kill himself. He just took a very big risk and he died because of it."

"Are you upset at him for taking the risk?"

Now he's the church shrink?

"Who are you?"

"I'm just a man. I saw you crying and it looked like you were really hurting and needed a friend."

My heart suddenly felt warm. I stared into his grayish eyes and I could see my reflection. "You're right. I do need a friend. Thank you."

"Tell me about your husband."

"I'm not upset at him for taking the risk. I'm upset at the universe for making it so hard for me to move on. And somehow that makes me angry with Cameron."

"So, Cameron is his name?"

"Yes."

"And you think he's gone?

"I know he's gone; I watched him die."

He looked disappointed. "You watched his body die, not his soul. Isn't that why you're here? To light a candle for him . . . for his soul? To keep his soul right there?" He pointed to my heart. "Isn't that why you still talk to him every day?"

My eyes shot open. "How do you know that?"

"Because we all do. We all talk to the ones we loved

and lost. That's why I'm here. I lost my Margaret twenty-five years ago, and I still talk to her. I still come down here every now and then and light a candle to remind her that she will never be forgotten."

Tears sprang into my eyes. "See, that's the hard part for me. So, you never move on? You just keep mourning day after day for the rest of your life?"

"No, dear. I moved on. I married and had two more children after Margaret passed. Now I have my Sophia, and she's a beauty, and we're just gonna love each other until one of us goes. And then who knows after that? You're still here, though, and you didn't die. Your Cameron lives inside you now. Go light a candle and talk to him. Let him know you won't forget, but you're here and he's not. And you have to live your life."

I patted him on the knee and said, "Thanks, Henry." As it turned out, Henry was just a well-meaning old man who wanted to help someone, and I was just a cynical brat who couldn't see that at first.

Still wiping tears from my face, I walked back into the church and put a hundred dollars in an envelope. Evidently, Red Bull had to carry a very plump insurance policy on their stunt people. I was rich now. I didn't put a deceased person's name on the envelope. I didn't need to. I lit a candle next to Saint Anthony, the patron saint of lost things, but I didn't talk to Cameron. I had been doing that enough lately. I just thought about him. I thought about his smile. I thought about his humor and his laugh. I thought about our moments together, and then unintentionally my mind wandered to Micah.

I thought about *his* shy smile. His easy demeanor, and

his light laugh that always came out in one quiet puff of air. I thought about how he felt in that club. God forgive me, I was in a church, thinking about the way he held my hips. The way he kissed me rigidly at first, but eased into it. How he pushed me against the wall, not gently but passionately, like he couldn't get enough.

I thought about whispering "relax" to him, and immediately feeling the tension in his body retreat. I thought about the way we made eye contact, and how I wasn't uncomfortable. How it seemed like he wanted to please me. How it seemed like he was enamored of me.

On the long walk home, I thought only about Micah.

When I got home, I realized my apartment was infinitesimally cleaner than it had been for so long. I had been getting things done without even really realizing it. The sink was empty and the blinds were open. I said, "Progress" out loud, and the moment I said it, my stomach sank. Getting over losing Cameron could not possibly mean progress.

I searched frantically for his phone. It had always been in reach before. I found it under a dish towel near the kitchen where I had mindlessly set it. I deleted forty-two voicemails I had left in the past so I could call and make a new one.

> "Cameron, I lit a candle at Grace Church today. Not for you, but for me. I lit it under the statue of Saint Anthony. You know, the saint of lost things? Because I'm still lost. I met an old man at the church. He moved on after his wife died. Should I? Why can't you tell me? Why can't you give me a sign that it's okay? Why can't you talk to me anymore, Cam? Why don't I see you in my dreams? Where'd you go, Cam? Are you still at the bottom of that ravine?

You know what I thought about today? I thought about how I had sex with someone else. I thought about how good it felt. I didn't do it to spite you. I did it because I could never get enough of you, and I missed you, and I wanted to feel you again, but I didn't feel you. I felt him instead.

Give me permission. Help me to stop hating; help me to love again. Help me, Cam. Will you let me?"

I hit *end* and threw his phone across the room, then immediately ran over to it. Of course Cameron's phone had one of those cases on it that essentially made it indestructible. I was grateful. Too bad he hadn't had a case on to make him indestructible.

That night I did actually have a dream about Cameron. He was smiling at me from the top of Mount Whitney. We were talking as though we were sitting in a room somewhere, except we weren't. We were standing on a rock slab with a sheer cliff next to it. It was a repeat of a conversation we had actually had in our apartment in San Francisco when he was alive. I think it was the fall after we had gotten married. I had wanted to take a trip to the Spanish Cave with him, but he told me he had to practice. In the dream, though, he said, "Laya, concentrate on your work." Cameron hated how much I worked. He never would have said that to me.

Was he sending me a message now? I just wanted to hear his voice say, "I'm glad you met someone. I want you to be happy," but every message seemed so cryptic. I wondered if diving into work really was the answer.

18. Pilaster

MICAH

"Melissa got hit by a car?" Devin said, shocked as he peered over my cubicle partition.

"How'd you know?"

"She posted a picture on Facebook with her knee and neck in a brace, all laid up in the hospital. Why didn't you tell me?"

"I don't know. I got busy on the Glossette model."

"Your sister got hit by a car, and you didn't tell your best friend?"

The truth was, I didn't exactly classify Devin as my best friend, but I probably should have told him so he wouldn't have to find out from Facebook.

"I got kinda hung up on the work."

"You're still working on that piece of shit?"

It wasn't a piece of shit anymore because I had altered the design and Steve had approved of it, so Devin was just being snarky, and it was too early in the morning for bullshit. Devin was always putting me down for giving in to Steve when Devin was doing the exact same thing. "What's up, Devin?"

"Were you there, when she got hit?" he asked.

"Yes, it was terrifying. Luckily Laya happened to live in the apartment right above where Mel got hit. I called her and she came running down."

He looked at me sideways. "You know where Laya lives?"

"We went to a movie. I walked her home."

"Wow, moving kind of fast, huh?"

I wasn't about to mention the club escapade.

"It was no big deal."

"I wonder how Jim would feel about that?"

I couldn't figure out what Devin's play was, but he was obviously jealous.

"Well, Jim encouraged Laya and I to go to lunch, so maybe he just wants someone to get her out of the house."

Devin turned and looked back at his computer and said under his breath, "Yeah, whatever."

"What's your problem, Devin?"

"I told you I liked her," he said.

"You don't even know her," I replied.

"Oh, and you do?"

"I'm not saying that, I'm just saying, I didn't really have a choice with the lunch thing. Jim suggested it. Was I supposed to say no? What would you have done?"

He shook his head and ignored me, so I sat back down and continued working.

I left the office around six and walked aimlessly around

New York. *Why hasn't Laya gotten back to me?* I walked down her street and stopped halfway. *What if she was looking out the window?* I thought. I would seem like a total creeper. I walked by anyway.

To my absolute horror, she was outside walking a dog. It literally was the ugliest dog I had ever seen. She looked up at me, surprised. "Micah, what are doing here? Don't you live in Brooklyn? Once again, just in the neighborhood?" She was smiling when she said it, but I knew it seemed weird.

Recover, Micah, recover. I remember my music teacher telling me to recover every time I messed up at a recital. He would say, "No one will notice your mistake." But I felt like this was just too coincidental, even though I honestly was just wandering, or maybe wondering.

"I actually wanted to come here and take some notes on where my sister got hit. She might file a case against the cabbie." It was a half truth. I did want to get notes and photos for Melissa but I volunteered enthusiastically just to have an excuse to potentially run in to Laya, though I didn't actually expect to.

"Ahh, I see."

Time for a subject change. "Who's this furry little creature?"

"This is Pretzel."

I smiled. "You named your dog Pretzel?"

"I actually just adopted him this morning." She bent and let him lick her face. He was some kind of mutant terrier. "He came with that name. I didn't want to change it and confuse him." She was still giving him little kisses, practically sitting on the ground. "And I kinda like his name. Isn't he adorable?"

NO! "Yes, he's the cutest dog I've ever seen in my life."

She laughed. "Now you're being sarcastic."

"But I made you laugh, didn't I?"

"You did."

"What are you doing tonight?" I asked.

She hesitated for way too long. "I don't know, probably staying in and letting Pretzel get used to my apartment. I also just got on a cleaning binge."

"It seems like a nice place. Maybe out of my price range, though. I really like this area."

"I'll tell my father to give you a raise," she said automatically.

"Ha! Does he always follow your recommendations?"

She cocked her head to the side. "I think that's actually Steve's department, but I'll put in a good word for you."

"Thanks. So, you're staying in?" I didn't want to push it and ask her about the following night. I would wait until she gave me a cue.

"Yeah. Gotta get this guy used to my place so he doesn't go peeing on the furniture."

"You should try crate training him."

"I think that ship has sailed. They estimate that he's six years old, and they found poor Pretzel in a dumpster, so I'm going out to buy him a big ol' fuzzy dog bed."

"Well, that makes sense. He deserves it."

She stood up. "Good seeing you, Micah. I was just at the hospital . . . they're allowing me to do my fellowship there." She rolled her eyes. "My dad pulled some strings. Anyways, I checked in on Melissa and she looked great. She's a character."

"I know." Now I was the one rolling my eyes. "I've known her since we were zygotes."

"She told me if I broke your heart, she'd cut my tongue out. And then she started laughing maniacally. A second later she said, 'I'm kidding, chill.' At least you know she has your back. She said you were a complicated person."

Gee, thanks, Melissa.

"Break my heart, huh?"

"Well . . . um . . . " She began stumbling over her words and I didn't want her to get uncomfortable and bolt.

"What else did Melissa say about me?"

Laya laughed. "She said you were her favorite person in the world even though you hung all her stuffed animals from a clothesline when you were six."

"In my defense, she had put hot sauce in my soccer cleats."

"Sounds like you guys really love each other."

"We do." My eyes froze on hers. I don't know what possessed me to blurt out my feelings but I couldn't help myself. My mind was racing with everything I wanted to say to her. "You . . . really . . . you're beautiful. You look amazing today. You always look amazing, but especially today. I don't know what I'm saying. Why can't I stop talking? I want to kiss you but I'm not going to, I'm just going to continue rambling about how good you look and how badly I want to touch you, and how I wish I would have taken you home that night at the club to sleep in my bed."

Her jaw dropped to the ground. She was speechless, which caused me to continue rambling. "I want you to lazily lie on top of me. We don't have to do anything, just lie there. You're staring. Am I making you feel uncomfortable? I hope not because I just wanted to tell you that the night in the club meant something to me. It wasn't just a careless screw,

I mean, that sounds terrible, but what I'm trying to say is that I really enjoyed it. I was completely awestruck by you and I didn't want it to end. I'm not usually this forthcoming. You just look . . . edible and sweet and lovely and wonderful."

"Edible?" she said finally.

"Yes, edible, but I want to feed you, too, and wash your hair and put your hands inside my shirt." I shook my head, shocked at my own words.

Laya looked at me with compassion. "Are you . . . feeling okay?"

"I could go on, actually."

She smiled. "I should say thank you. You're really sweet but—"

"No, please. Don't say anything." We were still standing awkwardly in front of the building next to hers. I wasn't ready to walk away. I scrambled and tried to change the subject. "What's your favorite movie?"

She quirked her head to the side. "Um, okay? It's, um, *Space Camp*, actually. What's yours?"

"It's a tie between *Willow* and *The Neverending Story.*"

"Really?" She looked amused.

"What? Is that weird?" I said.

"No . . . it's cute."

"What's your favorite color?"

"Orange."

"Now that's weird. No one has ever said that. Did you know your eyes are absinthe-colored?"

She didn't respond for a moment, watching me closely while Pretzel sniffed my feet. "Where is all this coming from. Micah? This is the strangest conversation we've ever had."

"I don't know. Maybe because I want to tell you that I'm

basically falling for you, and I really think you need to know right now." *Oh great, here I go again.*

"Micah—"

I felt something drop on my shoe. "Laya?" Pretzel had stopped sniffing—then took the biggest poop right on my foot. I was actually grateful. It interrupted whatever Laya was going to say. I feared it would be rejection.

"Shit," Laya said.

"Yep."

"I'm so sorry. What a mess."

"Yeah, way to spoil a moment, Pretzel. How did that much poop come out of such a small dog?"

"Let me run up to my apartment to get something to clean that," she said.

She didn't invite me up; instead, she appeared in a flash at the top of the stairs with a wet towel, jumped off to skip the last three steps, bent, and, voilà, had cleaned off my leather work shoes.

"These are nice shoes," she said. "Can I replace them? I don't think I can get them clean."

"Don't worry about it. Come on, stand up." When she stood up I could see tears in her eyes. "Why are you crying? They're just shoes. Don't worry about it," I told her.

"I have to go. I just . . . your confession. I just don't know if I can reciprocate right now, and my dog shit on your shoes right after you told me you were falling for me, and I want to tell you the same thing—not falling for me but falling for you. But I just can't get a handle on my feelings right now, and I do actually have to go, but I will replace your shoes and I'm so sorry about this." Her voice had gotten higher and higher. She glanced down, noticing that she was holding a poop-stained towel in her hand. But I didn't care about any of that. She felt the same as me. She was falling . . . for *me*. "My god, I'm so embarrassed."

"Don't be embarrassed. It's adorable."

"I really do have to go. Bye, Micah." She picked up Pretzel and was gone again, leaving me on the street with crap on my shoes. Even so, it was pointless to try to hide my stunned smile.

19. Tracking Station

LAYA

I knew I had to have Pretzel the moment I saw him. He was wounded and alone . . . like me. In front of the pet store by my apartment, they had an adoption day. There were two available adorable puppies—a happy jumping lab named Johnny that seemed way too much for me to handle, and then Pretzel, sitting patiently in the corner of a tiny fenced-in space.

He looked up at me with sad eyes. An hour later, I had a dog. I hoped it would help me focus on other things. When I walked him, we looked around for other dogs, or shot dirty looks at the people staring at him, wondering what the hell happened to little deformed Pretzel. I loved him for being so flawed.

When I thought about it, I knew my father would be happy if I started dating a guy like Micah. I mean, it would be his dream finally fulfilled, but I still didn't think I was ready, and I knew I would have to do it for me, not my father. It was also peculiar to me that I ran into Micah, and that each time he called it a coincidence. Was I going crazy, officially losing my mind and just trying to avoid having feelings again? I pushed the thought out of my head and chalked it up to being paranoid and having attachment issues, just a bunch of psychobabble I learned in therapy.

But I had Pretzel now, who I could try to fix first.

20. Rubble

MICAH

The only thing that kept me from feeling like a total fool during my run-in with Laya was that she finally admitted she had feelings for me, too.

From the office the next day, I called Melissa at the hospital to see how she was doing and to get my mind off Laya.

"What up? I'm happily jacked-up on pain meds," she said, slurring.

"How long are you gonna be in the hospital?"

"Dude, my night nurse is so fucking hot. He washed my hair last night and I wanted to blow him."

"Jesus, Melissa. Just get better. Quit flirting with the staff," I said, not at all in a nice tone.

"It's all I have, Micah. This is so mind-numbingly boring, lying here all day. I keep asking for more pain meds and they tell me I've hit the pinnacle more than once. That's what they called it . . . a fucking pinnacle. What does that even mean?"

"It means you can't have any more pain meds, Melissa."

She ignored me. "I saw your girlfriend. I guess she works here now. She said she remembered her mom dancing with good ol' Jim to the song 'Sweet Melissa' in their kitchen right before her mom shuffled off her mortal coil and went six feet under."

I held on to my phone a bit tighter, irritated by Melissa's drugged-up tone. "I have no idea why I tolerate you. That was so insensitive. Her mother died when she was a toddler, and then she lost her husband right after they got married."

"What's your fucking problem, Micah? You need to get laid so bad. Go get some lotion and fuck socks and bang city by yourself in your bedroom."

"How much pain medication are they giving you? That comment actually worries me. I don't even want to know what fuck socks are. After you get out of the hospital, we're dropping you off at Saint Peter's to have the demons exorcised from your demented soul. I can't believe I shared a womb with you."

Melissa was wrong. Getting laid was not the answer. Every time I thought about Laya, it involved something more profound. She wasn't just a woman I met in a club and had a one-night stand with. She was a surgeon who wore old NASA sweatshirts and pink Converse. She was a walking conundrum, and her complexities drew me to her.

Melissa was just being Melissa when she brought up my love life. She couldn't take anything seriously. It was a small miracle that she was able to stay with Kenny as long as she had.

"Mel, Laya told me that you threatened her."

"I was kidding, jeez. So sensitive. It's like you two are waiting for someone to offend you."

"She knows you were kidding, and by the way, I know you said it because you love me." I laughed. "I hope that makes you feel uncomfortable. I know how much you love me. You don't have to go around making death threats, though I do appreciate your commitment when you made the comment about cutting her tongue out."

"Be serious about what? I just got hit by a car. Isn't that pretty serious?"

"Melissa, the day you went to the hospital, you told the doctor with the horrible bedside manner that he was compensating for having a small dick."

"Well—"

"Nothing, never mind. I'll come visit you tonight," I told her.

I actually knew how to manipulate Melissa. She did have a good heart. It was just buried under a bunch of Medusa snakes, but it was in there. I guilt-tripped her often and it worked.

"Okay, tell me, baby boy. What's really bothering you now?"

"Laya has been posting these messages to her husband—"

"I know, I know, and . . . ?"

"And," I said, and paused.

"Oh my god, you still play Kill Your Loved Ones. And I'm the demented one?" She was starting to sound coherent and back to her normal self.

"No, I told you I stopped doing that. I kind of replaced it

with trying to fulfill Laya's posts by leaving stuff on her door-step. Stuff that sort of mimicked her life with Cameron."

Melissa didn't say anything for a long time.

"I think we should go to rehab after I get outta here," she finally said.

"For what?"

"I'll go for my demented soul, and you go for being a stalker before you get arrested."

"So, you're admitting you're demented?"

"Whatever," she said, "I'll just go to support you."

I laughed. "I don't think they have a rehab for that. Do you really think it's stalker-ish? What I'm doing?"

"A hundred percent yes. It would scare the shit out of me, and you know not a whole lot does."

My sister had worked at a haunted house as a character when we were teenagers. She was the guy cutting the woman's head off with a chainsaw. It started when we went to the same haunted house a year before and she didn't flinch when Freddy Krueger jumped out at her. She just calmly said, "Oh fuck off, Freddy. You suck at this." After we walked out, she said, "That acting was terrible. I should try to get a job here next year and show these wimps what scary is." So, yeah, nothing really frightened Melissa, not even getting hit by a car.

She was right about what I was doing to Laya. I already knew that. Emotionally, I was so cut off. I crawled in a dark hole for months and thought it was appropriate to start stalking a recently widowed woman.

"I know, Melissa, but what do I do? I want to be in her life."

"Just be yourself, Micah. Tell her the truth. You're a nice

guy, a rare breed. Stop looking at her Facebook page and just be in the moment."

"That might be the nicest, most sincere thing you've ever said to me."

"Come visit me tonight. It's boring as fuck in here."

"I will, I promise."

"I love you, Micah."

"God, Melissa, tell them to lay off the pain meds. You're seriously so looped."

"I'll see you, little bro."

"You're only seven minutes older than me. But I'll let you pretend. Get some rest."

We both hung up. We knew exactly when to hang up. It was a twin thing.

Against Melissa's advice, I scanned Facebook once I was back at my desk, and lo and behold, Laya had sent Cameron a message.

LAYA BENNETT to CAMERON BENNETT

I got us a dog named Pretzel. I'm not even completely sure what kind of dog he is. He's small and sweet and kind of ugly, but I love him. He keeps me company. He's a bit of a daredevil, go figure. He has a big-pup personality and will stand up to any dog that gets in his way. I want to get some of those Kong chewy things you used to buy for Jeremy's dog. I think Pretzel would like those. Three. Two. One. See ya.

Of course, after seeing her post, I couldn't resist. As soon as I was off work I went to the nearest pet store. They didn't have anything called Kong chewies. I went to three different places, all over the city until I finally found them. The store was called Pawfect Pet Store and *it was* pawfect, but they were about to close. The woman working there was actually locking the door when I walked up. I mouthed through the glass, *Please, please*. I shot her the best puppy-dog eyes I could muster. She looked at me sympathetically. Dog people are awesome.

"Hi, I'm looking for something called a Kong chewy."

She laughed. "Well, we have about seventeen different options for that. Which one would you like?" She pointed to a wall full of items with the Kong brand name on it. I was immediately overwhelmed, so I picked five.

I ran six blocks. Six New York blocks . . . in the dark, to get to Laya's. I quickly hopped up the stairs and hit her buzzer. This time I waited.

She slowly came toward the building's front door. Through the window I could see her hesitate when she saw that it was me.

When she opened the door, I started vomiting words, "Didn't you say, 'I'm falling for you, too,' after you left me today with shit on my shoes?"

She stared, blinking for several moments before she responded. "No . . . but—"

"It doesn't matter," I interrupted. "I need to tell you something." I handed her the bag of dog chewies.

"Okay." She set the bag down, folded her arms in front of her chest, and shivered. She was wearing a T-shirt and sweats, her hair twisted up into a messy bun.

I was searching for words. "Are you cold?"

"No, I'm fine. What's in the bag?"

"Chewies for your dog."

"You read my post." It was a statement, not a question, and her face held no expression.

"I did. I've read all your posts for a while." I was telling her finally . . . I was admitting everything. I had to.

She looked down at her slippers. "Do you know how fucking creepy that is?"

"Yes, I do."

When she looked up, I noticed her eyes were misting over. "So, it *was* you at the concert?"

"It was me."

"Why?" Her voice was shaking.

I was fumbling for words. "It's inexcusable. I don't know what to say."

She pulled her phone from her pocket. "Should I call the police?"

"Do you want to call the police?"

"You knew I'd be at the club. You left the damn flowers. To what? Remind me?"

"No . . . no, that's not it."

"What, you thought you could replace those memories with you instead of him." Tears were streaming down her face, but her expression was still blank.

"I did it because the first time I met you, there was a spark—"

"It's called static electricity. I was already grieving. Wow, I don't know you at all."

"You do know me. You do. I had good intentions."

"Very misguided intentions."

"Yes, they were misguided." It was going to be impossible to talk my way out of what I had done.

"Right now, I have a lot of words for you," she said. "But I'm not even sure I want to waste my breath."

"Talk to me, please. Just talk." She looked so sad. It made me feel like someone had reached inside my chest and ripped out my heart and threw it in the recycle bin. What was I thinking?

"I knew it was you." The tears stopped. "At least, I guessed it was you."

"What?"

"You're not very good at being a stalker. You live a million miles away from me and end up on my street . . . twice. You secretly leave shit on my doorstep and just happen to choose the ramen place I mention on Facebook. What sort of defect do you have that would possess you to do this? Why? Why do all of this? Do you have a sick curiosity to know how it feels?"

"Can we go inside and talk about this?"

"No way! Are you kidding?" she spat.

"Oh my god, Laya—"

"Don't fucking say my name; you don't deserve it."

"I care about you. I wanted to help. I wanted to know you more, and now I'm looking at you and I feel like the worst person in the world."

It was terrible what I had done. Did I actually think leaving stuff on her doorstep related to her experiences with her dead husband would help her? Or was I still really just trying to stay connected to her? I had opportunities to see her. I didn't need to freak her out; I worked for her father, for god's sake.

"You should feel like the worst person. You used my vulnerability to get close to me."

"No, I didn't mean to. That wasn't my intention. Please, you have to believe me." I was scrambling for footing.

"I don't want to believe this is true," she said. She still had her phone out, but she hadn't dialed anything yet. She pocketed it, looking tired, betrayed—I did all of this to her.

"Where does that leave us?"

"There is no *us*. Go home. I'm going to bed."

"Wait, please." She started to close the door. "I wanted to help put you back together. I wanted to build you up again."

She paused and stared at me. "We can't put people back together, Micah. And I'm not one of your projects to build."

"I had to try. And then . . . and then I fell in love with you."

She dropped her face into her hands and I think she was crying and laughing at the same time.

"This is insane," she mumbled. She took her tear-soaked hands and placed them on my face. I held her wrists. Both of us were shaking. "You're just like me . . . deluded," she cried. "You were way off the mark, Micah."

"I know. I figured it out. I'm still learning. Please give me another chance?"

She shook her head. "For what?"

"What do you need?" I asked.

"Time and space." She was still crying.

"I'm so sorry." I stepped back, clutching both sides of the door frame. I felt my body weaken. "I didn't mean—"

"Time and space, Micah. I know you're not a bad person. I remember that day in the office. I felt it, too." She looked away. "God, this is unbearably hard."

She glanced over her shoulder, as if checking for someone behind her. When our eyes met again, it was like I was seeing her sadness for the first time. The pain took my breath away. "There's no *us*. We can't be an *us* right now. Just a 'something,' which I can't define. We are just okay. And that's all I can give you right now."

A small part of me jumped like a drowning man who has spotted a lifesaver in his path. Stepping forward, knowing that it might cost me, I placed my hands on her hips, leaned in, and laid a soft, closemouthed kiss on her lips while she held my face and cried.

I kept my forehead on hers. "That's enough. I swear to god, that's enough for me. Just don't tell me I've ruined everything."

"You're the only person I know who hasn't told me to stop posting," she said.

"I never will. I know why you do it."

"Do you?" she whispered.

"It's your way, right?"

"Yes." She stepped back, wearing a small, sad smile. "Good-bye."

"See you, okay?"

She shrugged. "I don't know."

I walked away without looking back. It wasn't like the world was ending. She didn't say we wouldn't see each other ever again. I still had a desperate hope she wouldn't give up on me.

Telling her the truth was the right thing to do . . . even if it felt all wrong in the moment.

21. Suborbital

LAYA

Weeks rolled by . . . time and space. I threw myself into being Pretzel's mom and into my work at the hospital. I spent as little time as I could thinking about Micah. I couldn't decide if it was the most terrifying and bizarre thing anyone had ever done for me . . . or if he was my goddamn savior.

I tried not to picture his face as he stood in my doorway, telling me he had fallen in love with me and how sorry he was.

I tried not to feel his lips on mine. I tried not to think about what he and I could be, all mashed-up pieces glued together. Mosaics in the park.

Imagine.

One Friday, sitting in the cafeteria at the hospital, I checked Facebook on my phone. There was a message from Micah.

> Hi, Laya. I hope you're okay. So . . . I found a cool
> little French bistro that has a patio. I didn't know how
> to get ahold of Pretzel, so I wondered if you could ask
> him if he'd like to get breakfast with me?

I stared at the message for something like half an hour before I wrote back. While it was cute of Micah to frame the invite the way he did, I was still unsure of how I felt, knowing he had been spying on me. It brought me back to a place of fear and insecurity.

I was lonely and feeling isolated at home. Pretzel was helping me, but as far as I could tell, Pretzel didn't talk. Sometimes I felt like Micah didn't talk either, only choosing to talk when he meant it, like when he told me how beautiful I was, and how he wanted to help me. In those short little bursts, he came across as both thoughtful and well-intentioned.

Back on Facebook after eating an uncooked, dry bagel, I messaged Micah.

> Sure. I talked to Pretzel and he's OK with having
> breakfast. What time?

He messaged back almost immediately.

> Great! Is eight too early? We can beat the rush.

> That works for me.

> I'm glad you want to join Pretzel and me for breakfast.
> I'm excited to see you again.

A few moments passed by where I didn't respond.

> I'm sorry again, Laya. I hope you don't think I'm a
> complete psycho.

At that point I wasn't entirely sure how to react. I had married a guy who liked to jump out of planes and off cliffs, so could I really call Micah psychotic? I waited to respond.

He wrote back first.

> Well, I guess you left. I'll see you bright and early!

I replied soon after that, feeling bad for not reciprocating his nice comment.

> Sorry, I stepped away for a sec. Yes, I will see you.

I paused for a moment and once I saw the little light go off indicating he was no longer online, I typed . . .

> I'm looking forward to breakfast as well.

Toying with him was not my plan. I had to trust my instincts about him despite what he had done. I also had to get out of the house and be social.

At three a.m. I woke up sweating. I stumbled into the bathroom and took my temperature. It was ninety-nine. I made myself believe it was high enough to call off breakfast. I paced near the front window for twenty minutes, periodically looking out at the flickering street lamp and thinking it reminded me of my emotions. I was on and off again. I kept using Cameron's death as a way not to address what was going on in my own life. In the dim light of my bedroom I dialed his number again and again, hanging up each time after listening to his voice. Finally, I started talking.

"Cameron, every time I call you I feel I have less and less to say to you, except that I miss you. I've been watching the street lamp outside my apartment. I've been watching it for over an hour and it won't stop flickering.

"Off and on. Off and on. It's like my heart beating, slower and slower until it will eventually stop, so that I can catch up to you, wherever you are. Or it's my brain feeling conflicted about how I should move on. Off and on. Back and forth.

"Even saying the words 'move on' feels like I'm betraying you. What does it even mean? Is it like moving from one house to another, where we eventually forget how the wood floors felt on our feet? Or how the drapes smelled or what it sounded like when the front door was opened? We forget all the senses and just have a fading visual memory.

"The items I have left, belonging to you, have lost your smell. I've lost the last little "almost" tangible piece of you. All I have is pictures, and memories that are fading, turning sepia. Eventually they'll be black and white and I won't remember the vibrant spark that you were. The spark I tried keeping so bright only to watch it turn into the flickering light outside my window. I wish I knew what else I could tell you. I wish I could hear your voice telling me what I should do. It's all happening and I can't stop it."

Eventually, when I fell back to sleep, I was in a dream with Cameron again. We were in his tiny studio in California. I wasn't sure how I knew this but it couldn't have been long after we had met. We squeezed onto his twin-sized bed because his room was packed with skis, snowboards, climbing gear, you name it.

Cameron rolled on top of my naked body and started kissing me all over. His tongue was circling my nipple. He looked up at me and smiled. "I love your boobs," he said.

He had never said that to me in real life, and they weren't particularly special, but that was one part of my body I didn't hate.

When he started moving inside of me, he was looking down, into my eyes. He had a faint satisfied smile on his face as his breathing picked up. He came fast and laughed. He said, "Was that too fast?"

I replied, "No, it made me feel good."

He was sated and sleepy-eyed, smiling at me. "I love you."

"I love you, too," I told him.

"I have to go in a few minutes," he said regretfully. His callused fingers ran up and down my side, like he was touching the most delicate of objects.

I started giggling and he started laughing.

"I thought you weren't ticklish," he said. "You know why people are ticklish in certain spots? It's because our bodies are designed to automatically protect our important vital arteries and organs: under the neck, behind the knee for your femoral artery, under your arms for your head—"

"I know. You told me that already." But he hadn't. I had learned it in medical school.

He moved off me completely, taking away his warmth. "I have to go," he said, kneeling before me.

"Don't say that—you always say that." I started crying quietly, tears pouring from my eyes, down my cheek, and then dripping onto the pillow.

His eyes welled up, too. He never cried, but they were tears of empathy. "Don't cry, please," he said in a soft, soothing voice.

"Why are you leaving?"

"I have to, Laya. I have to go practice."

"Practice for what?"

"You know . . . I don't have to tell you."

He got up and started to get dressed. "But why?" I didn't understand. "Don't you want to stay with me?" His room seemed emptier; his equipment had disappeared. The sun was gone and a light outside—the moon, maybe—threw long shadows in the room, across Cameron's face.

At the doorway, he turned back, half-dressed. He said, "I can't." He didn't seem happy about my request.

"But we just had sex."

He shook his head. "Are you still using that as a bargaining chip?"

"I never do. I just want you to stay so bad. I didn't mean it that way. I meant that I'm emotional about it. Don't you feel the same way?"

What did he mean by "still" anyway? That was never my intention.

He stared. "Laya, sex is arbitrary. It's just an expression. But I love you, I do."

"That is such a contradictory statement."

He laughed. "Are you trying to outsmart me?"

"You're leaving me alone. Again."

It felt like the beautiful thing we had just shared, all feelings and emotions, him looking into my the eyes, drawing me in, telling me I was beautiful and that he loved me, meant nothing to him once he knew I needed validation in other ways.

"I want to stay, too, Laya. I don't want to leave you, but it's time. I'm sorry."

"I don't believe you want to stay or you would. All your sorrys are starting to blend together into a massive pile of disappointment." My voice sounded distorted—like it was coming through a PA system. It was my voice and it wasn't. "Where are you going to practice? I mean really, right now? What is so important that you have to leave right this second at two in the morning? You can't talk to me? Lie here with me so we can feel warm again? It means a lot to me . . . what we do, here in this room, Cameron. Sex isn't arbitrary to me. It always meant a lot to me."

Why am I speaking in the past tense now?

"It meant a lot to me, too, I just showed it in a different way. Please don't confront me about this now."

"You were always so busy; you hardly ever showed me any of your feelings. And you were rarely true to your word."

"You were busy, too, Laya. You shouldn't put all the blame on me."

"Why did we fight?" I asked him, my voice lower and becoming more passive and hopeless.

"Because we were different," he said.

The words felt like a gut punch. I always thought he appreciated our differences. "But we were so alike, too." I argued. "And our relationship worked."

He just smiled. "I want you to be happy, always, forever. I care about you and . . ." He hesitated. "And I love you. I'll see you on the other side. Count me down, Laya."

"What?"

"Honey, count me down."

Wind, from out of nowhere, was suddenly all I could hear. The room temperature dropped.

"No!" I yelled.

"Three," he said.

"No, please. Just a little more. More time, please." I was begging now.

"Two," he said.

Neither of us spoke. He was still near the door, looking sullen and penitent. It took me a while, but I finally said, "One." I let him go.

The wind roared, and the sound of ice collapsing—like it did *that* day—finally pulled me from my dream. When I woke up, my face was in my pillow. And I was crying again.

When I stopped sobbing, I mulled over the dream—because it was just that, a dream. It was perfectly clear; I remembered every detail. In real life, Cameron never looked me in the eyes while we were making love. What Cameron and I had was passionate, but he never made eye contact with me that way. Yes, it was a sex dream, but there was something in it, some kind of finality in his expression. He was a combination of who I wanted him to be and who he really was.

When the real Cameron started to come through at the end, I got sad. When he had a hard time expressing himself, and when faced with the idea that he might be hurting me, he retreated. He either made a joke out of it, or he claimed it was just his personality, when I knew it was a character flaw. We all have them. I wished he would have realized it.

I didn't want to demonize him. Thinking about him now was the opposite. I saw him clearly now. I didn't want to change Cameron; I wanted Cameron to grow up and to show me how much he loved me with actions, not words. I knew as long as he was making excuses and saying "That's just how I am" and "Nothing really matters," despite the fact that he was hurting me, then he would always be that way: selfish, not thoughtful or considerate of my needs, even though I followed him across the world and back, extending my residency far longer than I had planned. But he would say it's not "tit for tat, Laya." I bought into it that notion because for whatever reason, I loved him, and I wanted him to love me. It wasn't ever "tit for tat." It was just me asking for common respect and reciprocation between two people who claimed to have such a connection.

There were countless things I had made for him, or gifts I had given him, strewn throughout his room. It was as if I only existed in his thoughts when we were together, and nothing I did had meaning when he was practicing for a stunt. He would forget my birthday and say "I will get you something real nice, I will." Then he would laugh it off or tell me that asking was not a good way to get what I wanted. Or he would try to tickle me, having forgotten that I wasn't ticklish. These were things I couldn't let go of.

He would tell me, "You feel too much, Laya, and you have more of a capacity to address your emotions than I do. I can't express myself like you can."

I would argue with him and say, "But, Cameron, I had

no model for love, or self-expression, so I can't be those things any more than you can."

He'd respond, "It's just how you are, Laya. It's just how you are, and this is how I am."

Sometimes we can't really tell who we are in our twenties, or even thirties or beyond. It gets muddled up with ideals we've entertained. It's what we've been taught by other people and society, or what we've read in a book.

I didn't ever want to be in a committed relationship; it just happened, and once I was . . . I loved it. I loved spending time with him, even though it was limited and we fought often. Cameron and I fought because we were two independent people who, despite loving each other, were still figuring out how to share a life. We were used to the autonomous lives we had before we met. It took practice and sacrifice to make things work. Cameron wasn't always good at it, neither was I, but now in retrospect, it seemed like I made more of an effort.

When I had brought up issues to Cameron, he would tell me I was being paranoid or needy or that he couldn't handle the stress of me being unhappy. Since he had passed, I never thought this deeply about our dynamic. I always focused on his good traits, so it made me miss him even more. How can you bad-mouth a dead person anyway?

Before I demanded from him that my needs be met, I should have looked within. I should have searched for what my needs really were. My needs were not to be with some careless spirit so focused on doing dangerous stunts that he would forget I even existed while he was in *his mode*. It should have been a red flag when the person you're claiming to love chalked up sex to being an arbitrary action. It was immature and hurtful.

I would say, "Do you think of me when I'm not around?"

And he would always say, "Of course." He didn't know how he made me feel. He was too blinded by what *he* wanted.

If he was capable of forgetting I had called or texted and wouldn't respond for days, I knew he wasn't thinking about anyone but himself. The way he turned it around and placed the blame on me was selfish. He would say, "The last thing I need right now, while I'm practicing for the most dangerous stunt of my life, is another needy girlfriend." I was just a needy girlfriend. He probably married me to appease me.

Cameron hadn't even had a real girlfriend in his life, just a few "needy women" here and there. Had I ever asked him if he could recognize the common denominator?

Now I had to face that he was gone, and he wasn't perfect, and he wasn't my soul mate, and if he was, then we can have more than one in a lifetime. I hated the notion of soul mates anyway.

He was inexperienced when it came to relationships and every emotion attached to them. He had some words for it, but they would quickly lose their meanings when he wouldn't follow them through with actions. The dream made me remember, and deep down I knew it was just my subconscious speaking to me, not Cameron.

22. Buildings and Bridges

MICAH

My alarm went off at six a.m., and even though I was excited to see Laya, I mistakenly turned it off rather than hitting snooze. I stayed up way too late. Like a little kid, excited to go to Disneyland the next day, I couldn't sleep.

I imagined, over and over again, how our breakfast would go. In my mind there were at least five versions of what would happen. One where she tells me how good it feels to get out of the house. Another ridiculous version where she tells me she's been attracted to me since we met and was thrilled to be forming a deeper relationship with me. That was only silly because I knew it was a projection of my own feelings. The other three were extended versions of how she couldn't see me anymore, or how she never thought I was good-looking or interesting, even though she'd pulled me into a dark space in a bar and had sex with me. The worst version of all was her tearing into me again about leaving the gifts on her porch.

When I finally woke up, it was seven fifteen. I was running around yelling, "Shit, shit, shit!" I stared into my closet and wondered what to wear. I felt stupid. I didn't want to be overdressed, so I grabbed black pants, Nikes, a black T-shirt and a hoodie. I looked like a burglar, but I didn't really have time to try on a bunch of outfits like I was some teenager going on a first date.

I ran to the subway and quickly realized I would never make it on time. I knew a taxi wouldn't be any faster.

Glad I had my Nikes on, I literally ran to the restaurant from the subway stop. But when I arrived, Laya wasn't there. It was eight seventeen. Maybe she wasn't a punctual person. Maybe she'd changed her mind. After putting my name on the waiting list, I sat on a bench to text Mel.

Me: I'm going on a breakfast date with Laya. She's like fifteen minutes late.

Mel: That hot male nurse is cutting up my French toast.

Me: Do you pay attention to anything I say? You're like talking to a three-year-old.

Mel: Laya is damaged goods, Micah.

Me: That's a cliché. Just because her husband died doesn't mean she is damaged. She's young. She deserves a second chance.

Mel: What if you die a year after you
get married? What if you get sucked
into a tree cutter, or get hit by space
junk, or get your head caught in elevator
doors just as they're closing?

Me: Why do you have
to do that?

Mel: Because I love you.

Me: Thinking of all the morbid
and graphic ways I could die
is your way of showing
me you love me?

Mel: Oh, you're one to talk with
your creepy-ass omens.

Me: I don't do that anymore,
I told you! Oh my god, I think I
just saw her cross the street a
block away. I gotta go.

It *was* her. When she approached me, she was smiling
and it made me smile. When she got closer, she was still
smiling, except I noticed she had very dark circles under her
eyes, probably matching mine.

I bent and kissed her on the cheek. "Hi, beautiful," I
said near her ear. I wondered if I was being too forward.

Laya pulled back, squinting, but her smile didn't disappear. She said, "You're sweet."

I paused. "You're otherworldly."

Her smile turned to a full, beautiful, cosmic grin. She giggled and said, "You're full of compliments today . . . come on, we better go in. I think I heard your name." Before we went in, we stood there staring at each other for a few seconds. She finally grabbed me by the arm and said in a low, hesitant voice, "No one has ever called me otherworldly before. Thank you."

"Well, you are." I took her hand in mine and led her into the restaurant, praying we wouldn't revisit what I had done. "By the way, where is Pretzel?"

"He wasn't hungry."

I laughed.

We were seated at a booth and neither of us seemed able to find words to start the conversation. She spoke up first. "I've been here before. Have you?"

"Yeah, a couple of years ago, actually. I haven't been here in a long time, but I loved it."

She stared though the window, out into the distance, seemingly sad. God, I wanted again to profess how much I liked her in every way.

"This place is so cool. I can't believe I forgot I had been here with . . . " She paused. "I can't believe I forgot I had been here before, is what I meant."

I leaned forward. "Laya, I don't want to press you, or make you feel like you have to . . . but if you want to talk about what you're going through, I'm here for you. I know what I did was so wrong but—" I realized I was talking a million miles an hour.

"Stop. Just stop."

"I'm sorry. I don't want to make you feel uncomfortable. I just wanted you to know." It wasn't even five minutes into our breakfast and I had almost messed things up again.

She was staring directly into my eyes like she was trying to look inside me to see what I was made of.

"I'm going to be blatant with you," she said.

I took a deep breath. "Please do."

"I don't want to talk about Cameron. Cameron is dead." I wasn't sure if Laya had ever said those words to me. "I will miss him desperately, but the last thing I want to do when I'm out to breakfast with you is talk about Cameron, or his death, or how I'm handling it, or even the things you left on my stoop."

"I understand," I said immediately, feeling extremely relieved. I didn't want to talk about those things either.

"Do you?" she shot back.

"What?" I asked, confused.

"Do you truly understand?"

"No, no, I don't understand . . . I mean, I'm trying to."

She looked as if she wanted to cry again, and it'd be all my fault, so I wanted to do what I could to comfort her. I reached for her, laying my hand on hers.

"I'm sorry. . . did I say something wrong?"

"No. It's not anything you've said. There's something I should tell you. Something has been eating away at me and I haven't told a single soul."

"Go on, I'm listening."

"I lost my mother when I was three. I lost Cameron three years after meeting him. I'm a dark cloud, Micah. You should stay away from me. I'll probably put an expiration date on you the moment you get close to me."

"That's crazy, Laya."

"Yes, it is. I hadn't even said it out loud to myself but it's been a thought haunting me for months."

Taking a deep breath, she looked down again as though

she was trying to stifle a thought. When she looked up, she arched her eyebrows and that's when I was positive she was waiting for me to respond, but I couldn't think of what to say.

"So, Micah . . . if you feel like dying in . . . oh, about three years—"

I leaned over the table, grasped her from behind the neck, and interrupted her with a kiss. I kissed her slowly, delicately, and completely.

When I pulled away, her eyes were still closed. Quietly, I said, "I'm sorry to say, Laya, but your theory is horseshit. I don't care about your superstition. I'll take my chances."

She huffed and shook her head. "Another risk taker."

"I get a flu shot every year," I said, smirking.

The waitress came, forcing us to look at our menus, but it was hard to look away from Laya. I couldn't pretend I knew what she was feeling. The only thing I could tell was that she seemed stronger and stronger each time I saw her.

After the waitress took our order, Laya told me about her fellowship at the hospital, her nerves about going back into practice as a doctor, and also about the pains and joys of having a dog. I told her about my relationship with my sister, my parents, and the people in the office. When I told her about what I had been up to the last couple of years, the conversation turned again.

"Why did you lock yourself away outside of work? What were you going through?"

"I don't know, honestly. I've thought about it a lot and I can't pinpoint one thing."

She squinted like she didn't believe me.

"What?" I said.

"Nothing."

"Tell me."

"I'm guessing you have an inkling, or you know at least one of the factors," she said.

What I had said was true; there were a lot of factors, but I think I knew the one she was hinting at.

"What do you know, Laya?" I said humorously.

"I popped in to see my dad last week. I was in a bad place and Devin cornered me and—"

"This story already sounds like a very unhappy one."

"Let me finish." I nodded, prompting her to continue. "I asked where you were."

"You did?" I could feel my mouth turning up into a smile.

"Yes. I was roaming around the office, waiting for my dad to finish a meeting. I noticed the plaque with your name on it was still outside your cubicle but you weren't there. A minute later Devin found me by the water cooler. He asked if I wanted to go to a club or something—"

"Sounds like Devin," I interjected.

"Anyway, I told him no and then asked where you were. He said you were probably trying to be celibate." She started giggling, and when the words hit me, my eyebrows shot up to the crown of my head.

"What?"

"Yeah, his exact words were, 'Micah might be playing Unabomber in the forest and trying to be celibate.' He laughed, so I knew he was joking about the Unabomber part at least," she said with humor.

"Devin had no clue where I was at. I was probably at the hospital visiting Melissa. And frankly, the Unabomber comments were not only insulting to me, they were also insensitive." I hadn't even realized my food was in front of me getting cold. Even though I wanted to playfully dismiss Devin's comments, a part of me wondered when Devin would grow up.

"Whoa, whoa, whoa. Don't shoot the messenger."

I hesitated. "I just . . . no, I mean . . . I just . . . "

"You just what?"

Her beautiful green eyes looked translucent and her golden-brown hair framed her face in soft, long curls. I couldn't look away. It was like the first time I met her.

Finally, I said, "A few months ago I was spending a lot of time at my parents' cabin in the Adirondacks to just reflect on my life and what I wanted. Honestly, Laya, I was tired of the scene. I felt like I had put so much time, money, and energy into college and my career that I wasn't living the way I wanted to. I was taking shortcuts in my personal life. Any spare time I had, I was out at clubs with Devin and Jeff, just trying to find an empty promise for a night. And then I met you."

Her expression fell. Quietly, she said, "Is that what I was to you? An empty promise? Someone who was easy, hurting, and lonely? Someone who you knew you could do that with and not have to commit to later?"

"No," I said with fervor. "That's what I'm trying to tell you. You're the reason I was starting to come out of the dark, but—"

"But what?"

"But I still don't know how you feel. That night in the club, I thought *you* wanted to just feel good."

"I did, but I realized later how it had ignited something in me, too. Maybe I'm not wired the way I thought I was. I didn't date a lot, Micah. I had flings here and there, but they meant nothing to me when I was younger. I don't want that anymore. So, yes, I was testing the waters. I wondered if I could be with someone I was already attracted to and then walk away like I had done so many times before Cameron came along. I hate that it sounds like I was using you."

I nodded as if I totally understood. "You did sort of walk away."

"I didn't, though. Somewhere in the recesses of my sub-conscious I was aware of the change happening within me. Someday maybe I can express myself to you better, but right now I *am* trying to process it."

"You're softer than you think you are," I said.

She looked out the window and took a deep breath. "Are you gonna eat that French toast or what?"

"Why, do you want it?" I deadpanned, and placed my hand in front of my plate, protecting it. "'Cause you can't have any."

She quickly stabbed her fork into the French toast, pull-ing a heap of it away and shoving it in her mouth. I laughed. Still chewing, she said, "This is soooo good . . . even though it's cold."

"Well, I was busy and I forgot about it."

Just then the server walked up and asked if we wanted our coffee refilled. She looked exhausted, her hair flying everywhere and her frilly blue apron speckled with food stains. I noticed she had a piece of food or something on her cheek. Laya looked up at her, blinked, and then wiped her own cheek, signaling to the server to do the same. Laya cared about people. The woman didn't understand, so Laya very quietly said, "You need to wipe your cheek. This place is a madhouse; I don't know how you serve all these tables. I could never do it."

The woman wiped her cheek and said, "Thanks, honey."

After the server walked away, I said, "That was really

kind of you. I don't know many people who wouldn't feel uncomfortable saying that to someone."

"Well, who hasn't had mustard on their face without realizing it four hours after eating a sandwich and then talking to ten different people who said nothing." She cocked her head to the side. "Hey, maybe we can eat cold French toast sometime at my apartment."

"I would love that, though I do wonder why it has to be cold."

"Just in case we get caught up . . . in conversation, you know?"

"Yes," I said in a low voice. "Smart planning."

"Hey, are we flirting?"

"Are we?"

"Are we?" I said again.

"Well, it's hard not to flirt with me."

"True."

Just then our check came. We wrestled it back and forth until I finally yanked it out of her hand. I told her she could pay next time and she smiled. I walked her to the subway, and when we reached the top of the stairs going down, she turned around and hugged me. "Thank you," she said near my ear.

"You're welcome." I couldn't let go of her. She felt good in my arms. The top of her head fit perfectly right under my chin. I released her just a few inches so I could look into her eyes. "I want to kiss you again, Laya. Can I kiss you?"

I felt her shiver. She nodded. I kissed her softly, just for a few moments, and then pulled away. "You are gorgeous and you don't even know it."

She shrugged it off and said, "Where are you off to now?"

"Wherever you want me to be."

She laughed. "I have to go home to Pretzel; he has separation anxiety."

"Well then, I guess I'm going to church."

"Church?"

"Yes, to pray it won't be too long before I'm eating cold French toast in your apartment."

"It won't be," she said, and then she was off. I couldn't stop smiling as she skipped down the steps.

On my way back to Brooklyn, I called Mel. "Fuck, that hurt!" is how she answered the phone.

"What are you doing? It sounds like you're in a car."

"I'm in a cab."

"I thought you weren't being released until Monday," I said.

"Yeah, well, I hate it there. Taylor, the night nurse, isn't into me at all . . . figuratively or literally."

"Oh my god, Melissa. So, you just left? Who told you you could do that?"

"My brain," she replied.

"What is wrong with you?!"

"I just wanted Taylor to pay attention to me."

Not unusually, I was losing my patience with her. "You've had a boyfriend for years. Did you forget about kind, loyal, tree-hugging Kenny?"

"Why do you think I'm in a cab right now? Oh, wait, I forgot to mention I'm going to your apartment to stay until my flight tomorrow."

"Thank you for asking. Keep away from Jeff if he's there; he's a walking STD."

"I'll try, but I can't make any promises."

"Melissa!" I yelled, and then the phone clicked.

23. Spacesuit

LAYA

"You're not here. You're dead."

"I am here, Laya. You can see me; I'm right next to you."

"Cameron, you died. I watched it happen."

"No, I pulled the shoot. Didn't you see me floating to the ground?"

"Why did you say my name like that?"

"Laya, I said your name like this first. Have you already forgotten about me?"

"Of course not. How can you even say that?"

"Come on, why can't you figure this out? You're a surgeon, for god's sake. You should know these things. I have to go."

"Stop. What are you trying to tell me, Cameron? Why are you getting blurry?"

"Because I have to go."

"Are you coming back?"

"I'll come back when you know what you want."

*   *   *

MY SHEETS WERE drenched with sweat but the cold air in my room was making my teeth chatter. I couldn't get warm. I tossed and turned before finally switching on the bedside lamp. The moment the light went on, I remembered my dream: Cameron coming to me in the very spot I was currently lying in. He had never been in that apartment.

Before he left, he said he would come back to me. I couldn't figure out what he was trying to imply about me deciding what I want.

Getting up, I noticed a shard of light streaming through the opening in the curtain. It was still daylight. I never slept during the day, but after breakfast with Micah I had come home and collapsed onto my bed in a daze.

Looking at the clock, I realized I it was only three in the afternoon. I had only slept an hour. Just long enough for Cameron to haunt my dreams with cryptic messages. Or for my subconscious to send me on a dangerous journey back to a deep state of mourning. I walked to the kitchen and stared at the contents of the refrigerator.

Not long after that, I found myself on my living room floor, drinking wine alone. I knew it was wrong to deal with my emotions that way. I thought maybe if I drank until I passed out, he would come to me in my dreams again, but in the dark cavernous valley of my mind, I knew better. Don't we all?

The taste of the wine hitting the back of my throat made me buckle over and gag. What was I doing to myself?

The phone rang, jarring me. Unplugging it from the charger, I saw that it was Cameron's sister, Krista. I tried to evaluate how drunk I was and if she would be able to tell in my voice. The bottle was already close to being empty.

Something made me answer. Maybe it was fear that it would be someone else telling me Krista had died while climbing. The thought haunted me every day. "Hello?"

"Hey, it's Krista." I exhaled loudly into the phone. "What's wrong?" she asked.

"Nothing. I'm happy to hear your voice," I told her.

With an irritable tone, she said, "I haven't been climbing, so stop putting your negativity out into the universe." Krista was a tomboy through and through. She didn't sugar-coat anything.

"I wasn't doing that," I said.

"You sound like you've been drinking."

"Well, I'm not. And I'm sorry. I'm just worried about you."

"I can tell, Laya. I can tell when you've been drinking. I remember all the phone calls right after Cameron died. You sound like you're back in that place."

As I prepared myself for a Krista lecture, I quietly took the last swig directly from the bottle.

"I had a dream about him last night. He didn't die."

Silence overtook the phone lines for several seconds.

"He's gone. How many times do I have to repeat how dead my brother is? This is hard on me, too."

"I'm sorry. It was just so real. It felt like I could touch him. He told me I needed to figure out what I wanted."

"You're not responsible for Cameron's death, Laya. I don't know what exactly you're grappling with or what *figuring out what you want* means, but your dad told me you were easing back into your fellowship, taking steps in the right direction, and feeling better."

"Don't you have dreams about him?"

"Yes, Laya, I do, but it doesn't mean it's him."

"And?"

"The dreams about my brother are always happy dreams. They're memories I replay in my head. I don't dream that Cameron is coming to me telling me to do this or that. He never told me not to climb El Cap."

"Lucky you. I guess I still don't understand why you climb and want to risk your life at every turn."

"Did you understand why Cameron did it?"

"I never thought he'd die like that." Our conversation was curt but heavy.

"No one did." She paused and took two deep breaths. "That's not why I was calling you." For a moment I thought she was going to bring up Micah even though there was no way she would know about him, unless my father had mentioned it. "I'm pregnant. I wanted to tell you personally that you're going to be an aunt."

Saying I was shocked would be putting it lightly. I had never even asked Krista if she wanted to have children. I knew she had an on-and-off boyfriend, but they didn't seem serious. "Is it Brian's?"

"Yes."

"Are you happy, Krista?"

"I'm really happy. Climbing seems the furthest thing from my mind now. And if I ever do climb again, it will be with ropes and harnesses, and it has nothing to do with what happened to Cam. I admired him. He wasn't perfect, but he loved us. I only wish he were here to be an uncle to my kids."

"Hmm . . . kids, as in plural. Are you having twins?"

She laughed. "No, but I know I want more than one."

My brain was flooded with questions. Would I ever have a baby? Did I even want kids? Would life have been different if I had a sibling? And how did I not recognize before the bond Cameron and Krista had? It was so evident with Micah and Melissa. When I looked back, I realized Cam and Krista were as close as siblings could be.

When we hung up, I went to my computer and blew the layer of dust off the keyboard. My thumb hovered over the cursor. Five minutes passed before I finally began typing.

LAYA BENNETT to CAMERON BENNETT
Remember when . . . ? Three. Two. One. See ya.

There was nothing to say to him. I went to the kitchen and poured myself a large glass of water. I dialed my father's number and then hung up. I dialed Cameron's number and listened to the outgoing message.

Before the beep, I hung up quickly. It was six p.m.

I dialed Micah and got his voicemail as well. "It's Laya. I wanted to see if maybe you'd want to come over next weekend and have breakfast for dinner? I'll be in and out of the hospital this week but I'm free Saturday and Sunday. Give me a call back when you can."

Pretzel came up to me, sat, and barked once, breaking me from the nonproductive state I was in. After I fed him, I went on a cleaning rampage. I threw old clothes into a box along with some of Cameron's belongings. It felt liberating to get rid of his gear and, in a way, make space for change.

In the alley behind my apartment, I found a dumpster. Before I threw the box in, I said out loud, "Three, two, one, see ya." Liftoff.

Inside, I went back to the computer and transferred my money into a few different accounts. I invested in random stock I had never even heard of and I set up a fund for my little embryonic niece or nephew. The TV was on in the background, advertising a very extended St. Jude Children's Research Hospital commercial showing children and babies with childhood cancer. It made me cry. I had a real-world example to finally apply it to. I was going to be an aunt!

Maybe Cameron was also my real-world example. My experience with him would color not only my personal life but my professional life with more intense feelings. I hoped it would make me a better doctor. I had seen death in my profession. But witnessing my own husband's tragic demise was different. I understood grief, loss, compassion.

The commercial was still playing when I found the St. Jude's website, where I located the phone number. I called and set up a five-hundred-thousand-dollar transfer to the organization. It was for the children, but it was also for the loved ones who suffer along with them. There are always people left behind in the shadows, asking God *why*. People who blame themselves for something totally out of their control. I then donated the same amount to the space camp I attended as a child, to the neurosurgery department at the hospital, to a homeless shelter up the street from my house, to an abused women's shelter, and to a community-based project that helped the children of single parents.

At eleven thirty I checked my phone. There were no messages so I climbed into bed, dozing off and wondering why Micah hadn't called back. I set my mind to focusing only on the positive, and somehow, I fell asleep easily and peacefully.

24. Exposed Rafters

MICAH

Mel greeted me at the door of my apartment. "What's up, Pickle?"

"Is that my new nickname . . . and why?"

She opened the door wider. "Because you're so sour. Come on in."

"Thanks for inviting me into my own apartment. Where's Jeff?"

"Hell if I know. God, my leg is killing me." She wobbled over to the couch and plopped down. "Why don't you guys have a TV? This is lame. And this couch is disgusting. I don't even want to think about what has gone on in the very spot I am sitting. Have you gotten rid of that twin-sized bed you pretend is charming?"

"Maybe you should go back to the hospital where you belong. I actually got rid of the bed a long time ago and I never thought it was charming. Anyway, you should talk.

Don't you still have that stupid Elmo doll from when we were three?"

"Don't talk about Mo-Mo that way."

I grabbed two beers from the fridge, popped them open, and handed one to Melissa, who had already made herself comfortable in the spot where I always sat. "I'm thinking you should try a mental hospital this time."

"You're being sour again," she chided. "Aren't you glad I'm here?"

"No. I'm irritated that you jumped ship because you weren't getting hit on by members of the hospital staff."

"You try spending weeks in that place. You should see the scrambled eggs they serve. There is no way they're real. They come in the same exact shape every day. A perfect rectangle. I think maybe they make some kind of casserole and cut it with a knife."

"Our conversations are always so profound, Mel." I sat in the armchair next to her. "Does Kenny know you left?"

"I changed my flight and I leave in two hours. I'm gonna surprise him tonight. Oh, how was breakfast, by the way?"

"It was really good. I feel like I want to spend every minute with her but I have to give her space." I yawned loudly.

"Is baby Micah tired?"

"Yes, I'm exhausted from working on Steve's stupid Glossette apartment building. I've been putting so much extra time in on the stupid square box he designed. And I didn't sleep well last night."

"Well, I'll get out of your hair. Nice talking to you."

"Don't be snotty, Mel, I'm just tired. How are you getting to the airport?"

"Um, a cab, duh." She stood awkwardly and walked

toward the door. It was she who was wearing a sour face now. "Nice to see you, shithead," she said under her breath.

Despite her brattiness, I actually felt bad. "No, Mel, I didn't mean it like that."

She turned and scowled. "Why don't you ever come to Maine to visit me?"

"I've just been busy."

"You weren't busy when you were sitting in Mom and Dad's cabin trying to, quote, find yourself."

"Shut up. I needed that time away. It was self-care."

"I bet. Kind of like all the self-care you did as a teenager."

"I love you, too."

I walked her out to the street and hailed a cab. She got in and shut the door. When she looked up at me through the window, I mouthed, *I love you, jerk,* so she flipped me off as the car drove away. I walked back up the stairs, laughing.

Instead of working, I scrolled Facebook and saw Laya's vague post. I wondered if she had run out of memories. I listened to her voicemail inviting me over the following weekend, and I thought about calling her back then, but it seemed too late to return the call. I would respond in the morning.

At ten forty-five, Mel called. I figured it was to let me know she had gotten home safely or to apologize for being a child when I simply didn't want her to miss her flight.

"Hello?"

She was sniffling loudly. "Micah?"

"What's wrong, Melissa?"

"He's such an asshole. I came home and found him naked in the Jacuzzi with that yoga slut, Keri. He was . . . oh my god . . . she was . . ."

"Your friend Keri? The one who gave him that holistic crap to give to you?"

"She's not a friend . . . obviously." Mel's sobbing turned to a loud mewling sound. "I found them . . . hold on, I'm going to throw up."

"Melissa! Where are you? What were they doing? Isn't Kenny always naked?"

I could hear her throwing up. "Calm down, Melissa. Talk to me."

When she came back on the phone, she was still heaving between sentences. "He likes to be naked, yes, but he was sitting on the side of the Jacuzzi and she was sucking his dick." She heaved.

"Mel, take a deep breath."

"Then she said, 'Let's go against the tree where you like fucking me.' This wasn't their first time." She heaved again loudly into the phone. "I hope they get poison ivy on their genitals."

"Wow. Kenny went from tree hugger to tree fucker," I mumbled under my breath. God, I had totally misread him."

"He told her he loved her, Micah. I threw up in the bushes and then fell and they saw me. I looked like a Peeping Tom. I'm so embarrassed and disgusted." Now Mel was crying again. This Mel was different. She was truly and deeply saddened, maybe for the first time ever. "I screamed, 'Leave. Get your granola and scented oils and get the fuck out of here!' They left as fast as they could. They took my car even though I yelled at them to nature hike their way back to town. Kenny is the lowest of the low. He's lake scum with his stupid shorts and disgusting back hair. I mean, is it too much for him to go get a wax once in a while?"

"Okay, just stay there. I'm coming to see you. Jeff has his car right now; I'm gonna grab Dad's and head out there. I don't care if I have to drive all night, I'll be there."

Mel sniffed, sounding small. "Jesus, sorry. I'm being a baby. Aren't you exhausted? You don't have to come out. I will live through this. Hell, I just got run over by a taxi. I'll be fine."

"No, I'll be there. It's only a few hours. And, I want to kick Kenny's ass."

"He's gone; anyway, it wouldn't be any fun. He's a pacifist. He'd probably let you kick his ass." And there was Mel again. "Where *is* Dad's old Fiat?"

"In storage a couple streets away. I have the keys and I'll see you in a bit. Text me if Kenny comes back so I can stop and buy a giant slab of raw meat to throw at him."

"I hate how Kenny loves that stupid, one-dimensional set of legs and boobs. I bet she'd be able to wrap her legs around her head if her gigantic boobs didn't get in the way."

"What are you gonna do until I get there, Mel?"

"Double homicide."

"Just try and calm down. I'm leaving now."

"Okay."

I gathered some clothes and a toothbrush, threw them in a bag, and headed out the door. I was at my dad's storage unit in less than twenty minutes. The cabby agreed to wait until I started my dad's car in case I needed to jump-start it. Fortunately, the car started right up. I knew my dad occasionally sneaked away on the weekends to drive the piece of shit out to Coney Island. That was his little rebellion against my mother's packed retirement calendar.

I had a seven-hour drive in front of me. I thought about getting coffee, but I felt as if I was running out of time. A half hour in and I was fighting to stay focused on the road. Exhausted and bored, I let my mind wander to Laya's beautiful face. My eyelids began to close.

I pictured her lips mouthing the word *Hello.*.

25. Broken Wings

LAYA

On Facebook I saw my friend Izzy had moved into a new house. I felt guilty for not setting up lunch plans with her. She posted a picture of the house and I recognized it right away. It was on the corner lot of the street we grew up on and Izzy had always dreamt of living in it. I was glad for her.

I knew I needed to ease myself back into the world, and Micah was helping me do that. But he hadn't returned my call from the night before and I was trying my best to ignore that fact. I left a plant as a housewarming gift on the doorstep of Izzy's new place. Instead of calling or sending a card, she paid me a visit at the hospital on Monday.

It would have been too easy just to have someone tell her I'd be with patients all morning, so I sucked it up and met her in the waiting room.

"Laya, you're glowing," she said. "It's nice to see you in your element."

"Thank you, Izzy. But the operating room is really my element. I can't wait to get back in there."

"Well, I just came by to say thank you for the plant." She hugged me for an uncomfortably long time. "I really want to get together soon. I need a mommy escape once in a while."

Izzy wasn't a bad person. She cared about me and I cared about her, too. At the time of Cameron's death and the chaos that followed, I didn't seek out contact with friends. I shut down. I found ways to eliminate people from my life. I was scared everyone would drop dead around me.

"Yes, we can definitely plan something. Let me walk you out."

We headed toward the entrance when I saw Melissa standing near the check-in desk. When I got closer, I noticed she was crying on the shoulder of a man. The father, from what I remembered.

I grabbed my phone from my pocket to see if Micah had called or texted. "I have to go," I said to Izzy. I gave her an abrupt hug before turning quickly on my heel.

"Um okay. Well, bye, Laya!" she shouted, irritated.

"I'm sorry. I just have to go," I shot back.

As I approached Melissa, I noticed their mom was sitting in a chair behind her. She was sobbing into her hands and saying, "Why?" over and over again. The scene was all too familiar to me.

Melissa looked up. "Oh, Laya," she cried.

"What's going on?"

"It's Micah."

My heart dropped to the floor and my body followed soon after. The doctor in me was nowhere to be found. I had nothing left . . . no argument, no hope . . . I already knew what they were going to tell me. Of course the dark cloud that followed me would eventually produce a thunderstorm to wipe out anything positive in my life. Of course it was too good to be true that a man with patience, kindness, and a loving demeanor would come along and brighten the dark path I was on, only to be taken away just as fast.

His voice echoed in my mind, sending a whole new wave of guilt and regret through me.

"I'm sorry to say, Laya, but your theory is horseshit. I don't care about your superstition. I'll take my chances."

My eyes locked on the pain-stricken faces of Melissa and Micah's father as he hovered over me. He reached a hand out to pull me up, but I was shaking uncontrollably. "Miss, are you okay?"

Melissa knelt beside me. "What's happened?" I asked her.

"Micah . . . Micah was in a car accident. He was driving in the middle of the night to stay with me at my house." She burst into tears again. Still on the floor, I reached out and took her in my arms. I could feel her pain coupled with mine. Micah and I hadn't gotten a chance to really know each other. He'd never been able to scale the wall I had put up. Maybe only in his death would I realize how badly I wanted him in my life.

Once I was finally in a chair, trying to get my breath back, I realized how much Micah looked like his father. I could see all the love his family had for him. The love made them somehow so beautiful to me, even though they were all facing a major tragedy.

I wanted so badly to find the right words to say, but I couldn't speak. I couldn't console them. I didn't know how.

"We met when Melissa was in the hospital. I'm Peter and this is my wife, Leslie."

"I know," I managed to get out. "Where is he?" I needed to see him no matter what, even if they had taken him to the morgue already.

"He's in surgery right now," Peter said.

My eyes opened wider and a weight lifted from my chest. It was the unfamiliar feeling of hope. It's accurate to say I had expected something else; who would have blamed me?

"What kind of surgery?" I asked.

Peter, being the most composed of the three, began to explain. "His head smashed the windshield just before he was thrown from the car." As he spoke, a deep agonizing moan came from Leslie, who was seated behind Peter. "Micah has a brain injury. We're not sure how serious it is. Just praying."

"His leg is shattered. The same leg as mine," Melissa added.

"We're in the dark. We don't really know what his prognosis is. I don't know if my son will live or ever be the same." Peter finally broke down and started to cry.

I stood up slowly, my mind working overtime, logic pushing out the flood of emotions that passed through me. My doctor brain had returned with a vengeance. Micah wasn't dead. As horrible as his injuries sounded, he was alive. "They have to tell you the worst possible scenario. Any brain injury is serious and hard to predict," I said, trying my best to stay stoic and strong.

Leslie sobbed loudly again and sunk even farther into the dirty waiting-room chair. I wondered if I was saying the right words. I wanted to give them some kind of hope without false expectations.

"Which bone in his leg is shattered?" I asked, determined.

"His femur," Melissa said. I shook my head, knowing if he made it, he had a tough road ahead of him. Procedures started running through my mind.

"I need to go speak with the team treating him."

After asking around, I was pointed in Dr. Lee's direction. I had known Dr. Lee since childhood. He'd operated on my mother when she had the aneurysm. Dad always told me Dr. Lee worked tirelessly to save my mother the night she died, but it was too late. My father's firm eventually designed a special wing for neurosurgery in my mother's name. I never visited that wing. It was painful to be there, and now I had another tragedy to add as a reminder. I felt like a defective human being, a living bad omen.

In the operating hall, I caught sight of Joe, Dr. Lee's physician's assistant, who was removing his surgical gown.

"Joe, I need to know the status on the patient in surgery."

He scowled. "Why? What are you doing down here?"

"I know him . . . Micah Evans. I know him, do you hear me?"

Joe put his arms up to block me as I tried to push my way past him. "Laya, stop."

"I need to see him."

"You know the rules here, Laya. Lee is closing him up."

"I need to see him!" I said loudly. "Tell me what's going on."

"We had to perform a craniotomy. He had a subdural hematoma."

"Was he awake? Was he talking before you took him in?"

Joe shook his head. "He was stable but unconscious when we started the anesthesia. He coded three times."

"Jesus. What did you do?"

"The team brought him back, but he was down for a long time. It's hard to say what kind of obstacles he'll be facing if he makes it out of this." He paused. "Have you met with the orthopedic team?"

"No, I just found out he was here. When can I see him?"

Dr. Lee came into the hallway, looking composed but in deep thought. He was a pragmatic person . . . he always cut to the chase, sometimes abrasively, but he was a good man, a dedicated genius in his field. I had always admired him. And now Micah's life was in his hands.

"I know him, Dr. Lee."

"He's not out of the woods. I have to open him back up. Scrub back in, Joe," Dr. Lee said.

"Can you tell me anything else, please?" I said, still trying to catch my breath.

"The CAT scan just came back and we didn't get all of it. His brain is still bleeding. I need to get back in there, Laya."

"Can I scrub in?"

He looked at me like I was speaking a foreign language.

"I mean, can I just be in the room?" I asked.

"Absolutely not. You know the patient, and I can't have you emotionally compromised."

"I'm calm. It might help if I'm in there."

"No," he answered firmly. "I know you're worried, but you can't go in there. Meet with the ortho team; he's going to knee surgery."

I couldn't leave Micah now. I settled with pacing the

hall, eyes alternating between the floor and the door that separated us.

Come on, Micah, I chanted in my head.

After an hour my hands started shaking, I felt light-headed. A young candy striper walked down the end of the hall and I shouted, "Hey, do you have any candy?"

She walked up to me, smiling, and looked at my name badge. "No, Dr. Bennett, that's not really what I do. I'm a hospital volunteer."

"Oh right! It's just my blood sugar is low."

She dug around in her pocket and pulled out a piece of gum with a tattered wrapper that likely hadn't seen the light of day in months. "This is all I have."

"Perfect, thank you." I started frantically chewing it while the girl just stared at me.

"Is there anything else I can do?" she asked.

"Yes, can you please check on the Evans family in the waiting room. See if they need anything. Their son and brother is the one having brain surgery at the moment."

"No problem," she said before walking away.

After another hour of waiting, I slumped down against the wall, thinking I'd find a way to sleep here somehow. But right then Dr. Lee emerged. "How is he?"

He shook his head at the sight of me. In any other situation, he would have reprimanded me. "Laya, I know you've been through a lot, but you have to calm down. We did everything possible. We'll have to see when he wakes up." There he was—no nonsense, not quite completely devoid of emotion, just focused. I was embarrassed to think about my state a couple of hours ago.

"I'm sorry, Dr. Lee, for what happened before. I . . .

wasn't thinking straight. You were right; it wasn't a good idea for me to be in there."

He offered me a small smile. "I wouldn't say it like that. I didn't want you in the room because of your relationship with the patient. But for every other circumstance, I would have let you in." He paused, as if letting his words sink in. "I've studied your history in the operating room. You have a gift and you need to start using it."

"I have the gift of dooming all the people in my life," I mumbled.

He ignored me. "Come and talk to the family with me," he said. Behind him, I sighed in relief. Micah was okay for now.

Melissa, Leslie, and Peter were in the waiting room at the end of the hall. Through the glass windows I could see Melissa hunched over with her head between her knees, like she was hyperventilating. Leslie rubbed her back while Peter leaned against the wall. He stood up straight as soon as we entered the room.

"Please have a seat," Dr. Lee said. All three of them were staring intently at us. "Micah is stable, but we have a waiting game ahead of us now. I did everything I could to ensure Micah would have the best chances at making a promising recovery."

"What are we waiting for? How will we know that he's all right?" Melissa asked.

"We're waiting for your brother to wake up," I said.

"When can we see him?" Peter asked.

"You'll be able to see him by the end of the day," Dr. Lee replied. "Continue saying prayers. That's all I can tell you at this point." He reached out to squeeze Melissa's hand. I admired him for being both realistic and comforting.

Dr. Lee left, saying that he would check in with the orthopedic team. It was just the four of us now. Melissa said nothing to me. I sensed a shift in her—she had threatened me when she was a patient, but it was a joke, a part of her snarky personality. But now I felt like she wanted to attack me with words. "Let's go to the cafeteria," she finally said to her mom and dad.

"I can't eat, Melissa," Leslie said.

"We just need to get outta here." Melissa shot me a dirty look.

"Melissa, wait!" I said. I pulled her aside in the hallway, away from her parents. "I'm sorry."

She refused to look at me. I saw a bit of Micah in her profile. "I knew you were bad news."

Tears welled up in my eyes. Even though I said it myself before, it hurt a thousand times over to hear someone else say it. "I understand how you feel."

"You're leaving a path of destruction and my brother had to get caught up in it."

I breathed in, trying to contain myself. "I know how badly this must hurt and scare you."

"He's part of me, Laya!" she shouted. "This isn't fair! My life is falling apart and now I'm losing my brother."

"You haven't lost him. I'm going to do everything I can to help."

"No! Stay away. Far away!" She stormed off down the hall. Her parents followed, shooting identical looks of confusion, without saying anything. The first time we met, it was Leslie who didn't trust me, and now it was Melissa's turn. They went into the elevator, and as the doors shut, I saw Leslie holding her daughter close.

Dr. Lee broke my trance as he emerged from around the corner. "Laya, get downstairs. The orthopedic team is meeting now." I finally noticed a call on the speaker overhead requesting I report to the second floor. I pushed away Melissa's words; I couldn't let them affect me now.

But my steps grew heavier as I shuffled toward the stairwell. On the landing for the third floor, I collapsed onto the top step. *Why was this happening to me?* The sound of my cries echoed around me and a part of me just wanted to stay there, hidden.

In the back of my mind, Cameron's voice came through, surprising me. *Pick yourself up. Don't be scared.* He'd said this when I fell mountain biking. I was terrified, paralyzed by the idea of not being in control.

Fear was like a new feeling I discovered after I started dating Cameron. Growing up, even in college, I never felt that kind of fear so I never had to learn to overcome it. Cameron had taught me how to face it and stay strong through it.

Eventually, I did get up as the image of Micah came to mind. He wouldn't want to see me like this. I headed to the second-floor conference room. When I walked in, all the other doctors' eyes shot to where I was standing. "What's she doing here?" said one of the hospital administrators.

I squared my shoulders and said, "They called me down." I shouldn't have had to explain my presence in my own department.

Micah's car had hit a tree at high speed, I learned. He should have been dead. Police officers guessed he had fallen asleep at the wheel.

What were you doing, Micah?

During my meeting with the orthopedic department,

arguments and accusations were thrown around the room about how to handle Micah's injuries. The head doctor set up a team. I was to assist in a very limited capacity, as I was still only a fellow at the hospital and new on the staff. I guessed that Dr. Lee had put in a good word for me. I made it very clear that I knew the patient personally, yet they still added me to the team.

We would wait until status of Micah's condition came in after his brain surgery.

Micah was still unconscious in the recovery room when his family finally left for the evening. I kept my distance until they were gone, not wanting to disturb them as they kept vigil, or risk Melissa's anger again. I knew it was coming from a place of fear and love. Those two elements combined could make anyone go a little crazy. I should know.

When I walked into his room, his neurologist was performing an electroencephalogram to evaluate Micah's brain activity. She didn't acknowledge me as I stood opposite her.

"What does it show?"

"There's brain activity. I'll reassess in the morning." She removed the sensors from his head and walked toward the door. In the doorway she turned back. "He should have woken up by now."

It wasn't a medically induced coma. Micah should have responded to her touch, I knew that. "What are you saying?" I asked her.

"I'm saying there's isn't much you can do now. Pray, I guess."

In the medical world I was used to, praying was reserved for patients and family members. I never stood in an operating room and said, "Pray," to another doctor. It was an admission of powerlessness.

"Pray?" I asked her.

With her back to me as she wheeled the electroencephalogram cart toward the door, she said, "I'll check back later." That was it.

After she left, I pulled up a chair, rested my head on Micah's bed, and took his hand in mine. Throughout the night nurses came in and out, administering medication every couple of hours.

I opened my eyes slowly as the morning light pierced through the window curtain. The sun's warmth touched my back.

When I felt pressure on my hand, I practically jumped out of my chair. Micah's eyes were still closed but his hand was squeezing mine. "Micah," I whispered, voice wavering. "Micah, open your eyes."

His eyes opened for a moment and then closed. Adrenaline was pumping through my veins, my heart was beating out of my chest, my hands were sweating, and I was . . . praying.

"Micah!" His eyes opened again. He moved his hand to his mouth and tried to remove his breathing tube.

"No, don't do that; let me help you." I hit the button to call a nurse and searched for the instrument to remove the respirator. Once I removed it, he coughed and sputtered. When I ran a cloth over his chin and sides of his mouth, he wrapped a hand gently around my wrist. "Angel." His voice was scratchy, but I was relieved to hear it, and shocked at how clear his speech was.

"Micah, try to stay awake. Can you hear me?"

He nodded.

"You were in a car accident." I was even more shocked when he smiled. "You're hurt badly." His smile grew wider, alarming me. Did he not understand a word I was saying?

"I saw your face, angel," he whispered. His eyes were searching mine.

"It's me, Laya."

"Laya." My name came out like a breath on his lips.

"I'm here."

Still wearing a smile, he reached for my hand and began stroking my knuckles with his thumb. "Why don't you get in here with me?"

"Micah, you have broken bones. You're going to need surgery." I couldn't believe he was acting like nothing had happened.

"Are you going to fix me up, doc?"

"I think you need your head examined again."

"Why, because I'm in love?"

"You're on some heavy drugs. I don't think you even know what you're saying."

"You're my drug."

The nurse entered and started administering more medication before she said a word to us. I think she was pleased that he was awake and conversing with me. Amused, even. "Can you call Dr. Lee and tell him Micah's awake?" I asked her.

"I already have. He's on his way."

Micah lifted his blanket and examined his body. "Yikes," he said.

"They did emergency surgery on your femur two nights ago. I had no idea because you were taken to neurosurgery yesterday morning and that's where I found you." He touched his fingers to the shaved part of his head and felt the twenty staples running from back to front. "You're going to need at least two more surgeries before you go into recovery."

His eyes darted back to mine. "You were there." It was a statement, not a question.

"In the operating room?"

"Yes, I saw you."

"No, I wasn't."

"I saw you and heard you," he argued, though he still looked to be searching his memory. "You were there; I know it."

"What did you see?"

"I saw you talking to my parents."

"Micah, it was just a dream."

"No. My mother was sitting in a chair and you were explaining something to my father. Why was I mad at you?"

"You weren't." I was growing more and more concerned, but I didn't want to rile him up in his condition.

"Yeah, you cornered me at the end of the hall," he said.

Realization smacked me in the face. *Twins.* His eyes started to close. With a smile he murmured, "I'm not mad at you. I love you." And then he was asleep.

"Micah?"

"He's out," the nurse said. "I just pumped him with a pretty nice cocktail. He'll be out for a while."

"Thank you . . . I think," I said abruptly before dashing out of the room and heading toward the nurses' station. I caught Dr. Lee in the hall. "He was awake, but they just gave him more pain meds."

"Was he talking?" Dr. Lee asked.

"Yes. He just seemed a little confused but he was talking

clearly." *He said he loved me. God, he said he loved me again. He's doomed now.*

"That's good news. Of course he'll be a little confused."

"Is it normal that he remembers me talking to his parents when he was under?" I said.

"I think you would have learned by now patients often have strange dreams when they're coming out of anesthesia." He smirked.

"Yes. I suppose." Really, I didn't think it was a normal dream at all. I thought he and Melissa were impossibly invading each other's minds.

"Why don't you go steal a nap? It looks like you could use some sleep."

"I don't want to leave him," I said.

"You need sleep to be an effective surgeon."

I blinked several times, letting reality wash over me. As long as he stayed stable through the day and night, we would be taking him to surgery the following morning to fully repair his femur and knee.

"Okay," I mumbled.

I checked in on Micah before heading to an empty on-call room where I collapsed onto a bed and fell asleep praying I wouldn't have any visitors in my dreams.

26. Half-Timbering

MICAH

"She's the reason for all this chaos in our lives; I know it."
I heard my sister talking to my mom, but my eyes were too
heavy to open.

"Oh, Melissa, stop," my mother said.

"Seriously! Micah and I break the same freakin' leg
within a month of each other and we both end up in this
stupid hospital . . . where she now works."

"You got hit by a car. We taught you to look both ways.
This is New York City, for the love of god."

"Mom, stop blaming me for getting run over."

"I'm not blam—"

My eyes finally opened when I realized they were
talking about Laya. "Please do not fight while I'm on my
deathbed."

"Micah!" my sister yelled, "you're still an asshole, thank
god!" Melissa wobbled over to my bedside. "Show me yours

and I'll show you mine," she said, laughing and pointing to her leg.

I smiled when I remembered the moment Melissa and I had discovered how different we were. We didn't look alike, but I thought we were the same. We were four years old and had just gotten out of the tub when Melissa looked down at me and said, "What is that? Where is mine?" I don't know why at the moment it finally occurred to us; we had seen each other naked our whole lives. I think we were finally becoming aware of ourselves. Up until that point we had everything the same. If I got a fire truck, she got one, too. If she got a doll, I got one, too. Now, things didn't seem so different than back then. If she had a broken leg, I had one, too.

"Don't joke about your deathbed. We thought we were really going to lose you," my mother said.

"Well, I'm here to continue receiving Melissa's unrelenting insults. Speaking of,"—I turned my attention to Melissa— "how are you doing?"

"Fine. I'm okay. I'm glad you lived." She let a tight smile crease her mouth.

"Gee, thanks. What about Kenny?" I asked.

"Kenny who?" she said.

"That's the spirit."

Melissa grinned like she was hiding a big secret. "I got Taylor's number."

"The night nurse?"

"Yeah." She smiled wider.

"I guess you could use a semipermanent medical professional in your life."

"Look who's talking," my mother chimed in.

I began to laugh but stopped because it hurt my body and because I remembered what they were talking about. "About Laya . . . this has nothing to do with her. It's horrible to even think she had anything to do with this. And even worse, you two are chatting openly about it. She helped save Melissa's life, and it's terrible to blame her for any of this. If anything, you should be thanking her and blaming Kenny."

My sister rolled her eyes.

"Calm down, Micah. You need to take it easy," my mother said.

Just like that, I was thinking about the pain in my head and leg. "Fuck, this hurts. Can someone get a nurse and have her call Laya?

"No," my sister barked out.

"Melissa, shut up."

As if I had literally asked God, the heavens opened up and Laya walked in the door. She made eye contact with my sister, who was expressionless, and then she turned her attention to me after saying a brief hello to my mother.

"Hi, Micah. How are you feeling?"

"Like a million bucks." The pain was gone. She really was the best drug.

She laughed. "Wow, I didn't expect that."

"It only just happened a minute ago." I had tunnel vision again. All I could see was her.

My sister choked loudly behind Laya's back. When I glanced up at Melissa, she had her finger down her throat like a ten-year-old. I ignored her.

"Well, it certainly looks like the synapses are all firing well in that big brain of yours. You weren't quite all there when I saw you last."

"Oh, I was all there, believe me." I flashed back to her face willing me to wake up and speak. "Thanks for staying with me."

"You were in a coma."

"No, I knew you were here all night."

"Micah—"

My sister interrupted Laya. "I feel nauseous. I'm going outside."

"Hurry back," I said sarcastically.

My mother shook her head and followed Melissa out the door. Before going into the hall, she turned around and said, "I'm glad to see you up and smart-mouthing your sister again." She winked, then left the room.

"I think your sister is mad at me," Laya said.

"She'll get over it."

"It is sort of scary that people tend to drop like flies around me. She's right for not wanting you and I to see each other," she said solemnly.

I shook my head. "Don't, Laya. Don't do that anymore." *She just said we're seeing each other.*

She glanced down, playing with the thin blanket covering me. "Can I take a look at your leg now?"

"Is that all?" I said, smirking.

"I *am* one of your doctors."

"This is a dream come true."

"Either they tweaked something in your head or the drugs are a little too good for you."

"You're good for me."

"They must have pumped the romantic part of your brain with steroids."

"Did you?" I asked her.

"I still don't understand how you knew I was there yesterday."

"Neither do I. Who cares?"

"Let me look at your leg, Micah."

"Fine," I said with humor. When I pulled the blanket back, I expected her face to blanch at the sight, but she was all business examining me.

"Okay. It looks clean. You're lucky. They were really just trying to save your life, but they did a good job stabilizing your leg for your next surgery."

"You cutting me open?"

"Just your leg."

"I was really hoping you would have messed a bit with my brain so I'd have a new second language. Preferably a love language."

She laughed. "I didn't touch your brain, but it seems to me your love language is very well intact."

"But you touched my mind?"

"You are something else today."

"No, you are . . . something else. Kiss me; I'm hungry." She bent and pecked my cheek. "I'm starving now," I told her. Something about almost dying makes you want to blurt out your feelings to everyone.

"I hate seeing you like this. You've been so kind to me and thoughtful and I can't help but feel responsible for what's happened to you." I realized even though she had looked relieved earlier, I saw only sadness and exhaustion now.

"Don't let your mind go to that place, Laya. This had nothing to do with you. My sister caught her boyfriend cheating on her. I was driving to Maine, extremely tired, at eleven at night. It was a stupid thing to do." I wondered if

Laya would always feel like she was a dark cloud, like she was responsible every time something went wrong.

"I have to focus on your surgery now. I have to treat you like every other patient."

"Really?"

"Yes, of course." Laya was all business.

"But you're taking all the fun out of it."

"There is nothing fun about this. I'm going to meet with the head of orthopedics to check when you're scheduled for surgery." She squeezed my hand. "I'll come back after."

"Okay."

"See ya," I said, and noticed her smile turned immediately to a frown. "What? What's wrong?"

"Nothing. I have to go."

When she left, it finally hit me that I had almost died. I felt like calling Kenny and yelling at him, but instead I just lay there, staring at the ceiling. The nurse came in and upped my meds again. I hadn't even asked for more. About ten minutes later, in my drug-induced state I did actually call Kenny.

"Hello," he said, sadness lacing his voice.

"Kenny, you're a worthless piece of shit."

"I know."

"I almost died driving out to comfort my poor sister. Why did you do it?"

"Melissa texted me and told me what happened. She followed it up with an emoji story."

"An emoji story?"

"Yes. She basically compiled several emojis to explain how she was going to kill me."

"Sounds like something she would do. She's very creative. Sooo, why did you do it?"

"We fell out of love, Micah. Didn't you see it coming?"

"No, Mel was still in love with you. I know she's a handful, but she loves hard. You're going to miss it. It was totally selfish, what you did. You should have broken it off with her. You should have talked to her."

"I know. It's just . . . she was slipping away. She went out and bought a bunch of junk food to spite me." He said it as if it were the worst thing a person could do.

"So what, stupid. So she ate some candy and chips in front of you . . . what's the big deal?"

"We just weren't on the same page."

"Why am I having this conversation with you? Oh, I know. It's because I actually love her." As soon as the words came out of my mouth, I noticed Melissa standing in the doorway. She blew me a kiss and walked away. "Kenny?"

He had hung up, the spineless weasel.

Mel had never blown me a kiss, or shown me that kind of outward love. She didn't need to, but lying there in my hospital bed, it felt good.

I fell asleep shortly after that.

27. Flying Blind

LAYA

It was impossible to sleep, but Micah didn't seem to have any trouble. I popped in and out of his room throughout the night. I wanted to talk to him but I knew he needed the sleep. In the early hours of the morning Joe found me in an on-call room.

"Laya, go home and take a shower."

I forced open my eyes to reveal Joe's disappointed face. "You saying I smell?"

"Yes. That's exactly what I'm saying," he said. "You need to be at your best today."

"Why are you on this floor? Shouldn't you be up in neurosurgery?"

"Don't try to change the subject." I didn't know Joe well—I had only met him a couple of times since I had started my fellowship—but everyone told me he was the hospital comedian.

"I expected you to tell me some jokes. Everyone says you're funny, but you're letting me down right now."

"What do you call a tired and smelly doctor?"

"What?"

"A bad doctor." He smirked. "Get up. You're going into surgery in four hours."

"Okay, okay."

I rushed home, got to the top of the stairs where I saw my neighbor Esther standing on the landing with Pretzel. "Laya, I told you I could only watch him for one day. He pooped all over your damn apartment and I'm not cleaning it."

"Oh no, I'm so sorry. He gets anxiety when I'm gone."

Esther was a widow with no family. I thought she'd enjoy taking care of little Pretzel but I guess I didn't consider the poop part.

"I'm off to yoga. Here, take your dog," she said, practically dropping him onto my chest.

"Thank you for watching him. Sorry about the poop." I directed my attention to Pretzel. "Pretzel, now tell Esther you're sorry."

Esther rolled her eyes and went into her apartment.

My house was clean but of course smelled strongly of Pretzel poo. I found a big pile under my bed. I read somewhere that dogs poop under your bed when they're pissed at you. I don't know what made me think I could care for an animal when I could barely care for myself.

I cleaned the floor and quickly took a shower. Tying my hair in a bun, I headed for the door. Before I hit the stairs I stumbled over a large box that Esther must have brought in while I was gone. I bent down for a closer look; it was forwarded from Cameron's and my old address, and it had a large Red Bull logo on the side.

Hesitating, I slowly ripped the tape off the top and opened it. Inside I found one of Cameron's backpacks. I recognized it from the France trip. I pulled the contents out. There were notebooks with sketches of stunts he had prepped for, a pair of dirty socks—typical Cameron—and a letter sitting all alone in the front pouch.

Hands shaking, I hurriedly unfolded the letter.

To Laya, my girl with the magical eyes.

My legs suddenly went weak and I had to sit on the top step.

If you're reading this, then I probably took a ride and haven't landed. I don't know how else to say it. You were always supportive of me and the crazy things I wanted to do. You were my best friend and you know I don't use that term lightly. Every time I saw you, I wanted so badly to tell you how I really felt, but I was scared. Can you believe that? I know the Cameron you saw was confident, but that wasn't how I felt all the time. I thought I must be expendable for you. I didn't understand why you loved me.

When you agreed to marry me, I still thought it was too good to be true. I didn't realize what I had. I should have told you that you were always so precious to me. There is no one like you. I didn't have girlfriends not because I couldn't commit but because there was never any one person I wanted as much as you. That day when we were mountain biking, I told you to pick yourself up. I saw how scared you were. I wished in that moment I would have told you how scared I was, too. It terrified me to think you could have gone tumbling off that hill right in front of my eyes.

I can't imagine how you must feel watching me do stunts. Your strength makes me admire you even more. I know how strong you are, Laya. You make me want to be just as strong.

I don't want you to think you are the reason I'm not sitting next to you right now. You never made me do anything. I know sometimes I would act aloof or selfish or insensitive but inside I was always just trying to think of the exact right words to say to you.

There were times when I knew I was messing it up with you and that's what terrified me. I was still learning how to be, and I was still making mistakes left and right, but there wasn't a moment from the time I met you that I wasn't thinking about you. You would text me a cute picture of you in your scrubs at the hospital and I would stare at it for hours. Every time I went to sleep and you weren't with me, I would look at your pictures and daydream about having you in my arms.

As I write this letter to you now, I hope that I had enough time to make up for being a coward. I'm making that my goal now.

I'm sure you wonder what I wish for you after my death, but I think you already know.

I loved you and I know I love you still, wherever I am.

—Cam

The letter was dated two weeks before he died. *How did he know?* I wondered if he wrote a new one before each stunt. I felt angry thinking how easy it must be to tell a person everything inside your heart when you know they're not going to read it until you're gone. As if that's supposed to give a grieving widow solace. I wished he would have told me to my face how he felt. It would have changed nothing. It would have only validated my actions, my support of him, my devotion and outward expressions of love toward him.

I scanned the letter again, realizing that even in his death letter, he still couldn't let me go. He couldn't tell me all of those wonderful things and close the letter with "Please live your life, I want you to be happy." Instead he closed it with an "I think you already know."

"No, I don't know what you want for me, Cameron!" I yelled at Pretzel, who was sitting next to me on the stoop. The poor dog jumped at my outburst, then scurried back, trying to climb into my lap. I gently pushed him away.

Cameron had never expressed himself to me the way he did in the letter, but it was hard for me to overlook the fact that the letter was still missing the words I so desperately needed to hear. It was like he was conflicted and then just shut it down with an "I love you." If that was the last letter, the real grand finale, then it was a poor one at best.

I couldn't sit there all day, pondering Cameron's words, as much as they intrigued me. I had to get back to the hospital.

I picked up Pretzel and darted out the door. I knew it was a bad idea to take him with me, but what choice did I have?

THERE AREN'T MANY places to put a dog at a hospital. Everyone was staring at me. My pager was going off and my name was being called over the speaker. Pretzel struggled in my arms, trying to get a look at me.

"Pretzel, stop that."

I found a nurse. I didn't even know her name but she was one of those people who had a magnetic pull toward every animal, you could just tell. She approached me to pet him. "What a cutie," she said.

"Yes, he is very cute. Want to babysit him? I have to go into surgery."

"Are you serious?"

"Very."

"In my fifteen years here, I have never seen a surgeon bring their dog in."

"So, will you?"

"Well, I'm off in twenty min—"

"Here you go." I handed Pretzel over and said, "He likes water and peanut butter and long walks on the beach."

She took him reluctantly, and just like Pretzel, she seemed to be questioning my sanity. For good reason. It's not every day you get to read a nonaffirming letter from your dead husband.

On the orthopedic floor all the surgeons, nurses, and anesthesiologists were huddled in a group outside the operating room. The head surgeon was giving orders to the nurses about prepping Micah.

I turned to one of the other fellows and said, "Are you in on this surgery, too?"

"Yeah," she said before looking away in a dismissive gesture.

"What, do they need someone to babysit me?"

"No, you're off the surgery," she said, making zero eye contact.

Shocked, I turned toward the lead doctor. "Can I talk to you for a second?"

Once everyone else had left to go scrub in, the doctor pulled me aside. "Laya, do you even know my name?"

"Of course," I said. "You're Dr. Reynolds. I know everyone's name." That was a lie.

"I don't know if you're ready for this. You've missed several meetings."

"But . . . can't I just observe?" I didn't want to operate on Micah anyway, but I wanted to be there. I stood up straight and gathered myself. "I've studied this surgery for years and I assisted on it multiple times in my residency."

"But there are extenuating circumstances. The patient just had brain surgery."

"Micah is fine," I argued.

Dr. Reynolds squinted. "I think it's a conflict of interest."

Jesus, did everybody know about my relationship with Micah? "I'm well aware of the circumstances. And even though I personally know the patient, I'm going into this surgery as a doctor, not a friend."

"You should know how much personal feelings can interfere with a doctor's ability to make the right choices."

"Dr. Lee wants me in there."

"I need to make a phone call. I'm scrubbing in in five minutes."

As he walked away, I yelled, "So, am I scrubbing in or not?"

"Go ahead but you're not touching anything."

In the scrub room everyone shot me dirty looks. I could see Micah through the window, talking to a nurse. When I went into the operating room, we immediately locked eyes. "Hello, angel," he said. He was already out of it.

"Micah. I'm not assisting on this. I'm just observing."

"Does that mean you can give me a good kiss this time?"

"Shh, Micah. Don't."

"I wanna kiss from you, doc."

"Oh my god."

The anesthesiologist just smiled at me. She looked at Micah and said, "I'm going to start. Relax and count down from twenty for me. You can kiss him now," she said to me with a wry smile.

I pulled my mouth cover down and interrupted his counting with a good kiss. "Wow," he said before continuing to count down. "Three, two—"

"No," I said, but the words were already spilling out of his smiling mouth.

"One. See . . . " He was out. Tears sprang into my eyes.

"No," I said again, but it was too late.

"He'll be fine," the anesthesiologist said.

Doctors moved around the room as I stood out of their paths. Once they opened his leg, it was like I was in any other surgery. He was a patient. I was hyperfocused on what they were doing. Lessons I had learned about orthopedics were swimming in my mind. If they made one false move, I was going to jump in.

I watched with unrelenting concentration, glancing between the scans and the surgeons doing their work. The distal femur, a bone located just above the knee, was shattered, a common injury in high-impact car crashes. After seeing Micah's leg opened up, I realized the injury was much worse than I thought. He had intra-articular fractures, which meant the cartilage was damaged and the knee joint was in pieces.

The sound of drilling and putting screws in titanium started; I went in for a closer look. Dr. Reynolds paused, looked up at me, and squinted. He looked unsure for a moment. The other operating room staff said nothing.

He looked back down and continued with the intramedullary nailing, which involved attaching two plates to the outside of the femoral shaft. "Dr. Reynolds!" I pointed to the slow increase in Micah's heart rate on the screen.

A nurse said, "Oxygen saturation is dropping."

I immediately recognized signs of a pulmonary embolism. Dr. Reynolds blinked at the screen, eyebrows furrowed. I guessed his mind was mapping out the best options, but we also needed to act quickly.

"You need to push heparin," I said to the nurse. I didn't care if someone reprimanded me later; we had to act fast.

"Yes, give him five thousand units," Dr. Reynolds finally said. He glanced at me and nodded. "Help me close him up?" Micah's blood pressure and oxygen were stabilizing. I looked behind me as if the doctor were talking to someone else.

"Dr. Bennett?" he said.

"Yes, yes, okay." I moved around to assist him in completing the intramedullary nailing and closing up.

"Done," Dr. Reynolds said. Micah's leg was a mess, but I knew everything was where it should be. After we were through, I almost fell over from exhaustion.

"I helped put you back together," I mumbled to Micah even though I knew he couldn't hear me.

It wasn't long before fear overtook my thoughts. "Count the instruments!" I demanded to the scrub nurse. It didn't look like blood flow was returning to his leg. "Let's get a camera on this."

"No," Dr. Reynolds said. "He's good. The leg is good."

"He's not just a leg." I was starting to lose all sense. Another nurse grabbed my hand and pulled me out of the operating room. She removed my gloves and gown. I felt like a child. "We have to double-check . . . we have to triple-check," I told her.

"We were double-checking the whole time. That's our job. You did beautifully."

"What if he never walks again?"

"He will."

I finally understood the "conflict of interest" completely. It started doing on a number on my psyche. Would I be a doctor or would I be in love? How could I be both?

IT WAS FOUR o'clock in the afternoon when I realized I hadn't had a bite. My stomach gurgled as I sat in the recovery room, waiting for Micah to wake up. When I saw movement from his bed, I got up to check on him. He was groggy.

"Micah, you're in recovery."

He started laughing. "I am?"

"Yes. What is so funny?"

"I don't know." He was still delirious.

"Micah, you're just coming out of anesthesia. I'm going to get your family in the waiting room."

"Are you my girlfriend?" he said, wearing a huge grin.

"I'll be right back, Micah. Don't go anywhere."

He started laughing hysterically. As I walked away, I heard him say, "My girlfriend is a doctor." It made me smile. I got the surgery right; I knew it. The neurosurgeons were amazed at how well he bounced back after having his head cut open. And after assessing his knee and repairing his leg, I knew he would be just fine. Everything seemed right in the world.

In the waiting room, Mel was playing on her phone while Leslie and Peter were napping on each other's shoulders.

"Hello," I said softly.

Micah's parents woke up immediately and rushed toward me. "How is he?" Leslie said.

"Everything went well. He's awake and in recovery now. I can take you back to see him."

Mel brushed by me, which I ignored. She was worried about her brother. Once inside Micah's room, Leslie and Peter rushed to his bedside.

"You've taken about twelve years off our lives in the last few days," Peter said.

"You guys are overreacting. It was no big deal."

Leslie shook her head at him. "You had brain surgery, for god's sake."

"Mother, I'm well aware."

Melissa pushed her way through the group. "Thanks for calling Kenny. I'm having my stuff shipped down here. Oh, and congratulations on your stupid brain. They said you'd be fine. Well, as fine as *you* could possibly be."

"Did you say you're having your stuff shipped down?" Micah asked.

She smiled genuinely. "I'm a New Yorker through and through. Hey, I wanted to ask you . . . is Jeff still single?"

Micah just rolled his eyes at her. "Speaking of," his mother said, "Devin and Jeff are on their way."

Melissa raised a fist in the air. "Yes!"

"Melissa," Peter scolded.

Melissa gathered herself and said, "Wow, Micah, you have the same brace as me."

"We're twinsies," Micah said, smirking.

Everyone in the room started laughing.

Five minutes later Devin knocked on the open door and entered with Jeff following close behind. "Hello, Evans family!" he said boisterously. "Laya."

"Devin," I returned, and then smiled at Jeff.

"How's our baby boy Micah?" Devin had perfectly coifed hair like a Ken doll. You could tell he spent an unreasonable amount of time on it, and Jeff was just an average guy, wearing dress pants and a dress shirt rolled up at the sleeves. The men did a bro hug and Devin immaturely knocked on Micah's head. "Everything okay up there? You still gonna be the ladies' man you always were?" His sarcasm was evident and so was his competitive nature with Micah.

Micah laughed once and then said to Jeff, "Hey, have you met Laya?" Jeff looked at me and shook his head. "Jeff, meet Laya. Laya, meet Jeff."

We shook hands. "I thought you were his doctor for a minute," Jeff said.

"I am," I said. The room was quiet.

Micah was staring at us while Jeff tried to process what I had just said. "You mean you operated on him?"

"I did. Wasn't planning to, but it just happened. But more importantly, he's doing really well."

"Yeah, considering he drove my dad's piece of shit into a tree," Melissa chimed in.

"Melissa!" Peter scolded again.

"What? He did."

I shook my head. It was amazing how different twins could be.

"Hi, Melissa," Jeff said. She smiled at him shyly.

"Please, no," Micah sighed.

One of the nurses came in and shuffled around for a bit before asking the family to leave so Micah could get some rest. Devin didn't follow the rest of the family out the door. The nurse glared at him. "Oh, me too?" he said.

"Get the fuck outta here, Devin," Micah said humorously.

"Okay, okay. I was just going to stick around for a bit. Maybe escort Laya here to the cafeteria."

"Actually, thank you for the offer, but I think I need to get home. And Micah needs rest. And . . . and my dog is floating around here somewhere."

"Okay, okay," he said, smirking at me. He turned to Micah and said, "I'll catch up with you later, man." He gave Micah a brief awkward sideways hug before leaving the room.

I felt like the outsider. So many people cared for Micah, loved him. Melissa had joked with her brother before, but I understood the pain she was trying to hide. She'd almost lost her twin. Because of me. Because our paths crossed at the worst possible time in my life.

I stared at Micah, and he returned my gaze. I made up my mind. It started in the stairway when I broke down, but the fear grew stronger and stronger as I hovered over him in the operating room. I couldn't drag him along with me while I struggled anymore. It wasn't fair to either one of us.

"So you're really leaving?" he asked.

I nodded. "Yeah, I'm gonna go. I think you should focus

on getting better for a while, okay? I have some things to figure out, Micah."

He held a hand up to his stapled head. I felt sorry for him for a moment, but it was fleeting. I had to stay strong. He would be okay, possibly better if I wasn't in the picture.

I needed to get my head straight. It felt like everything was spinning out of orbit again. Reading Cameron's letter, operating on Micah. I made a pact with myself not to drag Micah through any more of my drama.

Our eyes were locked on each other. "I'm in love with you, Laya," he said.

"I'm not going away forever. You have your family and friends . . . and an awesome team here."

"You fixed me, Laya." He reached his hand out. "*You* did it."

"I just did my job." I squeezed his hand, bent, and kissed his cheek. The surgery could have gone either way. I could have totally blown it with my inexperience and jumping in when I knew I probably shouldn't have.

"But—"

"I hope you make a full recovery. I have confidence you'll do great."

"Please don't talk to me like you're my doctor." He squinted like his head hurt again.

I turned toward the door and started to walk out. "I am, though, Micah."

"Wait, please," he said. "You're more than just my doctor. You know that."

He was pleading but I couldn't think straight and I couldn't look at him in his condition.

So I left him. Thinking back to my childhood, I

remembered my dad sitting in his office at home, crying, sometimes. I'd walk in to comfort him and he would always say his eyes were watering from allergies. I believed him until I was about ten, when he had an "allergic" reaction to my mother's photographs. After that, I knew why he cried.

The last time we'd spoken, he'd mentioned how the waves of grief came fewer and farther apart as time passed. For him, maybe. But it hadn't been enough time for me. I wasn't ready and I couldn't take Micah with me on the roller-coaster hours after he had escaped death.

I apologized to the entire staff at the hospital in a quick email I wrote from my office. I was still holding Pretzel under my arm as I typed with one hand. I also asked to be taken off Micah's team, which was granted within minutes. As soon as I could, I was out of there and headed home, hoping I still had a job, and hoping Micah would understand.

When I got home, I tried to write Cameron a letter that wasn't stream of consciousness, like my phone messages had been. I needed to talk to him and tell him how I felt about the letter he had written me, about our short marriage and how I was barely keeping my head above water since I had lost him.

Hours later I found myself sitting on the couch, watching the flickering light again.

Everyone in my life had been constantly reminding me that I was *not* defective or damaged goods. But in measuring the choices I had made, I thought people had to be wrong about their assessment of me. Who seeks out a relationship with a person who likes to jump off cliffs? Who marries a person who puts their life in danger for nothing? When would I stop blaming Cameron for who he was? Or feel like he was still toying with me from beyond?

My mind was racing with thoughts, but each one brought me back to a place where I couldn't help but compare Cameron and Micah. I knew Micah had good intentions and there were so many qualities about him I adored. He was calm compared to Cameron's adrenalized energy. Micah was handsome, smart, and introspective. He was kind and gentle. But I questioned whether his actions were selfless or selfish, and whether my marriage to Cameron would always make me doubt everyone I formed a relationship with.

28. Structure Failure

MICAH

There was nothing I could do. I literally couldn't chase Laya down the hallway, begging her to stay. The only thing I could do was try to understand her and everything that had happened. I wanted to kiss the year good-bye, start over, meet Laya in a café somewhere, mulling over pastries. I wanted us to be strangers who didn't know each other's pain.

"If you love her, you'll do what it takes," came Melissa's voice from a darkened corner of the room.

"What does it take?" I asked. "And were you here the whole time?"

"No I just came in, but I saw her bolt down the hall with her ugly dog. She looked upset and I figured something had gone down."

Despite the disintegration of Melissa's relationship with Kenny, she actually had a lot more success than me in the

love department. She could be obnoxious and overly demonstrative, but she wasn't a fool.

"So what happened?" Melissa asked.

"She just said I needed to focus on getting better. I think
she meant that we can't be together right now. Everything is
starting to hurt."

"She's right. You both need the space. A lot of shit has
gone down between two people who don't know each other
that well. You were never officially together."

"I know," I said. Even though it felt like I knew Laya
well, it was true—we hadn't spent much time together.

"When you get out of here, I want you to come and stay
with me. I lined up an apartment near Mom and Dad."

"How are you going to afford that?"

"Pot is a lucrative biz."

"I guess so," I said right before Taylor, the night nurse,
walked in.

"Melissa, it's so good to see you. How are you?" Taylor
asked.

"Hi, Taylor. Did you get my text?" Melissa replied curtly.

I looked up at her from the bed, wondering why she
seemed confrontational.

"Yeah, you know, I need to talk to you," he said.

"I'm listening," she shot back.

Taylor glanced over at me, then back to Melissa.
"Maybe outside we can talk."

"Micah is my twin. He knows everything about me."

*Oh my god, is everyone losing their minds in my hospital
room as I lie here helpless?*

"Melissa, um, I did get your text. You are um, very sexy."
He was stumbling over his words.

"Melissa!" I barked. "Did you send him a pic?"

Melissa looked over at me, arched her eyebrows, and shrugged.

"I didn't respond, but I wanted to tell you, I hope we can be friends. I really enjoy your personality and now that you're out of the hospital—"

"I'm confused," Melissa said. "Are you gay or something?"

Very calmly Taylor said, "Yes, I am."

Melissa began to stutter, "I'm . . . I'm, ugh . . ."

"It's okay, Melissa," he said. "Happens all the time." When he winked at her, I burst out laughing.

"Zip it, gimpy," Melissa spat out.

"Pot, kettle much, Melispa?"

"I'm going to get some Doritos out of the machine. Sorry, Taylor, I feel like an idiot," she said as she left the room.

Once she was gone, Taylor said, "Your sister is a character."

"Yes, she is. Don't worry, she'll get over the embarrassment and probably ask you to lunch next week."

"Well, I hope so. Like I said, I really enjoy her liveliness, and I think she's a lot of fun."

I smiled and he smiled back. He was genuine and I had a feeling it wouldn't be long before he and Mel were inseparable.

After he left, Melissa returned with a bag of M&Ms. "How humiliating, right?" she said as she sat in the chair next to my bed.

"I think it's funny. I never would have guessed."

"Maybe you can date him now that Laya is out of the picture," Melissa said with a mouthful of M&Ms.

"Do you see the way Devin looks at her? He's shameless. He hit on her right in front of me." Melissa pulled a Kit Kat from her sweats pocket. I cocked my head to the side. "Really?"

"Fuck Kenny, I'm not giving up Kit Kats ever again. And you know what, fuck Devin, too. He's a shitty friend and a moron. Micah, why don't you just work on getting better? I'll do the same. At least we have each other."

A memory of Mel sitting in the rocker and me reading in the argyle jacket at our parents' cabin rushed through my mind and I grimaced.

As if she could read my mind, she said, "Not forever. Just for now."

"I really care about her, Mel."

"I think she knows that." Another nurse came in and pumped me full of more pain meds. Melissa continued eating candy next to me until I passed out.

Every hour after that a nurse would come in and ask me the same questions. "What year is it? Who is the president? What is your full name and birthday? How old are you?" It became redundant and annoying. I kept thinking, *I broke my brain; how will I ever design again? I fucked things up with Laya and she's never going to speak to me again.* It was unnerving to sit around obsessing over things I couldn't fix in that moment. My emotions told me to call her, but my brain told me to let her breathe.

At seven in the morning I could hear Laya's voice outside my room. She was talking to a nurse about not examining me anymore and how a new fellow was assigned to my case.

I texted her even though I knew she was right outside.

Me: I can hear your voice outside
my room. It's never sounded
more beautiful. I only wish
the words were different.

She didn't respond. Soon I didn't hear her voice any-more.

The rest of my time in the hospital was made up of more procedures, sleepless nights, and obsessing over the state of my life. But as my head and leg began to get stronger, so did my understanding of what Laya, Melissa, and I had all gone through in recent months. Our work woes and petty arguments with friends paled in comparison to the loss Laya had experienced, the deception Melissa had felt, and the self-awareness I realized I had been lacking. We'd all had a little brush with death, and for me, it made life seem louder, more delicate . . . more beautiful.

29. Jigsaw

MICAH

Weeks went by, then months. I was discharged from the hospital after daily intense physical therapy and weekly CT scans. I never saw Laya. I picked up where I left off at work. I was getting better and better physically, though I was still very much confused about where Laya and I stood. There was no question that I cared deeply for her, and though we didn't have many interactions, I knew I wanted her in my life. Maybe forever. I just had to figure out how to do that.

I asked Jim often about his daughter. I don't think he knew we had spent more time together, and I'm sure he wondered why I was constantly making inquiries. He told me she was doing well, diving into work and taking her life back. I was happy for her. I didn't want to interfere or cause her more distress.

My own life started to settle down. I was almost 100 percent back to normal. My job was picking up, and Steve and

Shelly were backing off. In April of that year I landed a huge job designing a building in the financial district.

All the pieces of my life were starting to come back together. Even though I was going through the motions and challenging myself to do better in every avenue of my life, I was still thinking about Laya nonstop.

Her. The woman who popped up on the screen of my life. She wasn't ever quite tangible. She was an image. Like one slip of the hand and I'd delete her. She wasn't made of plastic or glass, she was as real as they come, but still I felt like I never had a chance to reach inside, touch her heart, hold it, and let her know it was sacred to me and that everything would be okay. All I wanted was her trust, her time, but deep down I knew she needed the space more.

People around me knew even though I never said anything. It wasn't like I was walking around asking for love-life advice anymore, but people sure as hell wanted to offer it. They would tell me to find a distraction or go jogging in the park. Melissa tried to convince me to take a hip-hop dance class with her and Taylor, but that was a hard no for me.

Before I met Laya, I had no idea what a broken heart felt like. You tell yourself constantly, every waking moment, to stop thinking about her, but you can't. At some point you accept that the ramen place, the movie theater, an ugly dog, or some French toast will trigger an image that will make you miss her all over again. I guess on a much larger scale Laya had experienced the same phenomenon when she'd lost Cameron.

I did try to distract myself by diving into work, hoping, at the very least, that one day Laya Bennett would walk through a building I had designed and say, "Isn't this beautiful?"

30. Spacewalk

LAYA

I still talked to Cameron every day, on his voicemail, in letters, sometimes on his Facebook, but I was finding I had less and less to say. I stopped seeing him on the corner and in my dreams. It wasn't that I wanted the memories to fade; it was more that I wanted the pain and confusion to let up. Diving into work, fixing up my apartment, and taking care of Pretzel offered a nice distraction, but Micah was still on my mind.

He tried, and I took it for granted. He was a present, loving, and kind person. Part of me wished I hadn't pushed him away, but the other part knew I wasn't in the right state of mind to date or to give someone else a part of me that was still wrecked. Now I figured it was too late. I was sure he had moved on. Who wouldn't see all of his good qualities and want to spend time with him? I think the best part of Micah was that he was humble. I used to see that part of him as insecurity, but looking back it was actually confidence. He didn't need to talk about his talent; it was evident to everyone, including my father. And Micah certainly didn't need to worry about his looks. He was jaw dropping in old jeans, a sweatshirt, and messy hair.

I missed him.

When my dad called to say he was considering making Micah a partner, I was truly happy, even though it meant I would have to face Micah in the office at some point. I didn't know how soon it would be, though.

A week after the chat with my dad I was on my way to the firm to give him some paperwork on his rental.

When I got to the sixth floor, I was surprised and a little relieved I didn't see Micah as I made my way to Dad's office. The moment I sat down in front of him, I knew something was different. Lighter, maybe, but before I could ask, he said, "Laya, I met someone."

"Really?" I asked, my eyes wide.

"Yes. I want you to meet her."

"Wow. This is a first. What is she like?" I asked him.

"She's kind and funny, with a real zest for life. She has two adult children who I think you'd really get along with."

"Why is that?"

"They're intelligent and driven, like you." His words touched me. For so long it felt like everyone thought I was just a mess of a person and always would be. "Laya, you seem to be making a lot of progress lately. My friends at the hospital have been talking about how well you're doing."

I *was* doing a lot better. Still, every once in a while, a wave of grief, fear, and guilt would hit me. "He's getting further away. It scares me, Dad."

He smiled with sympathy. "You're not betraying him. He's not here—but you are."

"I know, Dad."

"You know, Laya, what shocked me most when you became an adult was how different you were from your mother."

In the past, whenever my father would start talking about my mom, my whole body would tense up. But that day it was different. I wanted to know more about her. "How do you mean?" I asked.

"Your mom was content. Looking back, it was like she knew."

I squinted. "Knew what?"

"That she didn't have long. Now I think of her as an angel who God let out for a little while to give me you, and to touch my life in a way no one else would. Now I don't look back with regret or sadness. I'm grateful I was the one she picked."

I started crying silently, without expression. It was like cleansing tears were rushing down my face to wash away the hurt, confusion, and sadness. Maybe Cameron was *my* angel, put here to show me that I was capable of loving.

After my father patiently gave me some insight, I left his office feeling a renewed sense of well-being. If I was going to hit the ground running, I was going to do it as Laya, wearing my dirty pink high tops from college and my old T-shirt from space camp. I didn't have to reinvent myself; I just had to reintroduce myself to life.

I walked toward Micah's new office. He wasn't there, so I went in. I started scribbling a note to him. Without noticing, I was saying the words out loud.

"Hi, I hope you're doing well. I was thinking—"

"What were you thinking, beautiful?" His voice startled me. I turned quickly and realized he was standing only two feet behind me. He wore suit pants and a dress shirt rolled up at the sleeves. He looked tan and healthy. I glanced at his muscular forearms and then up his body to his mouth. His lips were turned up into a tiny smirk and his eyes were clear and searching mine.

"Um, I was thinking about how you were doing?"

"Better now," he whispered. "Now that you're standing in my office."

"I shouldn't be nervous around you, but I am."

"You're not nervous. You just have some nerves. I might be able to help you," he said.

"I seriously doubt that."

He reached out to hold my hands between us. No, that didn't help my nerves at all. My heart rate spiked at his touch.

"Your office is nice, much better than the cube," I told him. There were miniature models decorating every open space of the room, and his window looked out onto Central Park.

"You're a really amazing subject changer."

"One of my many gifts," I said.

"That's for sure." He nodded at my half-written note. "So, were you going to sneak off after leaving me an unfinished letter?"

"Maybe. You look good," I finally said. I desperately tried to shake off the feeling of being turned on by his passive staring. He looked me in the eyes and waited, so I went on. "So, you feel like you've made a full recovery? Like you've really bounced back, and you're doing well, and everything is good . . . and life is good?"

"Still changing subjects, and poor syntax, Laya. To answer your question, I'm about ninety-nine percent. I had a great doctor." He winked. "And everything is well and good, as you would put it. There is just one thing I wish I had."

Oh no. "What's that?"

"Cold French toast," he said.

"Oh, um." His answer caught me off guard. "I'm sorry to hear that. Maybe your . . . girlfriend could make you that for breakfast?"

"Girlfriend?" he asked, his eyes playful.

"It's been a while, so maybe . . ."

He shook his head but didn't answer. Instead, he stepped forward. I hesitated before also taking a step, closing the space between us.

"What did you learn?" I asked.

"From us, you mean?"

I nodded but he just stood there, his eyes fixed on mine. "Why are you staring at me?" I said.

"It's hard to look away," he replied.

"So, you didn't learn anything?"

"I did. I learned that no matter how hard I try, I can't stop thinking about you."

He was beautiful, standing there, seemingly calm and collected. "What did *you* learn, Laya?"

"I learned that you say my name differently than I thought. You say it like Micah."

He laughed. "Well, I hope so."

"And I learned that I really do want to make you breakfast."

"What are we waiting for?" He took his thumb and gently tugged at my bottom lip. Without hesitating, he learned forward and kissed me softly. I was frozen. My hands found their way to his chest, which was hard and warm. He smelled like soap. It wasn't overwhelming, just a masculine smell that made my legs tremble.

"Micah?"

"Laya?"

"Can we go slow? Can we go back to zero?" I asked him.

He took a step back, releasing me from his hold. As he held his hand out to shake mine, I hesitated. I really wanted him to kiss me again. Would I ever be able to take things slow with Micah? There was an ease about him that made me want to crawl back into his arms and just burrow my head into his chest. He stood there quietly with his hand extended. He kept glancing down at his hand as if to say *Are you gonna shake it or what?* Micah knew who he was and didn't care what other people thought about him. He was okay with silence.

When I shook his hand, we both started laughing. "I'm Laya."

"Micah. It's nice to meet you. Would you like to go get a coffee with me?"

"Sure. When?"

"Now. It's usually the precursor to cold French toast."

Even though I wanted so badly to take him to my apartment, cook for him, and then get distracted with him, I couldn't. "I have to go into the hospital and do some paperwork."

"I'll take cafeteria coffee," he offered.

My dad came into the hall. He didn't bat an eye when he saw me with Micah. Instead he gave me a long hug. I think my dad always knew there was a spark between Micah and me.

Before leaving the office, I went to the ladies' room to take a breath and to get my thoughts in order. There are times in life when the pendulum swinging between happiness and sadness begins to slow. The powerful force of emotions goes dormant, we pause, look up, and realize we are finally content. I settled into the idea that I couldn't control what other people did. Surrendering to the notion that I was just along for the ride was freeing. Maybe that was what Cameron had always been searching for. The ride that would free him. Maybe in his death, he finally found it. Maybe in his death, I had found it.

31. Payload

MICAH

Time felt suspended in the cafeteria as we sat surrounded by tired doctors and nurses, patients and family members speaking in hushed tones, and the distant clanking of dishes from the kitchen. Laya cupped her coffee mug as she stared out of a large window that opened onto a courtyard garden. I didn't say a word because this was her time and I would listen to whatever she needed to tell me. Finally, she looked up; her expression was different from before, when she had been drowning in an ocean of grief. Her eyes looked clearer, more trusting . . . more earnest.

"I want to talk to you about everything," she said. "I want you to know who I really am."

"Go ahead; I'm a good listener. I'm ready."

"Do you want a muffin or a doughnut or something?"

I shook my head and laughed. "I thought you were going to tell me everything?"

"Right." She breathed in, then out. "I loved Cameron."

"I know."

"I never thought I would love someone like that. He took a lot of risks. He was spontaneous and wild, such a free spirit. There were times when I felt like he brought a new, exciting part of me out. It *was* thrilling."

"I bet."

"But, Micah, it wasn't always good," she said before looking away, out of the window again.

"It never is . . . always good. No one is perfect," I told her.

"I mean, Cam wasn't always good to me." She looked pained when she spoke.

"You don't have to have guilt for feeling that way."

"I used to. He was only human. After he died, I put him on this pedestal, like he did no wrong. I know he loved me the best way he knew how, but he loved the stunts, too. It was the lifestyle that always drew him back. He died doing what he loved. There aren't many people I can say that about."

"What would you say to him if you met him today?"

She chuckled almost as if she was laughing at herself. "I wouldn't change anything. He was exactly what I was looking for . . . then."

"What are you looking for now?"

"Nothing. I'm just living now. I'm trying to be the best doctor, daughter, and dog owner I can be. I'm staying in New York, Micah."

There was something buried in that statement. I didn't need to unearth it by asking more questions. "You seem different to me."

"I'm not different. In the last few months I've thought a

lot about the time we spent together. That night in the club, for one."

I shifted in my seat, feeling suddenly embarrassed. "Don't, Laya. We don't need to talk about it."

"I didn't do that out of spite for losing my husband, or because I was in pain, though I *was* in a lot of pain. I did it because I saw this gentleness in you. Right from the very start I knew you wouldn't hurt me. My dad would always talk about you being the pillar at the firm. He said he could count on you. He's very guarded about those kinds of things. I think when Steve and Shelly came on the scene, my dad was in a bad place. He let a lot slip through the cracks with them."

"Yeah, don't I know it. Why do you think he did?"

"Because the firm meant nothing to him once I said I had no desire to be a part of it. You ignited a new passion in him. He told me he felt like you were a son he never had."

Jim was always good to me, but I never would have imagined he thought of me as a son. "I've always admired your dad."

"And Micah . . . I knew that was you at the concert. Or I've figured it out, at least. I didn't want to acknowledge the feelings I had for you. We didn't even know each other then."

"Do we know each other now?"

"I want to know you more. I want you in my life. It doesn't matter in what capacity. We can figure that out later. I just know there is something about you that makes me feel calm and understood."

"You and I never got to spend moments like this together."

She squinted. "Moments like sitting in a smelly hospital cafeteria?"

"Normal life moments, is what I mean. Just the two us drinking coffee, having easy conversation. There isn't anything to confuse us now. I think we understand each other's boundaries."

"What's next, then?"

"Breakfast at your apartment?" I waggled my eyebrows. "I'll cook it, I don't even care."

"I guess it would be nice to just sit on the couch and not talk to each other?"

"You're very romantic." *Who said anything about sitting on the couch and* just *talking?*

"I mean, I just want to *be* and get to know you. Under more normal circumstances."

"I just want to *be* and get to know you, too." I knew I had to tread lightly with Laya. Even though I wanted to ask her exactly what she meant, I wouldn't pressure her about it. I decided it would be poor timing to tell her I wanted to be with her literally, physically, mentally, figuratively . . . and every other way possible. I'd tell her in time.

"I'll let you know my schedule for next week," she said. I heard her name over the intercom.

"You have to go," I told her.

"Yeah, I have to get back to work."

I stood up and stuck my arms out for a hug. I felt her lips touch my cheek. I didn't want to sit back and wait for her to change her mind so I bent my head and kissed her. It was a chaste, fast kiss, but it felt natural.

"Well, okay then. I'll text you."

"You better."

I CALLED MEL when I got back to the office, and she groaned before asking what was wrong now. I smiled and said, "Nothing at all is wrong." I described my conversation with Laya. "What do you think I should do? I mean, how do I really impress her?"

"She likes space" came a voice from the hall. Jim. He stepped in and leaned against the doorway, his hands casually in his pockets.

I quickly pushed the *end* button, paying no mind to Mel's protest of "Who said that?" I blinked at Jim, not sure what to say. I didn't know if he knew the extent of my relationship with Laya.

"Space, as in—" Jim pointed up.

"Um, yeah, I know," I replied.

"She likes doughnuts, too."

"Doughnuts?"

"Yeah, the twisty kind with cinnamon on top."

"Jim—"

"Micah, you don't need to say anything."

I coughed to buy time. "I want to make sure this won't interfere with my work here and the partnership."

"Not unless you hurt her. Then I'll fire you, wait a few days, and then I'll kill you."

"I can't imagine why anyone would want to hurt her." If I could have seen myself, I would have guessed I resembled something like a terrified meerkat.

"She's complicated, Micah. She's not a piece of cake."

"I definitely know that," I said.

"I don't think Laya is looking for quiet time locked away in a woodland cabin."

Whoa, Jim was pulling no punches now. "Let me explain that—"

"You mean the existential crisis you had a while back?"

"I had no idea you noticed," I said while my heart and nerves were running a 5K.

"The beard was hard to miss."

"Yeah, that. The beard was a bucket list thing. I'm over it now." Suddenly I was out of words.

"Am I intimidating you, Micah?"

"No—" I lied.

"Well, this might: What are your intentions with Laya?"

Intentions were not something I had necessarily thought about. My phone was buzzing on the desk. Melissa was relentless.

"How about a PowerPoint, Micah? To lay out why you think you'd be good enough for my daughter?"

"A . . . PowerPoint?"

He didn't crack for what felt like five solid minutes and then he smiled and said, "Relax, I'm just fucking with you. But I will kill you if you hurt her." He turned and laughed as he walked back down the hall. I said nothing.

"Hello?" I practically yelled into the phone.

"Jeez, what the hell?"

"Melissa, you heard Jim talking to me about Laya."

"It's cute; she likes space. What are you gonna do, fly her to the moon?"

"I have to think of something," I said.

"Why don't you take her to the Smithsonian Space Museum in Virginia?"

"Melissa, how do you know these things?"

"I don't know . . . I watch a lot of TV."

"That should have been a red flag for Kenny."

"Don't ever utter his name again or I will come and shove five pounds of granola up your ass."

"Charming. So, tell me about this museum."

"Well, it's in Virginia, and Virginia is for lovers. Maybe you guys can bone on a spaceship or something."

"I'll look into it."

Just then my phone dinged with a text from Laya.

Laya: I'm free Friday through
Sunday if you want to
get a real coffee.

Me: That sounds great.
I'll keep you posted.

"Micah! Did you hang up on me again?" Melissa yelled.

"No, I'm right here. I was texting Laya back."

"I have to go anyway, Taylor wants me to wax his back."

"You guys are so weird. I'll talk to you later."

"Bye, Pickle."

32. Reentry

LAYA

My door buzzer went off at exactly nine a.m. on Friday. I had worked pretty much all night, so I was exhausted. I wondered why Micah had never texted earlier in the week to make a plan. I thought maybe I would be bold and text him. I went to the door speaker.

"Hello?"

"Hi."

I knew right away it was Micah. My eyes shot open while I scanned my body. I was wearing yet another space camp T-shirt with a giant hole in the armpit and a pair of tattered sweats. At least my apartment was clean, except for a small pile of Pretzel poop near my bathroom door.

"Dammit, Pretzel." He looked up at me with sad, guilty eyes.

"Hi," I said back into the speaker.

"Hi," he said again.

"Good morning," I replied.

"Whattya up to?"

"Oh nothing, just sipping some coffee, walking around in my pajamas with bed head."

"I'm sure you look beautiful."

"Um, um, so what are you doing here?" I asked.

"I need you to get ready."

"For what?" I said into the speaker.

"Come on. Let me in, silly. I'm taking you somewhere."

I apprehensively hit the buzzer. He was up the stairs in seconds. When I opened the door, he leaned in, pecked me on the cheek, and said, "You look nothing short of gorgeous. Bed head and all. Okay, let's go, the plan is set."

"Are you crazy?"

"Yes." He held up a grocery bag. "I'll make breakfast while you pack."

"Pack?"

"What if I told you that you can wear your space camp T-shirts for the whole weekend?" he said.

"Not good enough. I need more details."

"What if I tell you I will devote several hours each day to kissing every inch of your body?"

"You might be onto something. Is this your idea of taking it slow?"

He maneuvered past me into the kitchen. "I would call waiting eight months to have French toast in your apartment taking it very slow. I exercised extreme restraint. Now get your butt in there and pack."

I followed him around in the kitchen and continued stalling. "Are you a good cook?"

He smiled while he whisked the eggs, milk, vanilla, and

cinnamon. "I can make like six things. My sister is actually a good cook. Three years ago she dated a chef and thought she should go to culinary school. She broke up with him and quit school after three months when the guy tried to convince her to eat a baby chicken still all slimy in the egg. I had forgotten about that."

"Gross."

"I guess they do it in other countries."

I couldn't take my eyes off him as he cooked at my stove. He set a plate of French toast and raspberries on the counter, cut a piece with a fork, stabbed it, and reached across to feed it to me. I think I almost passed out from how good it tasted.

"Laya? Where'd you go?"

"Food heaven."

We ate in relative silence, but it wasn't uncomfortable. I thought about life. Looking at Micah—smiling, happy, and content, just sitting in my apartment eating French toast—made me think about the life we choose. About Cameron, my mother and father, about the patients I had treated. Was I so self-absorbed that I couldn't give credence to the love that was all around me? When you look outside and compare a person's life to a flickering light on a post, about to burn out so that *you* can't see anymore, it's selfish. When you live alone and ignore all the beautiful humanity swirling outside your door, it's selfish. When you lie in your bed and cry because *you*, the one with a full life to live, have lost someone, it's selfish. It wasn't because I didn't have a right to mourn; it was because I was taking what Cameron no longer had, and I was throwing it all away. I vowed not to do that anymore.

"Laya, what are you thinking about?"

I shook my head, breaking the trance. "The future."

"Me, too," he said. "Now go pack. I'm serious, lady."

RUNNING AROUND FRANTICALLY, wondering what the hell to bring besides, of course, all my NASA T-shirts, I kept asking Micah and he kept giving funny replies.

"Micah, what do I need? What should I bring?"

"Your humor, please."

"Seriously," I said.

"Your undeniable beauty."

"Come on!"

"Your wit, your intelligence, your kindness, your determination, your amazing hands—"

"You. Are. Impossible."

"One more thing," he said.

"What?"

"Bring that pack of Skittles from your nightstand."

"That I can do," I told him.

At the door he picked up Pretzel and said, "We have to run by Mel's. She has my things and she agreed to watch Pretzel."

My eyes shot open with worry.

"It's okay . . . she's a vegetarian, sort of."

I shook my head and followed him to the street to hail a cab. When we got to Melissa's, she greeted us at the door. "You guys are freaks," she said. "But I think it's kinda cool."

She handed Micah his bag of things and we were off. "Thank you so much," I told her.

"Have fun. I guess you guys deserve it."

Micah leaned in, kissed her on the cheek, and said, "Thanks, Melispa."

She scowled and said, "Gross. Get outta here. Your car is parked on Fifth."

On the street I said to Micah, "Sweet Melissa."

"Not really," he said, "but she'll have to do."

"So, we have a car?"

"I rented one."

I literally didn't have a single idea where we were going, except that Micah said it would be a six-hour drive. We goofed off in the car. I didn't care about time. I didn't think about work, or Cameron. We ate junk food all the way to Virginia. After my sugar high wore off, I fell asleep.

"We're here, sleepyhead. Keep your eyes closed."

I could tell we were parking and then the car stopped. "You know what they say about Virginia, Laya?"

"Oh, you cheeseball. Virginia is for lovers?"

"Yes, but that's not what I was thinking . . . take a look. They say it has the best space museum in the country."

My eyes shot open. The entrance to the Smithsonian National Air and Space Museum came into view. "Oh my god. I've always wanted to come here."

"Well, let's go get our nerd goggles on," he said. I punched him in the arm. "Jesus, Laya, you are stronger than you think."

"Were you calling me a nerd?"

"Yes. Just another thing I love about you."

The first thing we looked at and went through was the Concorde. "It's beautiful," I said.

"An engineering marvel," he replied.

"Shame they had to decommission them."

"Yeah," he said, but he seemed distant. "Hey, stay here for a sec. I'll be right back."

He left abruptly, but was back in five minutes.

"Okay, Laya, it's time to see the shuttle." My eyes welled up. "Oh no, you're disappointed. Don't worry, we might get to see it take off."

I laughed. "I'm not disappointed. I'm happy to be here with you."

"I'm happy, too."

Our tour felt like forever. I relearned everything I already knew about the shuttle from my years at space camp. I was itching to go inside, but even just looking at it from the outside was fascinating. When we finally got to see the inside, Micah whispered something to the tour guide.

I marveled at the controls, the buttons and gauges. Soon the crowd cleared out. I tried to follow, but Micah took me by the arm and guided me to the front of the shuttle.

"The guide said we could sit in the front," he told me.

"What? Are you serious?"

"Go." He pointed to the pilot's seat. "Mission control is waiting."

"God, I always wanted to be the pilot."

"I'll be the mission specialist." He winked.

I sat down and felt my hands burning from the desire to touch everything, but I knew it wasn't allowed. Micah sat in the seat next to mine.

"So, mission specialist, where are we headed?" I asked him.

"Hold on, I need to tell you something."

"Okay."

"Laya . . . you are the most intergalactic, spacefaring terraform I know—"

"Now you're really turning me on."

He paused, pulled something from his pocket, reached over, and opened his hands. It was a cheap silver ring that had a tiny rocket on the top, clearly from the gift shop. "Will you go to the moon with me, Laya?"

I blinked several times, took the ring from his hands, and leaned over toward him. Just before our lips met, I said, "Yes, I will. Count me down, lieutenant."

He said, "Three. Two. One." And then I kissed him.

In the hotel room that night, I told Micah everything I knew about space. And he listened. I told him everything I could think of about being a doctor. I told him about my mom and my childhood and everything in between. And he listened. He tried to steal kisses every now and then, but still, he listened. I knew Micah wasn't asking me to marry him. He was just asking me to go on a trip with him. I was all in.

"What's on the agenda next week?" he said.

"I don't know. I do have to work, but I need to call Izzy and apologize for being a shitty friend. I definitely need to take Pretzel to the groomers. And I should call my sister-in-law, Krista, and tell her I support her no matter what. What about you?"

"Probably design some of those buildings you want to walk through, and other than that, find ways to kiss you in the storage closets at the hospital."

"I think we have a plan. Thank you for this weekend." I touched my hand to his cheek. "Micah?"

"Yes?"

"I feel alive and . . . I'm not scared."

"Me, too, Laya."

That night into the next day was a blur, I just know I

tore off my NASA shirt and everything else, and didn't put them back on for twenty-four hours.

Back in the city, nothing changed. We spent the next night together and the next night after that, even though we were both back and forth from work. One morning I woke up from a short dream. It was a memory of Cameron talking to me on the top of Mount Whitney. He had said, "I'm happy when you're happy, Laya."

When I woke up, I was sweating and crying. He had said it to me. I couldn't remember before, but he had said it. He *had* loved me, and I loved him, still do.

Looking over at Micah sleeping peacefully under my frilly peach comforter, I realized that I loved Micah, too, and it was okay.

I went to my computer, clicked on Facebook to Cameron's page, and wrote what would be my last post to him.

LAYA BENNETT to CAMERON BENNETT

Cam, I went to that space museum in Virginia where I always wanted to go. I sat in the pilot's chair. I felt brave, like I could do anything. You would have been proud, Cam. I miss you and I always will. I hope you're having a great new adventure . . . wherever you are. Three, two, one. See ya on the other side.

I clicked off my account, logged into Cameron's account . . . and I deleted it.

Epilogue

LAYA

The helicopter rotor thundered as it sliced through the air, parting clouds above the Mediterranean Sea. I peered down from my seat, my stomach churning at the thought of people actually skydiving from that height. No, thanks; I was good inside. Looking to my left, I saw that Jeremy was watching me with a wide grin. I hugged Cameron's urn close to my body, my mind at ease with what I was going to do next.

The summer after I started dating Micah, I told him I was going to Spain for a week because there was something I needed to do. Micah had an idea why I needed to go, but he didn't ask questions.

When I called Jeremy, who'd been with Cam and me that horrible day, he couldn't have been more surprised. "You want to parachute into the Spanish Cave? Sweet!" Jeremy was like Cameron in many ways. Getting a helicopter was no big deal.

"No, crazy. I want to fly over it. I want to spread the rest of Cam's ashes there."

He had hesitated. "Why the Spanish Cave? I didn't think you guys were ever there together."

"We weren't. I saw a wingsuit flight he had done there. I watched the video a few weeks after we had met. I always wished we had gone there together."

"I remember when Cam did that stunt. It was fucking awesome."

"He was happy, wasn't he?"

"Ahh, man he loved that day. He was also superstoked that he had just met you."

"Was he?" I whispered.

"God, he wouldn't shut up about you. It was annoying . . . no offense."

I laughed. "That's how I want to remember him, Jeremy . . . happy and alive."

"Let's do it, then."

Weeks later I was pointing out of the helicopter window to a familiar site I had remembered from the video.

"Right there?" I asked.

"Yep, that's it."

Right before Jeremy slid the door to the helicopter open, I pictured Cameron's face in the video. He was smiling from ear to ear, then he yelled, "Fuck yeah, see ya," while he simultaneously shot a peace sign to the camera man.

"Go for it, Laya," Jeremy said into the headset mic.

I took a deep breath and yelled, "Three. Two. One . . . see ya!!"

My nervousness and fear disappeared, replaced only with exhilaration. Was this how Cam always felt, being at this height? I turned the urn upside down, watching Cam's ashes fly away while Jeremy yelled, "Bye, buddy."

I was laughing and crying, smiling with relief, thinking Cameron would be so happy if he saw us. "I love you, Cameron Bennett!" I screamed. Somewhere, I was sure he could hear me.

Jeremy hugged me, both of us soaked with happy tears.

"He was a crazy son of a bitch, but impossible not to love. And he loved the shit out of you, Laya!"

"I know he did."

One thing I learned to do after I finally opened the blinds and came out of the dark hole with Micah by my side was to reframe the tragedies I'd gone through. I got to have two great loves in my life. One was a little nuts, a little unpredictable, a spontaneous spirit too wild to restrain, and the other . . . a deep and introspective, thoughtful being with magnificent eyes who loved the stars and space right alongside me. I will always look back and think of Cameron as that rocket ship, shooting for the stars, and Micah . . . well . . . he's like mission control, guiding me home.

Both easy to love, both loved me . . . and I never had to choose.

MICAH

I proposed to Laya for the third time two years after our weekend in Virginia. She finally said yes. She was right to take her time. I still don't know if she was waiting for some superstitious date to pass, but I didn't care. She said she just wanted to hear me ask over and over again. I would have asked for the rest of my life. Laya was life-affirming for me. Every moment we had was genuine and real. There is no one else like her; I'm sure of it. Maybe we both had to go away for a little while, to be alone, to get to know ourselves before we were able to know each other well. I don't know. But the planets did finally align and she eclipses them all.

Melissa was my best man in our wedding, and Pretzel was Laya's maid of honor. No one was confused. As our wedding gift, Melissa bought us a three-foot tall SpongeBob SquarePants doll dressed like an astronaut. And I'm the weird one?

A week after we got married, Laya and I got a brown-stone in the city. It has an amazing roof deck. We lie on lounges up there on all the warm nights and think about the stars and planets above us, even though we can't see shit over the city lights. It doesn't matter.

Laya's devoted to her job and she's quickly becoming the best surgeon in town. No surprise. I finally landed my own account and got to design a building. It was completed the spring we got married. It was mostly made of glass so that anywhere you looked, you'd always be able to see the sun and the moon rising and setting. Everyone asked me what my inspiration was.

I would just simply say . . . Laya.

Acknowledgments

Eternal gratitude to the family and friends who share my books, and who share a love of reading with me and the rest of the world.

To the readers, the lovers, and the dreamers: thank you for keeping love stories alive when there is so much negativity and hate in this world.

Allison and Jhanteigh, thank you for helping me get this book off the ground.

Everyone at Atria who works so hard to get my books into the hands of readers . . . thank you.

Loan, I am so grateful for your intense work on *The Last Post*. You brought so much to this story.

To the people who inspire me with kindness, talent, humor, and grace, thank you for helping me open the blinds now and then.

Sam, my little explorer: keep scouring that atlas; keep

reading and daydreaming. Your fortitude and curiosity amaze me.

Tony, you're definitely one of those people who makes me laugh on a daily basis. Your wit and humor bring such a bright light into this house.

Anthony, thank you for believing in me . . . still. I love you. Also, the French toast . . . THE FRENCH TOAST!

About the Author

Renée Carlino is a screenwriter and bestselling author of *Sweet Thing, Nowhere but Here, After the Rain, Before We Were Strangers, Swear on This Life, Wish You Were Here*, and *Blind Kiss*. She lives in the San Diego area with her husband and two sons. To learn more, visit ReneeCarlino.com.